A Thousand Generations

A Thousand Generations

Jane Lebak

Philangelus Press
Boston, MA USA

CHAPTER ONE

With his eyes glued to his handheld Grooz Capture game, Gage hunch-shuffled into the kitchen for a soda. Dad was pacing, rubbing his mustache as he spoke on the phone. "Honestly, don't. Can't you hear how dangerous this is?"

Gage paused his game and popped open the fridge door.

Dad's voice ticked up a notch. "I'm not sending him there—not for that. Don't you of all people understand? You think that's going to protect Jeff, but it's not."

Gage pulled the metal tab, and the soda can hissed. The mention of his cousin Jeff meant Uncle Zack was on the phone, probably doing something crazy. Again. And Dad would rant about it afterward. Again.

Although—protect Jeff? Was Jeff rock-climbing without a helmet? "Not sending him there" meant Uncle Zack had invited Gage to do whatever it was, and of course Preacher Dad would keep Gage from doing anything fun.

Gage sipped his soda before unpausing his game. The other eighth graders said the grey Groozes were hardest to snare, but Taylor had shown Gage the trick to predicting the shadowy figures' movements. She was already at level twelve, and she said it was all about seeing things you didn't ordinarily look for.

"You know the Lord explicitly commands—" Dad sighed, running a hand through his salt-and-pepper hair. "Because it's in the Bible, that's how, but you don't need to believe in the Bible to realize how dangerous what you're describing is."

A grey Grooz popped out. Gage missed. He selected the net tool and pursued the Grooz past the lake screen onto the forest screen.

"Listen—" Dad stopped. "Gage, could you leave me alone for a bit?"

"Sure." Dad's job frequently required private conferences. Gage was used to that. Usually Dad took these calls in his office, though—and that kind of call never came from Uncle Zack. Gage settled in the living room, trying to track the Grooz by using the background music. Taylor said that worked half the time.

Abruptly Dad's tone changed. "Zack! What was that? What's going on?"

Gage's chest tightened.

Dad's voice went frantic. "Get out of there! You're in danger!"

Then Dad was rushing to the front door, snatching his winter coat from the hook. "Gage, keep your phone open. Stay right here until I get back."

Gage dropped the game. "What happened?"

"Just stay here!" Dad yanked out his car keys and slammed the door behind him.

The Grooz music played like a carnival ride for a minute. With his long legs curled against his chest, Gage stared over the back of the couch as Dad's sedan sped out of the driveway.

Fading sunlight glinted on the snow-buried lawn.

"He's probably all right." Gage's voice sounded like a lie to his own ears. Uncle Zack was—well, he just was. He'd always been around. Dad said Gage's uncle was raising Jeff wrong, but Dad thought half the country was raising their kids wrong.

God, he thought in quiet confusion, *keep Jeff safe.* Whatever Dad had been on about, it had been something to protect Jeff. *He's my only cousin. Don't let anything bad happen to him even if he's being dumb.* That didn't feel like enough. *I don't even know what to ask, but You know what we need before we ask. Protect him. Please don't wait for him to ask.*

Yes, that felt right. *Please intervene for Jeff before he asks.*

Other than the cats, no one else was home. It should take Dad ten minutes to get to Uncle Zack's. The way he'd torn out of here, maybe five.

It wouldn't take Gage very long to bike there, either. What if Jeff needed him?

Uncle Zack. Gage untangled his legs from one another and sprang from the couch, then sprinted to the steps. He jumped down the first half-flight and stomped the rest of the way from the landing into the downstairs. Out in the garage, he freed his bicycle from the snow blower and the shovels, and then he stopped.

"Just stay here," Dad had said. Nothing unclear about that. But even so...

Pine branches sagged over the road, weighted with wet snow until they resembled Othello pieces, white moisture frozen hard over branches black with wetness. Power lines had the same effect, white over black, vivid against the graying sky. Gage hunched in his jacket and wheeled his bike toward the street. He could be at Uncle Zack's house in fifteen minutes.

While he stood, bike at an angle between his legs, a siren screamed through the nearest intersection, crescendoing and then blaring into a distorted wail as it hurtled over the hill. Then another siren approached. Maybe a second police car. Maybe an ambulance. Then a third.

Gage's hands clenched on the handlebars. *God...oh, God...*

He listened for a fourth siren, but that was the last. He looked at the top of the hill to his left, then back at his hands. The silence grew unbearable. Dad had said to wait at home. And anyhow, what could a thirteen-year-old do that the cops and an ambulance couldn't?

He walked the bike back into the garage while shadows lengthened across the yard. As Gage leaned it against the wall, his phone rang.

It was Dad. "There's a lot going on here."

Gage knew that tone of voice. When the church secretary had been in a crash at the railroad crossing...when one of the elders had lost his son to a drug overdose...when Grandma had been diagnosed with terminal cancer... That's when Dad got that voice. The strain. The used-up quality. The emptiness when he knew he had to be the one to replenish everyone around him.

Gage shoved his free hand into his jeans pocket. The air was so cold. "What do you want me to do?"

His voice sounded a bit like Dad's. Weary. Unnerved.

"You'd better go to a friend's for dinner, probably for the night. I'm not sure when I'll be back."

Voices cluttered the background, but Gage couldn't make them out. "Can you tell me what happened?"

"I'm still figuring it out myself. Pray hard, will you?" In his father's voice, Gage abruptly detected an emotion worse than grief. "I want you with someone, not alone. Where will you go?"

"Taylor's?"

"I'll call them to come get you."

Gage huffed. "I bike there all the time."

Silence.

Startled, Gage said, "What do you think is going to happen to me?"

"Well... Just get there quickly." A pause. "I've got to go. Text me when you arrive."

Numb, Gage ended the call.

Why quickly? First, Uncle Zack had to get out of his house, and now, Gage had to get out, too?

Gage turned on all the lights as he moved from room to room packing his backpack. He turned on the lights for the fifteen seconds it took to walk through the hallway, and again when he was in the bathroom just long enough to grab his toothbrush. At the last minute, he stuffed the handheld game into the pocket of his winter jacket. Then it was back onto his bike. For real, this time.

Gage lived a mile from the railroad tracks; Taylor's was the first farm on the opposite side. He still had half a mile to ride after crossing over, but Gage ignored the sting of the wind. The work of pumping the fifteen-speed hybrid bike kept him warm except for his hands. Every push of the pedals came as a wordless prayer for his uncle and his cousin.

The path to Taylor's front door lay beneath ten inches of hard-packed snow. Like many farm homes in Vermont, this one had grown both practical and impractical over the decades, as a succession of owners modified the house to suit themselves: additions built, ells added, wings closed off, bump-outs bumped out, chimneys turned into closets and closets turned back into chimneys.

To one side was a new barn for the dairy cattle, and on the other was the old barn that the local fire department should use for training new recruits, except they charged a hundred dollars to burn down a structure. But why pay a hundred dollars to be rid of it when time would do it for free? Taylor's house had a beautiful front porch no one used because using it meant more shoveling in the wintertime and muddy boots on the carpet, whereas they had a perfectly good attached garage that got plowed. A salt-encrusted dark blue Suburban sat in the driveway. Smoke rose from all three chimneys, scenting the road downwind. Gage left his bike by the dormant flower beds and texted Dad. "I'm here." No reply came.

Inside, Taylor's mother turned with a smile as warm as her oven-toasty kitchen. "Gage! What's going on?"

"Uh, nothing." Gage realized suddenly the ride had left him out of breath. He stood over the heat register and rubbed his gloved hands without unzipping his jacket. "Is Taylor around?"

"Stacking wood out back." Mrs. Greymore wore a baby in a sling and had a three-year-old boy underfoot. Her denim skirt swished around her ankles as she moved. "Would you tell her dinner will be ready in half an hour?"

Gage nodded. "Would it be all right if I stayed? Something came up, and Dad asked."

"No problem." Mrs. Greymore flashed a smile. "It's only chicken stew with dumplings. I'll throw on some extra noodles and make a salad. Is something going on at the church?"

Gage managed to say, "I don't know what it is."

"You look upset. I'm sorry." She adjusted the sling so the baby sat lower on her thick waist. "Why don't you go find Taylor?"

Gage headed through the living room to the steps down to the family room. Because of the steep slope outside the house, this became the ground floor in back. At the rear of the family room stood a pot-bellied woodstove on a raised stone hearth. Beyond that, a door led to the back yard, and in the entryway, Taylor was stacking wood.

"Hey!" Taylor grinned as he joined her. "Dad thinks it's going to storm again soon, so I get to load us up with wood. Go, me! And now, you're the one who gets to help. So, go you."

Gage put away his phone. "The weather didn't say there'd be snow."

Taylor dumped her armload with a clatter, then started stacking it. "But the cows are lying down, and cows don't watch the weather."

Gage sorted through words in his head, but they refused to congeal into sentences: Uncle Zack. Ambulance. Dad. Get out of the house.

It was easier just to stack wood. Gage zipped his jacket to the neck and joined Taylor on her trek to the shed and then back with armloads of split logs. Taylor had long since stripped off her jacket, relying on exercise and a lined flannel shirt to fend off the cold. Gage finally did the same. He'd grown up around the aphorism that wood warms you three times: once when you cut it, once when you stack it, and once when you burn it. It was an honest warmth. Behind the shed, echoes resounded against the heavy sky while Mr. Greymore kept thunking with an axe, chopping the logs into small enough pieces to fit into the stoves.

"Your Mom said dinner would be ready soon," Gage said during a breather. "And that I could eat here."

Taylor nodded, auburn ponytail swinging. "Pastor Jordan had something come up at the church?" Then, catching his expression, she paused. "What's wrong?"

He shifted. "Uncle Zack is in trouble."

"Not too bad, I hope?" Taylor waved to her father. "Hey, Dad? We're going in to clean up for supper!"

Just inside, standing before the woodstove, Taylor hung both their jackets on pegs. "What happened?"

Gage shook his head. "Uncle Zack was on the phone, and Dad lit out of the house. There were police cars and an ambulance. Dad said to find a place to go for the night."

Taylor's freckled face seemed grim as she added a log to the woodstove, then poked until it was in the right place to catch. "That doesn't sound good."

After clanking the lock on the door and detaching the handle, she closed her eyes and clasped her hands in front of her chest. Gage closed his eyes too, allowing the heat from the woodstove to dance across his windblown cheeks.

"Father God," Taylor said, "thanks for sending Gage to help with the wood, and thank you for letting him stay for dinner. But we're worried about his uncle, God. Please look after his Uncle Zack, and his cousin Jeff, and Pastor Jordan. And Gage, too. I know he's worried, Father."

Gage whispered, "Thank you for letting Taylor's parents take me on such short notice. And please let Uncle Zack be all right. Jeff needs him still. Keep Jeff safe, even if he doesn't ask. Please."

"We love you and praise you," Taylor murmured. "Amen."

"Amen." Gage looked at Taylor. "God wouldn't let anything happen to Uncle Zack."

It was almost a question.

"Rotten things happen to good people all the time." Taylor nibbled her lip. "That's why we pray for each other."

Before they made their way up the steps, Mrs. Greymore was already calling everyone for dinner. Gage thought his stomach would be too tight to eat, at least until she carried steaming homemade biscuits to the table, followed by a crock of stew with dumplings, a crisp salad, noodles in butter sauce, and fresh steamed broccoli. He ate until he was stuffed, but Mrs. Greymore kept ladling out more.

At home, he and Dad always used suppertime to catch up on the day, but the Greymore family transformed that same time into chaos. The baby needed constant attention, and Taylor helped out the preschooler and the five-year-old. The family dog lay beneath the table, hoping for good things to rain down from above (and frequently got rewarded for his patience). No one asked Gage about the situation at home. The omission felt like a fabricated silence, but still, Gage wished for real quiet.

While Taylor and Gage helped to dry and put away the dishes, Gage's phone buzzed. Dad.

Gage walked to the edge of the kitchen, his gut clenching up. "What's going on?"

Dad sighed. "It's not good. I don't think I should even explain to you."

How bad could it be? "How's Uncle Zack? How's Jeff?"

"Jeff doesn't seem to be hurt. Zack is— I didn't get here in time." Dad stayed quiet a moment. "I'm going to keep you out of school tomorrow, and I don't know when I'll be getting home tonight. I'd like you to stay with the Greymores if it's all right with them."

Taylor and her mother watched him sidelong as they cleaned. Gage faced away and whispered, "Is he in the hospital?"

Dad lowered his voice, as though even saying such a thing were awful. "Uncle Zack is dead."

Gage pressed his forehead against the wall and struggled to take a deep breath. Behind him, dishes clinked as they were lifted from the rack and hidden away in the cabinets.

Trembling, Gage said, "How'd it happen?"

"He was killed. Why does it matter how he died?" Dad sounded sharp. "Give Mrs. Greymore the phone."

Gage handed the phone to Taylor's mom, and she talked to Dad full of sympathy. Of course Gage could stay, and she could activate the prayer chain, and if there was anything else she could do—

Gage stalked to the living room. A minute later, Taylor joined him on the couch.

Taylor kept her voice soft. "That stinks."

It stunk to high heaven. "He won't tell me how it happened. It's my own uncle, but I'm not allowed to know? What am I, five years old?"

"You're pretty tall for five," Taylor quipped, then pulled back at Gage's glare. "Your dad's probably freaked out, but he should tell you. How's Jeff?"

"I guess he's fine." Gage folded his arms. "For an orphan."

"It must be like a nightmare." Taylor nibbled on one fingernail. "Does he remember losing his mom?"

"How could he? He was just a baby. I don't even remember my mom, and I was three." Gage bit his lip. "At least Dad's there."

"Is your Dad coming?"

"Not tonight." Gage swallowed. "Did Uncle Zack blow up the house? I hope Dad's not in danger."

Taylor drew her legs to her chest and wrapped her arms around them. "Your Dad's smart. He'll be all right."

Mrs. Greymore appeared in the living room with a mug of hot chocolate. She set it down on the end table, then handed back his phone.

Gage tried to do his homework but ended up staring at his binder and not solving a single geometry problem. Eventually he liberated a wrinkled deck of cards from Taylor's room and played solitaire. Taylor was reading a yellowed paperback called *The Making of a Surgeon*, but when he asked, she turned on her Grooz Capture game and networked with his. The handheld unit had other games, but none of them were anywhere near as good—nor were they multiplayer. They played a two-player hunt, relaying messages through the Wi-Fi, until it was time to put the younger ones to sleep.

Taylor's house didn't have a guest room, but the family room's pullout couch was plenty comfortable. Gage settled there, listening to the house creaking around him, the last sounds he heard being the dampened fire cooling down in the woodstove.

Still, he was restless. It never felt as though Gage truly got to sleep, although according to the clock, he must have.

Then came one moment in the long chain of half-dreaming thoughts when Gage started awake, certain someone was outside the house.

The Greymores' German Shepherd stood, nose to the window, tail still.

Uncle Zack was dead. And something was outside the house.

He heard nothing now, but maybe he'd been awakened by a sound? Or maybe by the alertness of the dog?

Gage slipped out from under the blanket to peer through the blinds, side by side with the dog. He could see no one in the field. "You shouldn't be here," he whispered to the shadows.

Something had killed Uncle Zack, so Gage ought to be terrified. There was no sense of danger, though. Even if someone were prowling the property, instead of feeling intruded-upon, the house—the land itself—seemed to welcome the visitor.

Gage didn't believe in ghosts, but maybe he was wrong. He ought to go back to bed.

Still, what was out there? Why had its silent approach awakened him?

The dog remained at the window while Gage tied on his boots, then crept past the woodstove to the back entrance. Gage lifted his jacket off the hook and stepped outside.

Dad wanted him to stay in the house. His heart wanted him out. His heart won.

A half-moon illuminated the snow. Stars gleamed in a sky undulled by city lights. Gage rounded the side of the house, then froze in place.

At the top of the hill, two children were digging in the snow. One glanced his way, but neither paid him any attention as he walked closer.

Although on second thought, they weren't proportioned like children. They didn't move like children, either. Gage had difficulty registering more than one glimpse at a time: either the moonlight or the sheen from the snow prevented him from focusing on the pair. He could see them perfectly with his peripheral vision, but looking directly made them vanish.

Only when Gage had walked halfway to them in a straight line did both regard him with a terrified stare. At this distance, he saw them clearly. They had straight shoulder-length hair and mismatched clothing. The nearer of the two wore a tank top and a pair of shorts, ankle boots, and half a dozen bracelets that chimed with every movement. The other had long pants and a large, loose T-shirt cinched at the waist with a string. Although shorter than Gage, they both had older faces with prominent cheekbones and turned-down noses. Their eyes reminded him of preschoolers on their very first day of church camp.

Gage whispered, "What are you?"

The bangled one nudged the other. "He can see us."

The second stepped behind the first. "What do we do?"

Gage breathed in little white puffs; they didn't. His legs shivered beneath his flannel pajamas, but the pair stood bare-skinned in the snow without so much as a goosebump.

He'd thought before that they shouldn't be here, but now his thought was, *I shouldn't be here.* As Gage took another step, the one in the T-shirt shrank back on itself. Gage asked, "Who are you?"

"I'm Mir," said the first, and pointed at the second. "That's Mek. We're looking for thread."

Gage frowned. "Thread?"

"You know, the kind God uses to hold the Earth together and tell it when to grow and when to freeze and when to get dark. Will-of-God-Threads." Mir bounced in place like a kid waiting to see Santa Claus. "One surfaced here, and we're going to pull it up. Not all of it. Just enough for Mek and me."

Gage came closer. "You're not people."

Mir said, "Who are you?"

"Gage Jordan."

The second figure gasped. "That sounds like what the other thing was called."

The first looked sad, then said, "No, no. It only sounded like that."

Gage said, "What? What other thing?"

Mir whispered, "There are demons around. They were hunting for someone. That's why we want the thread. Thread can help us hide."

If they wanted not to be found by demons, then the pair themselves weren't demons. They looked too scared to be running from one of their own. Gage said, "How can you hide from a demon?"

Mir regarded him, puzzled. "How come you can see us? Nobody else does."

"One did," Mek said softly. "A long time ago."

"Really?"

"She left us *treasure*."

Mir gasped. "Treasure?"

The pair carried on for a minute, machine-gunning irrelevant details atop other details and never making any more sense than before until Mek abandoned the conversation mid-sentence to kneel in the snow. Mir scraped a clear spot and then started to whistle.

Mek untied the drawstring of a cloth bag, then fished through its clattering contents until retrieving a scuffed plastic recorder. Puffing lightly, Mek created random squeaks, struggling to spread small fingers across the holes.

It was too cold to keep still, so Gage stamped his feet to get the blood going.

They started. "He can see us!" Mek shouted, dropping the recorder and darting behind Mir.

Gage picked up the instrument and handed it back at arm's length. "You just said that."

Mir pointed at the ground. "There's a thread here. Why aren't you playing?"

Side-eyeing Gage, Mek resumed the random notes.

Mir placed both hands atop the concrete-hard dirt. A frown

crossed the soft features, and Gage nearly asked again what was happening—but then Mir plucked something and pinched it between thumb and index fingers.

Mek smiled in a way that seemed to warm the night. "We're safe."

Mir nodded enthusiastically.

Gage said, "Give me some."

The pair jumped, then remembered who he was. Mek whispered something to Mir, who coiled the thread into three equal parts, then pinched. The thread parted easily. Mir handed one coil to Gage.

Gage examined his portion. "What do I do with it?" A yard long, it seemed translucent, much like the pair before him. In fact, as Mir braided one strand into the long locks of hair, it ceased to be visible.

Mek tied it into a loop and then coiled it into the string belt. "Keep it. It makes things the way God wants them to be."

Gage shoved it into his pocket. "How could things be any other way?"

Mir looked up. "The world is sad. Sometimes you can make it happy with a thread. Good things like the threads. They come to them."

Mek frowned. "Not angels."

"No. Angels don't need threads, and demons can't touch them." Mir beamed. "But the things in the middle know, and they love them."

Mek nodded as if this made all the sense in the world.

Mir said, "So use it right."

"Bye," chirped Mek.

The pair turned their backs on the house and skipped toward the road. Shivering, Gage watched until they vanished first from direct sight, and then from his peripheral vision.

What were they?

Gage returned inside with the thread.

CHAPTER TWO

Mrs. Greymore had learned many cereal companies contributed to a national organization of abortion providers, and consequently, the family boycotted every one of them. They either ate the generic or organic brands, or else Mrs. Greymore cooked an actual breakfast.

"I had such weird dreams last night," Taylor said around a mouthful of Crisp Treats of Rice, then turned to Gage. "Did your dad text you again?"

Gage felt exhausted, and he expected he looked it, too. The Greymore family was being extremely nice this morning, even by their own standards. He swallowed his Rings of Toasted Oats. "Nothing. I'll just bike home."

Mrs. Greymore still hadn't gotten a chance to eat her Unique J cereal. "If he's not there, come on back. You're always welcome."

The school bus came and went, leaving the house quieter.

Time for Gage to go, too.

Gage would have willingly forgotten last night's escapades, but in the sunlight, his own footprints were visible on the ridge. Placing his feet back into his own steps, he stalked his midnight self. The prints ended at a palm-sized circle of clear ground. There were no little prints.

Feeling as if he sliced a path through the chill, Gage retrieved his bike and pedaled back to his house. If Dad were driving to the Greymores' house to get Gage, he'd have to take this road, so they couldn't miss each other. A train was blocking the crossing, so Gage waited, rubbing his hands together, until it finally pulled through. Five cars idled on the opposite side, none of them Dad's tan Ford.

By comparison with Taylor's house, Gage's third-of-an-acre, cookie-cutter raised ranch looked boring, but he'd begun thinking boring was good. With all the lights dark, though, Gage hesitated, as if lights offered protection against monsters. Or demons, since those creatures last night mentioned demons.

Cold won out over vague anxiety. Gage opened the garage to put away his bike, and his father's car was tucked inside. He stepped into the house through the side door only to trip over two cats, tails straight up and faces tilted toward his own. Begging.

"No fooling around, guys," said Gage in a cajoling voice. "I'm sure Dad fed you." He scratched Salty behind the ears, then reached for Pepper only to have the black and white cat dash around the corner. Typical. A moment later, Pepper peeked back down the hallway. They looked so insistent (and desperate) that Gage fed them, and Pepper was hungry enough that he didn't flinch when Gage touched him. Well, if they'd tricked Gage this morning, it wouldn't be the first time. Probably wouldn't be the last, either.

When he refilled the water dish, Pepper came close, dipped his paw in the water, and then began to drink. That was a ritual with Pepper. As soon as any water came available, he'd rush for it, stick in his paw, then drink like crazy. Gage's mother had rescued the skeletal kitten at six months old, but their vet said that in those six months, Pepper must have endured a lifetime of abuse. Based on this behavior, the vet had guessed Pepper's previous owner denied him water for days, then set down a bowl of boiling water.

It wasn't fair. Pepper was an awesome cat—not that any animal would have deserved that. If Gage ever ran out of "enemies" to pray for, he could pray for whatever monster did that.

Gage tried again to pet Pepper, but the cat skittered away. It had been ten years. He prayed, *I hope that when Pepper's previous owner gets to Judgment, you take the form of a very large, very angry mother cat.*

Gage slipped up the hall to Dad's room and listened at the door: steady breathing. Dad usually didn't sleep until seven. It must have been a really late night.

In the living room, Gage stopped at the key hook, but as his fingers reached into his coat pocket to hang his keys, he started.

His cousin Jeff sat on the couch, staring out the window. And the God-thread was hot.

As Jeff turned to him, Gage gripped the thread. "I'm sorry... about Uncle Zack. Dad told me."

Hollow-cheeked, Jeff watched blankly, then stared back at the road.

For a moment Gage wavered beside the kitchen. The thread was still warm, but no longer burning, so he took off his coat to hang it on the hook. He ought to move the thread, just out of respect. But where to? And with Jeff watching—watching so strangely—Gage didn't dare explain. To remove something so insignificant-seeming and then treat it with reverence would only invite questions.

Regardless, Jeff took no further notice of Gage, so he

emptied out his backpack in his bedroom, then turned off the sound and resumed his game of Grooz Capture. He couldn't stop thinking about Jeff, though. Dad always said you don't abandon people dealing with something huge, even if you have to get out of bed to help them.

Leaving the game, Gage returned to the living room. After another minute of staring into the grey road, Jeff turned his head toward Gage. He looked like a dead man with his listless grey eyes, his limp blond hair, and the way he slumped like a rag doll.

Gage sat on the arm of the couch. "I'm sorry." Why wasn't he great with words like Taylor? She'd already have had Jeff feeling better, and instead all Gage could do was come out with an apology for something that wasn't his fault.

Keeping his voice low, Gage continued, "Dad told me what happened. Well, not everything. But the important stuff. Are you going to be staying with us?" When Jeff still didn't respond, Gage shifted in his seat. "Um, maybe, ah...I was going to get something to eat. Want anything?"

Awkwardly he walked to the kitchen. No sounds followed from the living room, so when he turned from the fridge and found Jeff at the table, he started.

Heart pounding, Gage tried to smile. "If you're going to stay with us, Dad will tell you to make yourself at home. The cereal's up here," he opened a cabinet, "and the bowls are there. I'll get the milk. What do you want?"

Jeff stood still. He must be famished, though. He hadn't eaten this morning, and probably he hadn't wanted to last night.

Gage propelled Jeff toward the cabinet. "Pick something. Anything." At least Dad didn't try to make a political statement in his cereal purchases. Jeff would recognize the choices. Eventually he took the closest box.

Gage set him up at the table, then picked an apple from the crisper. By the time he'd washed it and seated himself, Jeff had shoveled in half the food. Before Gage finished the apple, Jeff had polished off a second bowl.

While Gage loaded the dishwasher, Dad showed up in the doorway. "Thanks," he said, a little raspy. "I didn't mean to sleep so late."

Gage nodded. "No problem. Jeff and I had breakfast."

"Oh?" Surprised, Dad smiled at Jeff, but the boy studied a spot in front of him on the table. The smile faded, and Dad set up the coffee maker while Gage put out a bowl for him. Dad always ate one of two cereals for breakfast, so Gage took a guess, then seated himself across from Jeff. The percolator was spitting the last of the steam before Dad's troubled gaze.

As Dad poured the coffee, Gage said, "Can you tell me what happened now?"

Jeff's eyes registered an emotion too fleeting for Gage to name, and he left the room. Dad watched him go.

Dad whispered, "We think Jeff saw what happened, but he hasn't spoken to anyone. Not me, not the ambulance, and not the cops. He wouldn't write it out. He won't even make gestures."

Gage's throat tightened. "How did Uncle Zack die?"

"We're not sure. I told the police what I knew, but they're understandably skeptical." Dad drank some coffee black and unsweetened, then paused, figured out the problem, and added milk and sugar. "I found Jeff huddling under the basement steps. Even with the cops there, Jeff refused to come out for an hour. Zack was murdered—and you don't need to know the details. I wish I didn't know."

Gage swallowed hard. "There's no clue who did it?"

Dad sipped some more coffee. Then, barely audible: "Demons."

Goosebumps stood under Gage's shirt sleeves.

For a long minute, Dad added nothing. Then he sighed, a weary sound that verged on a groan. "I didn't say that to the police. They're investigating it as a homicide."

Gage slid a chair very close to Dad, and he lowered his voice. "Demons?"

"I'm not sure what other interpretation there is." He rubbed his mustache. "Zack was inside a magic circle. There was no mark on him, but he had a unique book that's currently in the custody of the police." Dad's face crumbled. "He didn't leave much room for other explanations. They're going to do an autopsy."

Gage's mouth twitched. "Maybe he worked himself up until he died of a heart attack."

Dad muttered, "Wouldn't that be a much nicer alternative?"

Gage glanced at the door, but Jeff hadn't returned. "You were yelling at him over the phone. What was he doing?"

Dad's mouth twitched. "He admitted he was working white magic. Don't believe that white part. Smearing vanilla frosting over a cow pie doesn't make it dessert."

Gage wouldn't meet Dad's eyes even as Dad wouldn't meet his. "Isn't there anything between angels and demons? Other than human beings, that is?"

Dad shook his head. "We're not in between them. We're a completely separate species. If it's an angel, its orientation is decided. There are none in the middle."

With a shiver, Gage thought of the pair of creatures in the field. "What was Uncle Zack trying to do?"

Dad chuckled softly. "Protect him and Jeff. From demons. Calling on demons to protect them from demons is all it amounted to. Once the demons had entry to his house, they flooded in."

There didn't seem to be anything to add to that. Mir had claimed demons prowled the area, but without knowing why. Well, now Gage knew why. His uncle had summoned them.

Dad said, "Jeff's going to stay with us, at least for the time being. After, I'm going to push for us to adopt him, assuming Zack's will didn't specify otherwise." Gage watched the moments play out in his father's eyes: documents, probate, death, adoption, his brother-in-law, murder, and one very hurt boy. "I can't see anyone objecting. We're his closest relatives, and it's better if he stays local. He can go to the same school, and all of his friends are here."

It made sense. Their house had an extra bedroom, since every builder assumed each family would have exactly two children. Taylor's family, with no plans to stop, or Gage's, which consisted of himself and his father, had no clout with a hundred contractors and a town planning board.

Dad paused. "Is it all right with you if he lives here? There was no time for a discussion last night, but he needed a place to stay."

"Of course." Jeff would be a great brother. He and Gage were only a month apart, and they attended the same school, and saw each other frequently, being the only family each other had in the area. Well, the only family on speaking terms.

The next thought hit Gage hard: Jeff and Uncle Zack had no quarrel with Grandpa Rivers. If Dad adopted Jeff, maybe Gage would see his grandfather again.

Dad said Grandpa Rivers was a bad influence. He never gave a reason, but he also never let Gage visit him. He even screened the man's Christmas cards. Dad would never stop Jeff from visiting Grandpa, though. Not when Jeff had already lost so many people.

Two calls came in while they ate breakfast. Dad had the ringer off and the volume turned down, but every so often Gage heard their answering machine click into action. The old machine wasn't nearly as efficient as voicemail, but Dad kept it because by using the speaker, he could triage calls in the background to hear if someone's mother was dying versus if someone wanted to complain about the milk choices at coffee hour. Gage had come to think of the machine itself as a member of the congregation: *Pastor, can you pray for my next-door neighbor? Pastor, I can't find my son's dog. Pastor, can you jump-start my car?* This morning, as word got around, the calls would all be the same. *Pastor, I'm sorry. Can I help?*

Dad said they'd have to go back to get Jeff's things. Jeff's house was a crime scene, and he'd brought out only a few things, so the police would have to let them back inside. Gage's eyes traveled to Jeff's empty seat. How would it feel if his own father had been murdered, and Gage had needed to go live with Uncle Zack? How would it feel to walk back into a home where he'd seen his father die?

Gage and Jeff had grown up side-by-side. Mom and Uncle Zack were sister and brother, but Uncle Zack's wife had resembled Mom, making it a family joke that the pair were twins. Even their names were similar: Gage's mom was Jeannine and Jeff's was Jenna. Dad said once it was funny until both of them died.

"Maybe you can get through to Jeff." Dad kept his voice hushed. "Don't do anything different. Just spend time with him. You'll be sympathetic anyhow, but I'm warning you it's hard being near someone in the middle of a tragedy when there's nothing you can do to fix the problem. Just stay close. When he talks to you, listen."

After Dad headed to his downstairs office to return all those calls, Gage retrieved the God-thread from his coat pocket. In his room, after making sure Jeff hadn't appeared at his door with that unnerving silence, Gage set the coil in the neck compartment of his guitar case along with his picks, capo, and tuner. That should keep it safe until he figured out how to use it.

Come to think of it, there would have to be a funeral—a wake and a funeral, both—and Gage might get asked to play guitar at one of them. Did Uncle Zack have a favorite hymn?

Did Uncle Zack even know any hymns?

On an unseasonably warm night a week before Halloween, Uncle Zack had invited Dad and Gage to his townhome for a cookout. An early frost had killed the mosquitoes, so everyone could linger after dark on the concrete slab that served as the back porch. Gage had finger-picked through a song while Jeff played Frisbee with two of the neighbors. "You're pretty good," Uncle Zack said while he put more hot dogs on the grill. "What's that song called?"

Gage hadn't even looked up. "*Now the Green Blade Rises.*"

"Hah!" Jeff tossed the Frisbee back to the other kids and leaned against Dad's chair. "Who's the Green Blade? Some kind of ninja?"

Gage laughed out loud. "A Christian environmentalist ninja! 'Beware the wrath of the mighty Green Blade!'"

"Or he'll *mow* you down!" Jeff smirked, and Dad groaned. "No, seriously, who's the Green Blade? A comic book character?"

Gage frowned. "It's Jesus."

Uncle Zack announced in an artificially deep voice, "Jesus Christ *is*...the Green Blade!" and Jeff had concocted the Adventures of the Green Blade until Gage, with his cheeks burning, put away the guitar to join the game of Frisbee.

In the spare bedroom, Gage found Jeff sitting up by his pillows, his knees tight to his chest while he stared at his socks.

Gage said, "Dad says you saw it happen." When no response came, he walked into the room. Resisting the urge to flip the light switch, he sat at the bed's opposite end. "Do you know who did it?"

Terror flitted over Jeff's eyes, and his hands clenched his elbows.

Gage said, "Someone you recognized?"

Jeff buried his face in his arms, but not before Gage saw the terror transform into a fear even more primal.

He inched forward on the bed, leaning close enough to extend his arm and touch Jeff on the leg. "They told you not to tell?"

Jeff tightened.

"Dad will keep you safe."

Jeff's head popped up like a jack-in-the-box, eyes glistening in the light permeating the curtains. He drew breath and opened his mouth, but after a moment of choking on words that couldn't emerge, Jeff cocooned around himself again. That was the last response Gage got from him all day.

Chapter Three

Right after school, Taylor biked to the church where Gage was shoveling snow. She retrieved the second shovel and set to work alongside him.

"Thanks." Gage didn't look at her as they dug. The grounds crew never used the snow blower on the entrance because of the two sets of steps. Only the front door of the church got any attention. If Dad wanted people to get inside, he needed to do the shoveling himself...or press his son into service. At least Taylor would make it go faster.

"So what happened to your uncle?" Taylor tightened the gloves on her hands and kept working as she spoke. "No one at school had a clue."

"Uncle Zack got murdered. Jeff saw it, but I think they threatened him because he's not talking. He's going to stay with us."

"Whoa." Taylor chopped at the ice with her shovel blade.

"Do the police know who did it?"

"Dad says demons."

Taylor's shovel struck the ice and didn't come up again.

Gage looked right at her. "I don't know what to believe. Uncle Zack admitted he was working magic, but would they really kill him?"

Taylor balled up some snow and tossed it at a nearby bush. "I've read about people who work themselves up into such a frenzy that they believe something's about to kill them, so they die."

"He started the magic himself. Obviously he didn't expect to die."

Taylor underhanded a second snowball at Gage's head. "I'm so glad you value my medical advice."

"You aren't a doctor until you graduate college and go to medical school, so yeah, I want a second opinion." Gage leaned on his shovel. "The thing is, I saw something, too. Last night. Not demons. But they weren't angels either. More like children, only they weren't human."

Taylor's eyes widened. "Where?"

"On the hill beside the old barn." He shook his head. "They were looking for something they called a Will-Of-God thread because it would protect them from demons. They gave me part of it."

Taylor raised her shovel, then moved closer. "What were they?"

Gage frowned. "They didn't say. They were surprised I could see them at all."

Taylor returned to ice-breaking. After a few minutes, she said, "I can look through the used bookstore and see if they have any mythology books. Maybe I can bug Dad to take me tonight. He doesn't always check what I drag out of the quarter bin, as long as I don't ask him to pay."

"Is that how you get all these medical books?"

Taylor laughed. "After I read the entire 610 section in the

public library, yeah. I assume you can't ask your Dad. You'd get in trouble for speaking to them, whatever they were. Do you think they might have been ghosts? Saul called Samuel back from the dead."

"I didn't summon them. They didn't curse me." Gage frowned as he started cleaning off the set of steps by the front door. "They weren't even scary. I mean, it was weird to see them because they weren't like us. But they were more scared of me."

Taylor laughed suddenly. "I always knew you were more frightening than a ghost!"

"Very funny." Gage tossed a load of snow at a nearby bush. "I didn't think I was dealing with demons. But what if I was?"

Taylor shook her head. "You'd have to tell your dad."

"He says there's no difference between white magic and black magic."

"If all you did was talk to them, that's not magic." Taylor's shovel scraped hard against the stone step. "I think if someone's working magic, it's about controlling things. No one would do magic to cross the street, right? But they sell spell kits at that weird shop in the mall to make people fall in love with you."

After a moment, Gage said, "That makes sense."

"I always make sense. Your uncle must have been bonkers, though." She paused. "What if Jeff's not talking because he's under a spell?"

Gage's mouth opened. "Now you're being bonkers. Jeff's just scared."

"You said you don't believe your uncle gave himself a heart attack by the power of suggestion, but now you want to believe your cousin went mute by another psychological process gone awry?" Taylor shook her head. "If Jeff saw his dad killed by demons, then he saw demons. I don't know what a demon can do, but the angel Gabriel made John the Baptist's father mute."

Gage blinked. "Then what ends the spell?"

"I have no clue. John the Baptist's father had to name his kid what the angel said." Taylor shrugged. "Could we break the spell by praying over him?"

Gage opened his hands. "Like I've ever done this?"

"Praying over him can't hurt, can it?"

A Jeep pulled into the lot, and Gage played the game he'd been playing all day, Guess the Visitor: lawyer, detective, doctor, or social worker? The Jeep was encrusted with too much salt to belong to a lawyer, and the menthol green paint probably ruled out a detective. A gentleman wearing a green canvas winter jacket stepped from the car, supported by a cane and walking with such care that Gage went to assist him.

Even before Gage reached him, the man squinted his iron-grey eyes. "Well. You got big."

Most people in this church recognized the pastor's son, but usually Gage recognized them back. "Can I help you? I hadn't finished shoveling yet, and it's still icy."

"You sound a lot like your mother." The man huffed as he planted his cane and continued navigating the ice. "You've got her eyes, too."

Gage escorted the man to the entrance. "Are you here to see Dad? I'll get him for you."

Taylor gave Gage a look he couldn't read, but he suspected she was certain of the stranger's identity—the same way he was. Inside the foyer, Gage offered to take the man's coat, but the man refused. "I won't be here long. Just point me to his office."

When Gage opened the door, Jeff looked up from Dad's couch with shining eyes, but Dad's face hardened. "You can go now," Dad said to Gage, and he ushered Jeff out of the office as well.

After Dad shut the door between himself and the boys, Gage whispered to Jeff, "Is that Grandpa Rivers?"

Jeff watched the door with what Gage imagined should be

yearning.

Dad had soundproofed his office, so Gage and Jeff never heard the grandfather speaking. Eventually they heard Dad, though. Just the tone, but not the words. Jeff went to sit by the front window, resting his flushed cheek against the chill glass.

After five minutes, their grandfather exited the office and aimed for the main door. "I'll show myself out. Don't trouble yourself."

Dad glared from his doorway. "It's no trouble."

Jeff launched from the window and hurled himself at his grandfather, wrapping his arms around him. Grandpa Rivers rested a hand on Jeff's hair and pressed the boy's cheek into his chest. "I'll be back, even if it takes a court order. I won't let you be endangered." Then he looked at Gage. "It was nice to meet you again."

Gage stood rigid. With Dad so close, he didn't dare do more.

In the church parlor, Taylor and Gage drank Cokes and looked out the window. This room with its comfortable chairs usually served as a meeting area for Pastor Jordan and families in crisis. They'd made the walk reasonably snow-free, at least until the wind redistributed the piles.

Taylor tucked her feet under her legs. "If my grandfather lived so close, we'd see him every weekend. We see Grandma Greymore all the time, and she's in St. Albans."

While Gage never pretended to read minds, he knew what she wasn't asking. "Dad and Grandpa Rivers don't get along. Dad says he believes the wrong things."

Once more, Jeff sat against the door, cheek against the glass, as if to be as close as possible to the last place he'd seen his grandfather. Gage said, "Dad can't keep Jeff from him, though. Grandpa made threats about grandparents' rights. And I'll definitely see Grandpa at Uncle Zack's funeral. We'll all have to be at that."

Taylor tilted her head. "What would you say to him?"

Gage shrugged. "I might ask what my mother was like. Dad tells me a ton of stories, but I bet Grandpa knows more."

Taylor nodded. "That doesn't sound unreasonable."

"Dad thinks he'd say other things, too. They have a weird view of God. I heard Dad tell Uncle Zack once that God doesn't roll dice."

"My dad says that. Then Mom shoots back that someone said God throws the dice where we can't see them, and then Dad lectures all of us about gambling. I've got the routine memorized." Taylor rose from the sofa to look around the corner at Jeff. She whispered, "I wish there were something we could do."

Didn't Dad say that was the worst part about helping someone in crisis? "I wish he'd talk to us."

Taylor shook her head. "You said he's scared. He'll speak when he can."

Gage said, "Even if he's under a spell?"

"Did we just flip our scripts?" She met Gage's eyes for a long moment. Then her eyes narrowed. "It doesn't matter how powerful Satan is. Jesus beat him once, and the gates of Hell will not prevail."

"They may not *prevail*," Gage said, "but the Bible never says how close they'll come."

Taylor shivered. "Now you're frightening me."

"Then you weren't listening before, because it's already frightening."

She sprang off the couch and glided out to Jeff in the hallway. For a moment she crouched at his side, and then with a touch on his arm, she got Jeff walking. When Jeff reached the parlor, Taylor brought him to the center and gestured to Gage to shut the door.

Keeping Jeff in front of her, Taylor and Gage stood on his opposite sides. They extended their arms around him and joined hands.

Taylor whispered, "Dear Father God, where two or more are gathered in your name, there you are in our midst. Please be here with us. Please be our protection and our shield. May the name of your Son be our armor and your Spirit our sword."

Gage said, "Drive off the snares of the evil one, and purify all within these walls."

Taylor swallowed. "Jeff, you're safe. You're protected in God's light. You can talk freely."

If Jeff had any words left, he clamped down so none escaped.

Gage closed his eyes. "Father God, please heal Jeff. We—"

He couldn't go on. Trying to voice it, he just couldn't. Death. Murder. Demons. It was too big. Too much.

Maybe that's what Jeff felt, only he felt it about everything. Words wouldn't form in his mind because Gage couldn't even encapsulate the thoughts.

Taylor took over. "Lord Jesus, this is beyond what we can do. There are some places we were never meant to go, and Lord, Jeff's been on the brink of those places."

In the silence that followed, they waited with closed eyes and tense spirits.

Taylor whispered, "Jeff, why don't you add something?"

Jeff stared at the carpet.

Gage took over. "Please answer all our unspoken prayers. You know what is in Jeff's heart and what he needs before he asks."

As he said the words, Gage's throat tingled. The words ricocheted around his head: *Before he asks. Before he asks. Before he asks.*

"Amen," whispered Taylor.

"Amen," replied Gage.

Even then, Jeff kept his silence.

Minutes before midnight, Gage put on his coat and crept outside. The house had long since subsided to stillness, and even the cats had settled to sleep.

With his hand on the God-thread, Gage crossed the back yard. He hadn't asked Taylor her opinion on this because she'd have said no. Or even worse, she might have said yes. Whatever happened tonight, it needed to happen to him alone.

If Dad would have listened, Gage would have talked to him first. Maybe he should have anyhow. Those creatures last night weren't demons. They hadn't left behind the indelible terror Jeff wore every moment. They'd wanted this "treasure" for themselves but then given Gage a part of it without any second thoughts. They said it was protection. Jeff seemed to think he needed protection. Grandpa, too.

It was time to find out how a thread protects you.

First Gage inspected it in the moonlight. It seemed translucent along all three feet of its length. Although it had spent all day in a coil, it didn't cling to that shape once he unwound it.

Next he ran the thread between his thumb and middle finger, its smoothness never once snagging against his skin. It felt colder than the air, and it didn't warm with contact.

This held the world together? Was Gage supposed to believe millions of these things told the world when to get green and when to get brown? Then, assuming that was true, he should also assume demons wouldn't touch them, yet "things in the middle" liked the threads and wanted to be near them?

That pair had to have belonged to the "things in the middle." Angels and demons were smart. Even the dumbest angel would make a Nobel Laureate seem like a second grader, so angels or demons would have used a different vocabulary. Demons would have used complicated words and emotional venom to describe the world they hated. Angels would have been expressive and clear. By contrast, the pair of creatures had said, "The Earth is sad."

They'd implied these threads made the world happy. Would a demon think things were happy near God? Wouldn't a demon instead believe God's will head-locked a creature and subdued it?

Gage tried to snap off a portion of the string, but it resisted his tugs and twists. Mir had pinched it, and when Gage tried that, a fragment parted from the end. On his palm, that quarter-inch segment shimmered.

Back when Mom died, Dad had planted a rosebush, and when they'd moved from Milton to Colchester, Dad had arranged for the bush to come, too. Although the plant hadn't died, for the past five years, they'd had no roses at all. Gage couldn't even remember what color they were.

Dad had set the trellis out by the woodshed, so that's where Gage went. If whatever he did with the thread killed the bush, Dad would feel sad because it was Mom's rosebush. But on the other hand, if the plant thrived, Gage would know what this thread could do. Roses had no soul. He couldn't endanger them, and this rosebush had room for improvement.

Gage cleared the snow from the base, and once he reached the ground, he crumbled the bit of thread between his thumb and forefinger, sprinkling particles over the roots and base of the bush.

Gage stepped back. The bare branches looked exactly the same in the shadows of the moon.

"You shouldn't play with that."

Gage pivoted to find himself staring at a white-clad man about his father's height. He had beige skin and sharp features, and his dark hair glinted like the God-thread.

Gage dropped to his knees in the snow.

"Get up." The man's eyes shone green, like a cat's. "The one you should worship is God, and there's no reason to be afraid. I'm not going to hurt you, but you shouldn't be handling that thread."

Gage glanced over his shoulder. "Why? It didn't do anything."

"Didn't it?"

It came to Gage like a wave that during winter, God's will for roses was to stand dormant. Come this spring, however, he could envision the rosebush rioting with growth, devouring the trellis and then climbing the shed, sending shoots off its base and exploding with dozens of yellow buds on every branch.

It would be thornless, Gage realized. The new shoots would have no thorns.

Wide-eyed, he turned to the man. "The thread did that?"

"Now you understand how powerful even a fragment was." The man's deep voice sent shock waves through Gage's heart. Gage wasn't sure he was hearing it as much as feeling it in his chest. "You've been entrusted with a dangerous strength. Don't play with it."

Gage's hands clenched. "Who are you?"

"My name would mean nothing to you. God is our only protection."

Gage edged backward. "Are you an angel?"

"I am what God made me."

Gage caught his breath. "The things that gave me the thread...they weren't demons, were they?"

The man didn't shake his head. In fact, now that Gage knew to watch, the man lacked any kind of "body language." His form was immobile, and he conveyed everything through words alone. "They were jinn, and they wouldn't hurt you intentionally. But they do make mischief." The angel's voice lowered. "They shouldn't have pulled the thread at all, and they certainly should have known better than to give it to you."

"Jinn." He'd need to look that up. There weren't any jinn in the Bible. But then again, cats weren't in the Bible, and he fed two of those every day "What killed Uncle Zack? Were those demons?"

The man darkened visibly. That was enough of a yes for Gage. "There are some things no one should know. God forbids some acts for a reason."

Gage's hand tightened on the thread. "What should I do with the thread?"

Gage had half-expected the man would tell him to give it back, but the man didn't extend a hand. "If you were to leave it for the jinn as treasure, they'd remember you forever." A light crossed the angel's eyes, but just as quickly it vanished. "Don't try to force it to do anything. God allows things to happen without forcing. Don't manipulate the world. Are you willing to wager your family or friends' physical lives—or your own eternal life—on your ability to compete with demons?"

Gage shivered violently. "No."

The sound carried far. Abruptly he was talking to no one.

A prickle crossed the back of his neck, and the thread tingled with heat. Looking to the house, Gage saw Jeff's face in the kitchen window, staring right at him.

Chapter Four

Dad spent the next morning driving around town, talking to police and lawyers and a funeral director. Jeff hadn't indicated any desire to join him, so Dad let him stay home. Gage chose the same. The lawyers wouldn't have been so bad, and the detectives might even have been fun. It was the last he wanted to avoid. Dad knew every funeral director in the greater Burlington area, so they wouldn't give him a hard time, but even so, there would be a thousand decisions and funeral parlor smell.

Jeff turned on the TV, but the television kept making senseless sounds that in reality were probably cartoons, the news, or talk shows. Eventually Gage tuned his guitar and sat in his room practicing his favorites, singing under his breath.

He'd returned the thread to the guitar case. It would have been better off in a wall safe, but his suburban home was fresh out of those.

Jeff showed in Gage's bedroom doorway. In his hands he held both his own and Gage's Grooz Capture units.

"You want to play?" Gage set his guitar in its case. "I'm on level six. I hope you're not miles ahead of me."

Jeff didn't so much as shrug. Even though they could do it over Wi-Fi, Jeff plugged a cable between the units and set up a two-player game. Together they started laying snares for the various Grooz types that inhabited their electronic world.

Gage sent Jeff's hunter messages through the game, but Jeff's hunter didn't reply. Gage opted instead to create strategies within the game and let the two hunters enact them.

Gage's unit and Jeff's sounded off their carnival-type tunes in synchrony. When one or the other made a capture, the individual units chimed. Gage cheered his little figure as it made its virtual hunt; Jeff concentrated with deep furrows in his forehead.

In the upper right-hand corner of Gage's screen, the messages light flashed. Gage opened it.

"Help me."

Gage's hands went tight on the machine. Sick inside, he dared to look at Jeff.

As if he hadn't sent that message, Jeff was pouring all his attention into the hand-held game.

Help me.

———◦———

Taylor came over after school, and Gage brought her to the wood pile at the side of the house. In a hushed voice, he related the events at the rosebush.

Taylor bit her lip. "Were you scared?"

"He said not to be." Gage's eyes dropped. "Was it really an angel?"

Taylor's cheeks whitened. "How would you tell?" When

Gage shuddered, she added, "You need to go over it with your father."

Shaking his head, Gage said, "He'll go ballistic."

Taylor closed her eyes hard. "That's bonkers. You're more afraid of your Dad than Satan?"

Gage laughed loudly, then smothered it with a nervous glance toward the house. Dad had returned an hour ago and taken Jeff into his office.

"Jeff's terrified," Gage said finally. "I'm afraid to tell you how I know."

Taylor swallowed. "Then don't say anything."

"That's the problem with invisible enemies. You never know when they're listening."

"I wish we knew how to drive them off." Taylor took a step toward the road. "Jeff thought even prayer wouldn't do the trick."

"There's the thread." Gage clenched his fingers around it in his pocket. "I wonder how the jinn use it to keep evil away?"

"It's got to be more than just holding it." The Vermont chill had no trouble penetrating their jackets, and their breath came up in clouds. "If you really saw a demon last night, then they can get close enough to observe you."

"What if it was an angel?"

Taylor's eyes narrowed. "Are you willing to bet that's what it was?"

"Not really." Gage swallowed. "I wonder how I could find out."

"Do you think you could find the jinn again?"

Gage folded his arms and squinted at the ground. "Apparently treasure is important to them."

"And naturally, we have treasure."

"Rolling in it." Gage grinned. "I stuff my mattress with jewels and pieces of eight."

Taylor giggled. "Must make it lumpy to sleep on."

Gage swallowed. "I wonder if Jeff would know. He spoke to

Grandpa Rivers and Uncle Zack all the time, and this sounds like something wrong-headed enough that Uncle Zack would be involved."

"Except Jeff's not going to talk to us."

Gage shook his head. "All I know is, Jeff wants help."

"Interesting. And he saw you use the thread. So—"

"—so I'm willing to try," Gage said. "But this is getting into dangerous territory. I don't like involving you, but I need someone with common sense."

"If he's under a spell by a demon, we can hardly make it worse."

"Of course we can!" The angel had asked if Gage was willing to risk the souls of everyone around him. "We could get him killed like Uncle Zack."

Taylor cocked her head. "That's his body, not his soul. I say we try it."

Gage lowered his head. "Then the demons find out he can talk, and they kill him? Maybe us, too?"

"We never gave them permission—"

"Maybe he did!" Gage's cheeks flushed. "Don't you think I've thought about all this? I could crumble a bit of thread and put it on his tongue hoping he can talk again, but then what happens? It can't possibly be God's will that he can't communicate at all. Give me a little credit."

She shoved her hands in her pockets. "You're right."

"There are some things we were never meant to do."

"In this case, you still have to do them because you're the only one with anything like the right kind of tool."

"A tool without an owner's manual. Remember Mike Bellingham who played with a gun and shot his dog? What if I pulled out that thread and 'shot' my dad? Then what?"

Taylor shrank back.

Gage walked toward the house. She followed without protest.

"I'm sorry," he murmured. "I'm frustrated, and you're

trying to help. I just wish I could have a test run. Or a reset button for when I mess it up and make things worse."

"The rosebush was your test run." Taylor hummed. "The thread enacts the will of God. How could it make things worse?"

Gage shuddered. "The visitor said it might."

Taylor dropped her backpack on the floor by the doorway. Gage had instinctually lowered the volume of his voice as they entered the house, so Dad hadn't caught the last thing he said, and she matched him, quiet for quiet. "Everyone has something they'd like to forget."

"I'm not going to experiment on you," Gage said.

They set up shop at the kitchen table, and they attacked their homework assignments along with apples and soda and a bag of tortilla chips. Taylor explained the math lesson Gage had missed, and afterward they both read their history chapter and worked on the essay question. They ignored the phone, which sang out at regular intervals and which Dad picked up from his office downstairs. By five, Gage had caught up on homework, and Taylor was reading the novel they'd been assigned for English.

Jeff had joined them with a notebook and pencil to sketch a narrow semi-detached house. Then he sharpened his pencil to an armor-piercing point and poked holes in the paper.

"Don't do that," Gage said. "It's better than anything I could draw," but Jeff continued until the page was a series of punctures.

Dad emerged from his office and asked Taylor to stay for dinner, possibly thinking her presence would relax Jeff. Dad wasn't a chef like Mrs. Greymore; dinner came out of a box, just add water. Taylor was thrilled. In fact, halfway through the meal she thanked Gage's father because she felt like a "real American."

"How so?" said Dad.

"Real Americans eat things that come out of boxes," Gage

said with a smile.

"Or bottles." Taylor had a calculated smile. "I think cool things come that way."

Gage felt his inner antennae go up. Dad chuckled. "I appreciate your enthusiasm, but this isn't a cool dinner."

"You know what I mean, Pastor Jordan." She didn't give him a chance to protest that he didn't. "All the coolest stuff comes that way, like Coke and chocolate sauce."

Gage wasn't sure if he should call Taylor's bluff. "Boring stuff comes in bottles, too. Ketchup."

She shrugged. "How about a genie in a bottle? I'd take three wishes any day!"

Dad looked grim. "I thought you read 'The Monkey's Paw' in fifth grade. I distinctly remember asking your teacher to find a different story, but I guess that was a waste of time since you didn't take any of the message away from it after all."

Taylor frowned. "Stories aren't real."

Dad said, "Fiction has to be even more real because it's telling universal truths. In both cases you have magic, three wishes, and people getting what they asked for in the worst possible way."

Taylor wore a thoughtful look. "Does it have to be bad? What if the genie—or would it be jinn?—actually wanted to help?"

Gage's sidelong glance caught a very interested Jeff, but Dad was beyond tense when she said the word "jinn." Gage said, "Come on. Why would a genie want to help us? We're just people. What kind of things could we have that they'd want?"

"Jewels?" Taylor shrugged. "Treasure? There must be something, or why would the legends have us interacting?"

Dad flattened his tone. "Jinn, or genies, don't exist."

Taylor looked so breezy that Mrs. Greymore would have known in three seconds she was up to mischief. "But if those stories were true, what kind of treasure would a jinn want?"

Gage said, "What would a jinn remember for a generation when they can't even remember you're standing in front of them?" When Dad looked really startled, Gage sputtered, "In the stories, they never figured that out."

"You're reading the wrong stories." Dad wore darkness across his eyes. "I'd like to change the subject, please."

There was only the sound of Jeff's fork against the plate. Gage said, "What color was Mom's rosebush?"

Dad laughed. "When I ask you to change the subject, you really do change the subject. It was yellow."

Gage snickered, then caught Jeff looking right at him with a curious expression.

⸺◦⸺

After Gage and Dad finished cleaning the kitchen, Dad drove Taylor home. Gage remained so Jeff wouldn't be alone, but he might as well not have bothered. Jeff sat on the couch, buried in Grooz Capture. In his own room, Gage played his guitar.

When Jeff entered Gage's room holding an empty bowl, Gage never stopped doing scales. Jeff set the bowl on the desk, then poked through Gage's desk drawer and under his bed, then into the bottom of Gage's closet, depositing things into the bowl with periodic clinks.

When Jeff left, Gage looked in the bowl to find...treasure?

A metal admission tag from a third-grade class trip to the museum. A rusted whistle on a green string. One of Taylor's red plastic-ball hairbands—how had that even gotten in here? A push-pin. Five cat's-eye marbles, one of them a shooter.

Treasure?

Before going to bed, Gage set the bowl on the front steps. First thing in the morning, he checked again. Except for a light crust of frost, the bowl stood empty.

Jeff continued his long quiet, the vow of silence he'd had no opportunity to refuse. Dad arranged to take him to a psychiatrist because the lawyers expected it. Gage suspected that Dad felt the same as he, that Jeff would talk if he could, or at least cry or sigh. It wasn't just selective mutism: Jeff wasn't communicating nonverbally, wasn't writing, wasn't gesturing.

Gage tagged along when Dad brought Jeff to the psychiatrist. In the back seat, Gage stared at the trees overhanging the road. This therapist worked on the outskirts of Burlington in a development that tried to mingle strip malls and stick-frame housing. You could get a gallon of milk without riding in the car, but there were no corner grocery stores.

Dr. Dasson's waiting room consisted of two couches and two chairs, plus a table with magazines. Gage poked over those while Jeff marched to a seat and planted himself there. Dad paced, but Gage only pulled out his handheld game and took up residence on the other seat.

"I'll be with you in a minute." Dr. Dasson came though the room briefly, using the restroom off to the side, unlocking a filing cabinet and looking in it, then heading back into her office. That was the whole facility: her office, the waiting room, the bathroom, and the closet with the filing cabinet. How good could she possibly be? He was all for using Christian doctors and therapists, but they should be at least remotely competent.

"Jeff, go inside. I'll be with you soon." Dr. Dasson ushered Jeff into the other room. Gage couldn't see inside except a glimpse of her desk. She kept it neat. As soon as Jeff turned the corner, she guided Dad to the side and asked a few questions. Gage couldn't hear either. Shortly she and Jeff closed the office door to remain there for the rest of the session.

Dad said, "They'll be in there for forty-five minutes. Come with me."

Gage had gotten good at manipulating his game without pause even while walking to the car and buckling his seatbelt, and he was lucky that focusing on close objects never made him carsick. He didn't look up until Dad stopped the car.

Uncle Zack's house.

It was a narrow semi-detached townhome in a subdivision with curving streets. No chimneys here, and no fences. They'd entered a land where the HOA board decided if you were allowed to plant a bush or take an axe to your rotting tree.

For a moment, Gage imagined a respectable gentleman convening an HOA board meeting to tackle the request of the Rivers family to summon demons in their basement. Oh, and for the next agenda item, the Millers wanted a koi pond.

A police detective got out of a cruiser as they approached. Gage slipped his game into his jacket pocket, then shook hands with the detective. The detective cut the yellow tape across the door (*Pardon me, officer, but this shade of yellow crime scene tape is not approved by the HOA board...*) then peeled down the tape on the doorjamb to usher them inside.

As Gage's foot touched the carpet, chills shot through the length of his body. He stopped in the entrance, eyes wide, breaths rapid.

Dad and the detective kept walking, oblivious. Gage felt numb, paralyzed. *Dad, get out of here—get out—*

He couldn't scream. Invisible hands clutched his throat, squeezing out the air, crushing his voice box. As his lips tingled, his vision grew pixilated like a digital image expanded to a thousand times its right size, and then everything turned to blackness. Gage staggered backward—

—and as his foot hit the ground outside the front door, his sight cleared up, his balance returned, and the whistling stopped in his ears.

"Dad?" he called. His voice was shrill. "Dad?"

Dad turned back from the kitchen. "You okay?"

Dad wasn't being asphyxiated, acting nauseated or getting devoured. Trembling, Gage tried to steady his voice. "Are you sure we should be in there?"

Gage raised a hand to the door frame, then drew closer. The hairs on his neck arose, and goosebumps traveled to his shoulders from fingertips gone suddenly numb.

As far as Gage was concerned, that was as good as a neon sign flashing, *"Don't go in there."*

Dad looked sad, but otherwise undisturbed. "If you're feeling uneasy, you can stay outside."

What on earth had Uncle Zachary done to this place? Whatever he had started wasn't over, even beyond what had been done to Jeff. What had they promised, and what debt remained to be paid? Why could Gage sense the residue when Dad, a pastor, obviously couldn't? Dad would never have brought him here if he'd thought Gage would end up compromised by an evil presence.

A third time Gage moved toward the house, and a third time, the pins and needles returned. He rushed back to Dad's car.

Dad had been here just after it happened. Shouldn't that presence, that wrongness, have been strongest then? Or did evil ferment like hard liquor?

In the back seat Gage slumped so he rested on his back, head jack-knifed up and his knees resting on the seat in front of him so his feet dangled.

The jinn's presence hadn't consumed him like this. The visitor in the back yard had left no impression on Gage's body-sense whatsoever. This felt more...more instinctual. Gage imagined a rabbit scenting the wind. Maybe a rabbit couldn't know what she smelled was a coyote, but she reacted with fear, with adrenaline, with puffed-up fur. This was the same. God must have equipped human souls with the ability to "scent" evil. Sometimes. The blatant kind.

God, help me. Gage wrapped his cold fingers around one another but didn't reach for his gloves. *What did Uncle Zack do? What's happening to us?*

Dad and the detective returned, bolting the front door and replacing the caution tape. Dad carried a bulging duffle bag, and the detective walked with Jeff's backpack slung over one shoulder. Dad tossed both into the trunk, saying, "Have you got results yet from the autopsy?"

Dad must not realize Gage could hear through the open trunk.

"A preliminary report, but the medical examiner asked for a second opinion."

Dad sounded startled. "Why would he need that?"

"Yeah, the guys in homicide wondered that, too." The detective huffed. "The early report is inconclusive. There wasn't a mark on the outside of him, but his internal organs were a mass of crush injuries."

Gage fought nausea.

"Broken bones?"

"The bones were fine. But his spleen was crushed, his kidneys, his stomach—internals like you'd expect from a motorcycle crash. The examiner wanted his results double-checked before he filed a final report."

Dad dropped the trunk lid. If the detective continued talking, Gage could no longer hear it.

Crushed. Crushed from the inside out.

After another few minutes, the front door popped open, and Dad settled into the driver's seat. "Weren't you cold out here?"

Gage hadn't felt a thing. Could fear do that to you? "I was fine. What happened in the house?"

"I wanted to get some of Jeff's things."

"Did you sense anything strange?" He didn't know how to

ask. "You didn't get an odd feeling?"

"A bit." From the way Dad started the car without elaborating, Gage knew he hadn't felt a thing beyond the awareness of a tragedy. "A bit" didn't describe being in the sight of a preternatural sniper rifle, numb and unable to breathe on your slide toward unconsciousness.

On the way back to Dr. Dasson's office, Dad listened to Duke Ellington. Light snow was falling, swirling and spreading and dancing over the blacktop like the caps of ocean waves. The wind of the car's passage blew them apart, and then the wind of the weather herded them together again.

They returned to Dr. Dasson before Jeff's session ended. Dad tried to ask Gage about his schoolwork, but then he had to take a call, and Gage continued his game. The carnival music filled the room.

Would Jeff talk to the therapist? Could he? Was she working a magic of her own in there, navigating the labyrinth of Jeff's mind with little more than one smoldering torch held high?

What made a therapist particularly Christian, as opposed to a Christian who gave therapy? Could you specialize the product that way? Dad said magic was bad whether a Christian did it or a pagan or a Satanist. If psychotherapy was good, shouldn't the same standard hold? Since the idea was that magic would corrupt your soul no matter your motives or your faith, good therapy should benefit the mind no matter the therapist. When they went to McDonalds, Dad didn't ask if the guy at the grill was a Christian. Hamburger's hamburger. Fries didn't harden your arteries any less if you prayed while they sat in the deep fryer.

So that thread—could it be used the same way, as a tool or a skill?

Then again, some things really were better done by certain people than by others. Married people could do things unmarried people shouldn't. Some Christians didn't mind when the state killed someone for killing someone else because killing was wrong. Taylor's mom had no problem with spanking the five-year-old for hitting the three-year-old.

Even the angel had indicated the thread could be used in the right way. Don't *play* with it.

Gage came to himself abruptly when a hand closed over the screen of his game.

"It's like you're on another planet," Dad said. "Come on. We're going."

Jeff had emerged from Dr. Dasson's office, his face a mask. He'd already put on his jacket, and he held several papers and a booklet. Gage said, "When did you come out?"

"About five minutes ago," said Dr. Dasson. "You were so engrossed, I thought you'd never notice us."

Gage shut off the unit. "Sorry."

"Don't be. Everyone needs to be able to do something that stops time." Dr. Dasson smiled broadly. "That's what makes life worth living."

Dad frowned. "I wouldn't go that far."

"I would." The doctor gave Gage a wink. "Not that video games replace a relationship with God, but what you're doing when you get into your game is a gift. It's a state of mind called 'flow.'" When Gage squinted at her she shrugged. "I know you think I'm the bonkers doctor-lady, but the mental escape of flow gives us the energy to go on with life. Some people get it exercising, praying, painting, singing... But God gives each of us a skill that when we exercise it to the best of our ability, time stops."

"So for me it's the game?"

"It's not the *only* way, but yes. You enjoy it enough that you tune out the world and recharge."

Gage smiled at her. "That's neat."

She turned to Jeff. "See you next week, buddy."

In the car, Jeff kept the stack of papers face-down on his lap, but Gage could make out a few words on the back of the green booklet. Trauma. Stress. Fear. Flashbacks. Jeff wasn't looking at them, only staring out the window while rubbing the heel of one hand with the thumb of the other.

Wow, God. It must have hurt so much to see his dad get killed, to see it and not be able to respond, not be able to stop it. Worse, to know you yourself were the indirect cause, or maybe even a participant.

Gage said, "Can I see the booklet?"

Without expression, Jeff handed it over. Standard stuff. Green cover, white print. *Kids and Trauma. Grief and the Teenager.* Inside the pages were the freehand drawings he'd come to expect in a supportive pamphlet, lots of curves, kids and adults interacting in "typical" situations that never really happened.

As Gage handed them back, he caught a glimpse of the other papers. Jeff and Dr. Dasson had been drawing. Unlike Gage, Jeff had always had a talent for making pictures, and now Gage felt his throat tighten.

Jeff had covered the papers in bold lines that made no sense. He'd drawn streaks of red against a black background, layered on so thick that the crayon shone in spots. Darting through these were slim needles of grey, pressed in so hard they gleamed silver. All in the same direction, as if swept by the wind.

"What's that?" Gage said, but Jeff snatched back his booklet and stacked it on top of his drawing, then turned everything face-down on his lap.

CHAPTER FIVE

That night, Gage showed Jeff more treasure: a rectangular pink eraser, a tea-light candle, five plastic-covered paper clips in bright colors, and a roller skate key. Jeff walked away, but later he returned and handed Gage a needle. Gage put the loot in the bowl and left it outside, but before bed he kept thinking about it. He checked the bowl and found it already empty.

Thrilled, he ransacked his room for more junk. Maybe the jinn were skulking around the house under cover of dusk. If he left something else, he might convince them to return tonight.

Gage put on his coat and snuck outside with one of his die-cast metal cars and two guitar picks. He placed them in the bowl and sat perfectly still.

Shortly, he felt the same prickly sense of intrusion and welcome that had awakened him the first time. On the night of the rosebush, the angel—or demon—had come unawares on his spirit, but not these preternatural creatures. For them, the land welcomed them even as human establishment resisted their presence.

They returned as a pair, Mir followed by Mek. Mir wore the metal museum tag as a hair clip, and Mek wore the whistle as a necklace.

Gage waited with the bowl of treasure between his feet. Mir studied him momentarily, then edged closer. Mek stayed by the brush.

"You see us?" Mir whispered.

"I saw you before." Gage hoped his smile reassured them. "You gave me part of your Will-of-God thread."

Mir looked puzzled. "Really? When did we find one of those?"

Mek edged closer. "I think it's here. See?" Tiny fingers strayed to the rope-belt. "You should have one too."

"In your hair." Gage forced himself to take a deep breath. Mir's fingers moved into the morass of blond hair and tugged it free. The pair smiled at the shimmering thread, and Gage tried to get their attention again. "You said the thread was very powerful."

Both jinn nodded.

"If it's that powerful, what do you use it for?"

They watched blankly.

A sudden heaviness sank in Gage's stomach. "You don't know?" Perhaps a different approach would work. "You said demons were on the move."

The pair shrank toward each other, and Mek wove slender fingers like a basket. "Maybe they were. But we have the thread, so they leave us alone."

The nighttime figure had said the jinn wouldn't hurt anyone intentionally, but that they were mischief-makers. It must be an accidental sort of mischief, the kind that comes from not paying attention. "Demons don't avoid you just because you have the thread. There's something you need to do with it. What do you do?"

Mir looked suddenly worried. Gage tried to keep the frustration out of his voice so the jinn wouldn't bolt for cover. In a lower tone, he repeated, "What did you do with the thread?"

Mek said, "It came up out of the ground, right? It makes the earth happy. The demons stay away."

If this was all the jinn could do, Mek and Mir had no reason to fear the demons. Why would demons attack something so ridiculous? The jinn might dig up the thread, knowing its power, and then attribute their safety to the thread rather than to being beneath notice.

Gage said, "Who told you about the threads?"

Both jinn shrugged.

Abruptly Gage remembered what the nighttime stranger had said: *Leave it for the jinn as treasure. They'll remember you forever.*

Probably not what the angel intended, but it might work. "Who else used to leave you treasure?"

Both jinn brightened. "On her front porch!" Mir blurted out, even as Mek said, "She had a dog, and she could see us!"

Quite the difference. If that person still lived in the area, maybe Gage could find her, and she would know how to use the thread. "Do you remember her name?"

"Water," said Mek. "She moved like water."

Mir said, "Stream or River or something like that. Sunlight glinting."

Gage squinted. "Rivers?"

Names mustn't matter to jinn. Whoever it was, they remembered this person as an entity with a name as a useless attachment, like knowing the month of her birth. In their minds' eyes, they could recreate this person's soul and never once care what series of syllables other people attached to that persona.

Mir was jumping in place. "Rivers full of life! Rivers of

trout, something you can't stop, rushing downhill and then merging with other rivers...so much fun! She left us feathers and pretty rocks. And we gave her that thing, too."

"What thing?"

Mek and Gage said it at the same time. Hands clasped, Mir stared at the moon. "You remember. She said she'd keep it. She said it was treasure from us." Abruptly Mir fumbled with the belt-pack. "Isn't this something from the water-girl?"

Mir pulled out a small pile of treasure, much of which must have come from the roadside. Pine-cones, small sticks, Gage's old die-cast car, some pennies, and a pull-tab from a can of soda. How much could one bag hold? Mek stared in amazement at all the wonders emerging from the pouch. Gage sighed. The piece Mir finally settled on was a metal barrette, three inches long and rusted in spots.

Why did I think they'd help? Gage wanted to believe the jinn would have helped if they could. Keeping information in their heads wasn't their nature: wandering and collecting was. "Could I use the thread to break a spell?"

The jinn paused in the act of stuffing all the treasure back in Mir's bag.

Gage said slowly, "I know someone cursed by demons. Could the thread set him free?"

Mir's eyes brightened. "Jesus can set him free."

Mek nodded. "You have to ask Jesus."

This wasn't working. The words stuck in Gage's throat, but he improvised. "I asked Jesus. Jesus wants me to do it myself."

Mek's nose wrinkled. "Weird."

"I think the thread is the way to do it. That's why you were sent to me."

Mek stood straighter. "God did that?"

Mir's eyes shimmered. "God sent us to you?" The jinn bounced in place again. "That's wonderful! God used us! God used us!"

Mek said, "You should use it."

"How?"

Mek beamed. "If God sent us, then God will send someone else to tell you more things. That's how it goes."

Mir stuffed the rest of the treasure, including the thread, back into the belt-pack. "I want to tell the birds!"

Mek brightened. "Me, too! Hey, wait!" Mir had already run through the brush, and Mek took off in pursuit.

Gage slumped forward. With any luck they were right, and God would send someone in the morning.

Rivers, Gage thought as he lay in bed.

Jeff's last name was Rivers. The water-girl might have been Jeff's mother. She might, for that matter, have been Gage's own mother, except while Aunt Jenna might have been mixed up in this demon-stuff, Mom had been a Christian, not a cultist. Although...

How had Dad known what Uncle Zack was doing would kill him? Dad must have some kind of experience he wasn't talking about. That's why he was so vehement that Gage shouldn't even read books with jinn. This situation had hurt too many family members already.

Aunt Jenna had died right after Jeff's birth. Gage remembered her condition had a long name that made it sound like an explosion. Jeff himself had been very sick and stayed in the hospital several weeks. Gage wasn't even born when it happened. A few years later, Mom died in a car accident. They were both normal deaths, nothing like an eldritch entity emerging from a yellowed tome. Nothing to put fear in Dad's voice.

Whatever Dad wasn't sharing, it might save Jeff. Mom and Aunt Jenna couldn't help. Uncle Zack couldn't help. That left only one family member who might understand, and him

Gage had been forbidden to contact.

Not exactly forbidden. Dad never said it in so many words. Dad just assumed that if he cut ties with Grandpa, Gage would have no option but to do the same. But really, after luring jinn to the house with bowls of goodies, why not break the rules big-time and track down his grandfather?

─────◦─────

Chapter Six

─────◦─────

Breaking one rule would require breaking several.

After a fitful sleep, Gage pulled himself out of bed and whispered a plan to Jeff. Next he prepared for school. Dad seemed concerned that Gage wasn't ready to go back, but Gage claimed he shouldn't get too far behind. Although Taylor could share her notes with him, that wasn't the same as listening to the teacher's explanations. Dad finally agreed.

Before the bus came, Jeff appeared in the kitchen dressed and wearing his backpack.

Dad said, "I don't think you should go."

Jeff didn't put down his backpack.

Gage said, "Maybe it would take his mind off of things."

Dad frowned. "You're not ready."

Gage said, "If I go to school and he doesn't, he'll be alone in the house all day."

Gage had meant to be just as ambiguous as he sounded

when he used that tone of voice. If Dad was afraid Uncle Zack had summoned demons, he might be afraid Jeff would summon them himself. After all, if Taylor and Gage could discern the presence of a spell from Jeff's behavior, certainly Dad as a minister would.

Dad finally shook his head. "I'd rather he remain home alone. The church isn't so far that I can't drop by from time to time."

Gage noticed the way Dad didn't mention using the phone, either speaking or texting.

Right before the bus came, Gage texted Taylor and asked her to bike to school that morning. Then Gage got on the bus while Dad warmed up his car. Jeff watched from the window.

At the school, Gage met Taylor and took her bike. "Thanks. Even if it's a girl's bike."

Taylor rolled her eyes. "I want it back in one piece." She looked around at the other students congregating around the main entrance. "What's up?"

Gage stared at his feet. "I don't want to involve you any more than I have to."

"You're involving my bike." Taylor closed her eyes. "Okay, have it your way. Just be careful. You're scaring me."

"I already said you're supposed to be scared." Gage swallowed. "Remember when David wanted to cover up what he did to Bathsheba? David disobeyed God and had Uriah killed. But in order for David to disobey, everyone beneath him had to disobey too. Joab the general had to do things differently than David ordered. And then the messenger Joab sent didn't even deliver the message the way he was supposed to."

Taylor snorted. "You lost me about five 'disobeys' ago. Quit being the preacher's kid and just talk normally."

"This keeps snowballing. We're cutting school. Well, I'm cutting. Jeff's not supposed to be here anyhow." Jeff had just now neared the school on Gage's bike. "Everyone will think

I'm still out because of my uncle." Gage mounted Taylor's bike. "Wish me luck."

"Where are you going?"

Gage forced a grin back toward Taylor as he biked into the street. "Away."

Jeff and Gage biked to the closest bus stop and rode to downtown Burlington. There weren't many other passengers, so no one complained about bikes in the aisle. At the station, they dumped Gage's school books in a locker, then bought more bus tickets to Rutland and wandered the stores until departure time. Gage bought a video game magazine, but once they were on the bus he didn't read it, only linked his game of Grooz Capture to Jeff's so they could hunt together on the trip. Distracted and worried, Gage couldn't immerse himself in the game, and Jeff sent no messages, not even the ones customary in a two-player game.

Like most Vermont vehicles by late February, the bus was covered in salt, sand, and dirt. Greenish light filtered into the windows while telephone wires moved up and down like a sine curve. The fields, which should be brilliant with snow, looked only grey. *Like my soul,* Gage thought. *I wonder how much light's getting in there, and how much the salt is distorting the brightness I see outside.*

In Rutland, they retrieved their bikes from storage beneath the bus. With Jeff in the lead, they biked over the bumpy, curving roads.

"You do know where you're going, don't you?" Gage called to the figure ahead of him. Jeff maintained that difficult pace until the roads turned to dirt and gravel. Shortly afterward, he stopped before a square New Englander, then walked his bike up a driveway of packed snow. As the deer longs for running streams, so this house yearned for a gallon of paint.

While Taylor's house had grown in incoherent spurts, this house seemed to have been planted exactly as it stood. No bump-outs, no ells, no raised roof, just the ubiquitous square foundation and double windows on either side of the front door. A chimney stood from the center of the building like a needle in a pincushion. The only addition seemed to be a carport where Gage would have expected a garage, and it sheltered the green Land Rover.

Jeff stopped at the front door without ringing the bell. Was even pushing a button forbidden? Gage did it instead.

A minute later, the door opened, and Jeff wrapped around their grandfather, eyes closed, breath hard. Grandpa held him tight, so tight.

Then Grandpa put a hand on Gage's head, too. Firm. Strong. Almost like a blessing, except Gage didn't know if Grandpa gave those.

The sweet scent of burning wood hung in the air briefly before suffusing Gage's body. Birch? Ash? It was the same perfume he'd come to associate with wintertime at Taylor's house.

Grandpa looked past the boys to the driveway. "You two got here alone?"

Gage said, "Dad doesn't know." It was about eleven o'clock. "We need your help."

Grandpa brought them inside. Looking about to cry, Jeff drank in his surroundings, staring at all the furniture and decorations, even the carpet, as though he'd never see them again. Gage touched Jeff's shoulder, then sat on the opposite end of the couch.

Their grandfather went into the kitchen. "I'll put on the kettle so you boys can have some hot chocolate. I know Jeff likes his without marshmallows. You can add what you like, Gage."

The furnishings and one window were recognizable from photographs of his mother. She and Uncle Zack had grown up in this house, quite possibly had walked on this carpet and sat on this lumpy couch. Were there bedrooms in back maintained just as they'd been when she grew up, shrines to memory? Or had Grandpa turned them into storage, Gage's mother's childhood bed buried behind boxes of books, an end table he meant to get around to fixing, and empty plant containers?

On his return, Grandpa took a seat in the upholstered chair facing the couch. "What's happening?"

Gage swallowed. "I'm not sure if it's safe to talk, with everything going on."

Grandpa Rivers said, "You're so young for this to happen. Sometimes I wonder if God's love isn't a curse."

Gage's eyes bugged.

Grandpa raised himself from the chair and took careful steps to the bookshelf to retrieve his Bible. An orange and white cat meandered into the room and curled up in the warm spot of the seat Grandpa Rivers had just vacated, only to get forced out when Grandpa returned. Gage noted his grandfather's trim grey hair, the neat appearance of his clothing, and the care he'd taken to look well-groomed even though he hadn't suspected anyone would visit. Nothing he wore was extravagant, including his watch and his plain gold wedding band.

Grandpa opened the Bible to one of the bookmarked pages, and he read carefully, "*Again I say to you, if two of you agree on earth about anything they ask, it will be done for them by my Father in heaven. For where two or three are gathered in my name, there am I among them.*" He paused, and Gage prepared to pray as well, but his grandfather continued. "Lord Jesus Christ, Son of God, defend us in battle. Be our protection against the wickedness and snares of the devil. O God, rebuke them, we humbly pray, and do thou, Creator of the heavenly host, by your own divine power, cast into Hell Satan and all the evil spirits who prowl throughout the world seeking the ruination of souls."

Wide-eyed, Gage said, "Amen."

Grandpa left the book open on his lap. "Now, son, talk

freely."

Gage looked at Jeff. "Is it safe?"

Jeff didn't respond.

Grandpa said, "If Jesus says it's safe, who am I to say it's not safe?"

Gage frowned. "Jeff doesn't think it is, if he's still afraid to talk."

Grandpa snorted. "He's not afraid to talk. The poor boy *can't* talk. They've put a geas on him—a spell."

Gage looked uneasily at Jeff. "How do we break a—a geas?"

Grandpa took a deep breath. "I've been praying over it, but God hasn't given me an answer." He turned back his Bible one page and read, *"Lord, have mercy on my son, for he has seizures and he suffers terribly. For often he falls into the fire, and often into the water. And I brought him to your disciples, and they could not heal him."* Grandpa shook his head. "You know the rest."

Gage said, "Jesus says the disciples couldn't cast out the demon because of their unbelief." He opened his hands. "How much faith is the size of a mustard seed?"

Taylor would have added, "And how do you measure faith? Is it size, weight, volume...?" She'd have been asking all the right questions and then slipping the details into all the right slots of the puzzle. Instead, Gage just had her bike and his muted cousin.

"This kind of exorcism isn't about faith alone, no matter what your father told you. Jesus gave us a road map." Grandpa Rivers said, *"But this kind never comes out except by prayer and fasting."*

Gage gasped.

"It's interesting, demonology. Too interesting. Some Bibles omit that line. Maybe they thought it was too dangerous."

Gage said, "Is Jeff possessed?"

Grandpa looked squarely at Jeff, who never flinched. "Invite a demon inside, and sometimes it moves in. If you don't exorcise it right, it'll come straight back and invite a few of its friends along. Our Lord said no less." Grandpa sighed. "Son, whatever else is to blame, you've got a mute spirit."

Gage said, "Have you ever heard of a Will-of-God thread?"

Grandpa's eyes widened. "Your father told you about that?"

"A pair of jinn gave me one, the same night Uncle Zack died." Gage winced even as he said it because it might remind Grandpa that Uncle Zack had died, but Grandpa only nodded. "The jinn couldn't tell me how to use it. I want to try, but I'm scared."

"If you've got it, then God wants you to use it."

Gage sat back a little, involuntarily thinking of a half dozen things humanity had acquired that God probably didn't want people to use—the atomic bomb, for starters, or crystal meth.

All this time Jeff had been turning his head toward each one as he spoke. Now, though, he turned his eyes toward Gage and didn't take them off.

Gage said, "I tried to use it on Mom's rosebush, the one that won't bloom any longer."

Grandpa prompted, "And—? Did it work?"

"Somewhat. Something came to me and told me the thread was too powerful to play with. It said I might lose my soul if I did it wrong. Or Jeff's."

"Jeff wouldn't lose his soul because of something you did. Only something he did could hurt him in God's eyes." Grandpa lowered his gaze. "Your soul...? That's yours to lose. I guess you're not sure if it was an angel or a demon. Obviously it said it was an angel."

Gage chuckled. "It certainly wasn't the same as the jinn."

"Jinn are completely different." Grandpa cocked his head. "They're like animals, only they don't have animal bodies. They're smarter than animals but not as clever as they think they are. Their souls are innocent, like a cat's soul. It's not that they've been tested and passed, but rather that they're not put to the test in the first place. Jinn aren't good or evil.

They're just themselves."

Gage straightened. "So it's okay to talk to them?"

"Of course, but you'll never get a clear answer." Grandpa sat forward. "Is the thread in a safe place?"

"I guess."

Grandpa Rivers scowled. "Maybe you ought to do better than that."

Gage's stomach tightened. "Have you got a demon-proof safe?"

"Take it easy. I want to make sure it doesn't go missing."

"I didn't leave it lying on the carpet." Gage looked over at Jeff, who remained impassive. He'd have felt better if Jeff's eyes had shown even a twinkle of amusement. "The whole reason we came was I thought you could tell me what to do with the thing. I don't want to use it wrong and find out the whole world's going to end."

Grandpa Rivers chuckled. "If it's God's will that the world ends, who cares what tool He uses? One force is as good as another in His hands."

"Judas was an instrument of God's, but it would be better for him if he'd never been born. We need to do something for Jeff. Quickly."

"Not too quickly. You're right that he'll need it done *correctly*—perfect on the first try." Grandpa Rivers might have caught a sudden terror on Jeff's face. "Yes, Jeff, they might try to harm you bodily, throw you into a fire or give you convulsions. You haven't had any problems yet, have you?" Grandpa made a face. "That's dumb to ask. You can't answer." He moved over to Jeff and started examining him, raising his shirt-sleeves and looking at his arms, then at his stomach and chest and his back. "You look intact. They're not sporting with you." Grandpa returned to his chair. "I wish I knew what they promised your father."

"They promised to protect Jeff." Gage swallowed. "That's what Dad said. I think Uncle Zack wanted me there too, to protect me. Dad said it wouldn't work."

Grandpa sighed. "Stupid, stupid... Of course it didn't work, and he lost everything trying to make it work."

Gage said, "Why did Uncle Zack think he needed to protect us?"

Grandpa shook his head. "If I tell you this story, your father will send a mob after me."

Gage clenched his fists. "Don't you think I need to know? If something is galloping around Vermont killing my family members, shouldn't I at least know why?"

Jeff shifted on the couch so he was nearer Gage's seat. Gage didn't even look at him. "I can see jinn. Do you think that's normal? I had an angel or a demon come to me—I can't tell which—and it told me my soul was in jeopardy if I did the only thing I can to free Jeff, and now you're holding out on the truth?"

Grandpa looked aside. "Your father isn't sure it will help."

"But he's sure I'm in danger. When Uncle Zack said he wanted to protect me, Dad said it wouldn't work, not that I didn't need it."

Grandpa sat back, folding his tough hands. "I won't interfere with the way he's raising you. He thinks he can pray you into safety. Maybe he can."

"Prayer didn't save Mom, did it?"

Grandpa looked stung. "Son, are you saying these forces are more powerful than God Almighty?"

Gage grabbed his coat. "Forget it. Dad's right about you. You're more dangerous than Uncle Zack."

Grandpa sighed. "I have to go by your father's wishes."

Gage stalked to the door.

"Do you want your hot chocolate?"

"No, thanks. I'm supposed to fast this thing away, remember?"

Grandpa shook his head. "Don't be like your dad."

Not replying, Gage pulled on his coat.

Jeff stood, then stopped.

"I know. You can't ask for it." Grandpa closed the distance between himself and Jeff and treated him to a long bear-hug. Jeff melted in the old man's embrace. "But you're still my grandsons, and I'm doing everything I can to help you."

● ━━━━━◆━━━━━ ●

CHAPTER SEVEN

● ━━━━━◆━━━━━ ●

What   stank was that Gage would get in trouble for today without having learned anything.

He and Jeff made it back to school by two. Gage hoped Dad hadn't come home to an empty house or gotten a call from the school. Dad would look disappointed after he finished looking angry. Of course, he might look angry for a long time. But eventually that let-down glimmer would flicker across his eyes, and this would put the final punctuation mark on the lecture. Dad wanted to protect Gage. Dad wanted to believe the best about him.

It's not as if I'm working magic myself, Gage thought. On the other hand, if he was summoning jinn, even if only by leaving junk in a bowl, wasn't that close to the real thing?

Still, Grandpa's admonition worried him. Gage checked his guitar case to make sure the thread remained where he'd left it, an innocuous-looking coiled wire. Once he had the guitar in his hands, he settled on his bed and warmed up with some scales. Without thinking about it, he started strumming "Now the Green Blade Rises," then switched at the end to "More Precious Than Silver," one of the hymns they opened with at the church youth group. Was youth group really tonight already? He ought to go. Dad would ground Gage for life, of course, but maybe Dad might think exposure to decent kids would help straighten out his own son. Or he might think Gage would corrupt them. It could go either way.

Gage let his hands strum the guitar, but he turned his heart toward God. *I'm afraid Jeff's suffering. I don't know what he did, but I know you can forgive it. I'm sorry I cut school today. I'm sorry I saw Grandpa without permission.*

Even as he prayed that, though, he knew he wasn't sorry to have seen his grandfather. He was only upset that he'd had to defy Dad to do it, and further upset that it hadn't given him any useful information. It felt good to hear Grandpa's voice, see his face, and inhale the scent of his house. He was part of Gage's history, and until now an unknown.

As Gage played, Dad stood in the doorway. Gage couldn't read his father's face as he said, "How was it today?"

Dad went to sit on the edge of the bed. Wondering if Dad could hear his heart pounding, Gage shifted the guitar so Dad would have more room. "I don't know what to tell you."

"Are you feeling okay?" Dad paused. "You don't look okay."

Gage stared at his lap. "My stomach is upset."

"You're under a lot of stress. Sometimes I think I treat you too much like a little adult." Dad took a deep breath. "You don't have to go to youth group tonight if you don't feel up to it."

"No, I can go." Dad didn't know he'd cut school after all. Gage lifted the neck of the guitar. "They need music."

"They can do without a guitar for one night. Maybe Brandon's parents will have let him have his back by now."

The youth group's other guitar player had gotten his hard-body electric guitar "seized" when his parents came home to find him playing a song so forbidden that Brandon wouldn't even reveal what it was. It was Brandon's private opinion that Jesus would have to give it back at the Second Coming.

Seeing the expression on Gage's face, Dad chuckled. "Well, maybe not. But someone will have music on their phone."

"Jeff might come if I go." Gage shook his head. "He's not ready yet for school, sure, but it might help to be around lots of other kids. Especially if he doesn't have to join."

Dad nodded. "I was thinking it was important to share the Word with him, now that he's alone. What he's been through has got to leave him empty, and I know better than anyone how God rushes in like sea water to fill that space. After a while, Jeff might like to come to youth group. Now might be too early."

Gage said, "What if only God can heal him?"

"Then pray for it to happen." Dad rested his hand on top of Gage's on the guitar body. "When Jeff reaches out to God, God will have been waiting for a long time. Never forget that."

When Dad lifted his hand, Gage strummed a chord. "We can help it happen."

"We can also hinder it. Reaching out to a soul in need is crossing a tightrope. Fulton Sheen said we don't make converts—God does. It's too easy to pretend it all depends on us." Dad stood. "I have to be there tonight, but you don't. Think about it."

The more Gage thought, the more he felt called to attend. It wasn't just maybe seeing Taylor and getting a few minutes to tell her his deception had netted him nothing. He wanted to see everyone: Brandon and Sydney and Luke and Jessica... The house would be so quiet with only him and Jeff. Him and Jeff and who-knew-what-other-beings he couldn't see? The silence itself would roar at him until Dad returned. Gage wasn't certain he'd be able to sleep even with Dad in the house, thinking Jeff might actually be possessed.

When it came time to leave, Gage carried his guitar case to the car, and he was surprised to see Jeff waiting, too. Dad stopped behind Gage. "Are you sure you want to come?"

Jeff rested a hand on the car. Dad put the guitar in the trunk, then let both boys into the back seat. Gage's skin crawled. Looking sideways at Jeff, he wondered how it might feel to share a body with something that hated you.

In the church, Dad flipped on the lights and raised the thermostat while Gage set up his guitar and music stand. Youth group met in the basement, a large room with acoustic ceiling tiles, a scuffed floor, painted cinder-block walls, and very few distinguishing features. Every church group used it, but the vastness echoed when only a handful of people filled it, like now.

Jeff scraped the chairs into place once Dad showed him where they needed to be. Shortly the early-birds arrived, and then a line developed by the sign-in sheet. For whatever reason, Taylor didn't show. Dad stood nearby, reviewing his notes.

Brandon, the disgraced guitarist, came over during the chat time to ask how things were. Gage shrugged. The high E string kept wandering out of tune, but it ought to hold for the rest of the night.

Brandon pulled a chair closer. "Trouble tuning?"

"Yeah, but it ought to hold."

"So when do you think you'll be coming back to school?"

Gage said, "Uh...tomorrow. I'll be there tomorrow."

Brandon said, "There was a running bet at lunch today when you'd come back. If it's tomorrow, I'm going to win."

Gage offered a nervous laugh. "Glad to be of service."

A hand landed on Gage's shoulder.

The E string snapped with a ping, shuddering through the guitar even as Brandon jerked back from the waving steel string. Dad closed his hand around the neck of the guitar, bringing the string back in line with the others. "Gage, come with me for a minute."

"I need to restring—"

"That can wait."

Brandon took the guitar from him so he could go.

Gage's heart thrummed like an engine in high gear. He followed Dad into one of the storage rooms, then stood his ground as Dad faced him.

Dad looked shocked. "You skipped school today?"

Gage's voice was gone. He might as well have been Jeff.

"Was Jeff with you?" When Gage nodded, Dad took a deep breath. "I was wondering where he'd gotten off to. I knew he'd taken your bike." Dad's eyes narrowed, and then came the anger. "I told you that you could stay home if you wanted. If you wanted to come home, you could have called. But you didn't even go in?" And then, "Why did you lie to me?"

"I'm sorry." That was nowhere near enough. Dad was going to demand the whole story—he wouldn't stop until he had it. "Look, it was the first time, and you would have let me stay home, but then you'd have wanted me with you. I only wanted to help."

"You aren't making any sense. Where did you take Jeff?"

Gage swallowed. "Rutland. Dad, don't get mad."

Dad's hands were shaking, but remarkably, he kept his voice down. "You went to see your grandfather." He didn't wait for an answer. It hadn't been a question. "Jeff's in enough danger as it is. After saying you thought he needed God in his life, you're telling me you— Or did you know only God could heal Jeff because you found out that garden-variety black magic couldn't?"

"Grandpa prayed over him. It wasn't magic. The first thing he did was get out his Bible! I have to find out why these things are happening to our family, and you won't tell me. I want to know what happened to my Mom and Jeff's Mom."

Dad folded his arms. "Was your grandfather's version interesting enough that you failed to see how wrong it is?"

Ascending notes played in the background: Gage's guitar was being tuned. Instinctively he turned toward the sound, but the door blocked his view. "Grandpa refused to tell me anything because of you, but I know enough to realize something's happening. I want to fix things."

Dad started to fire back, then took a deep breath. "Get out of here. We'll talk after we get home."

Gage clenched his fists. "Can I still play for the group?"

"As long as you're not trying to work any sorcery." Dad didn't sound as if he were joking.

Gage's heart stabbed him, and he followed back to the hall, unable to raise his eyes.

Brandon was the one tuning his guitar. "Don't say thanks." He laughed. "I replaced the string and then I couldn't resist. I've been wanting to play anything at all for weeks now."

As Gage's fingers closed around the neck, he felt the God-thread, warm. He gasped.

The E-string shimmered like a steel string, but it was definitely the God-thread. Brandon had knotted the bottom where it ought to have had a steel circlet. The top end waved, a little too loose. Gage rested his fingertips on it, trembling.

This had to be a sacrilege. If God didn't strike him down, it was pure mercy.

Brandon stood. "I'll go find scissors."

"I'll take care of it." It was too late to restring the guitar. If he said the string wasn't right for the guitar, Brandon would wonder why Gage had kept it in his guitar case. Gage was wondering that himself. That and why Brandon had used a loose string rather than one of the ones in the envelopes. "Is it staying in tune?"

His voice was so strained, it almost sounded like a croak.

"Perfectly. It didn't even need to relax."

Gage plucked the string, and a high E filled the room.

He went to the supply room and pinched off the end of the thread, then returned with the leftover thread in his pocket.

Dad asked one of the girls to open in prayer. Gage lowered his head, and only then did his hands begin trembling.

The angel had said not to play with the thread. And what was Gage about to do with the guitar? Oh, right, play it.

Gage hoped God had a sense of humor. Otherwise, Gage would be in a worse place than Jeff.

Dad's voice had a peculiar tightness as he asked for the opening song. Gage quivered with his fingers on the neck of his instrument, and in his right hand, the pick felt awkward.

The first strum sounded normal enough. So did the second, and the third. By the time he got through the intro, Gage regained his confidence. Demons hadn't poured up through the basement to devour the Milton Community Bible Church junior youth group. The kids sang without recognizing anything was different. Even Dad, still stern, sang alongside the others.

Everyone except Jeff.

Where is he? Scanning the room, Gage couldn't see his cousin.

As the first verse continued, the guitar sounded richer. The longer Gage played, the more the wood acquired a deeper reverberation, a sweeter resonance. The guitar vibrated against his arm and his stomach, and it was the very wood of his guitar changing. Contact with the string had obliterated the flaws of machine craftsmanship and transformed it into a Stradivarius of acoustic guitars. A hand-made violin plays its best notes a hundred and fifty years after the craftsman's hands apply the final touches, after the wood has fully seasoned, and so the instrument acquires its truest resonance. Gage's guitar aged under his hands as the notes vibrated through it. Gage's throat ached. His eyes burned. He was in the presence of a miracle only he recognized.

By the time he reached the second chorus, Gage didn't dare take his eyes from the sheet music. With the guitar coming alive like a songbird, the song itself felt like a surging wind, poised to carry him away if his concentration lapsed.

The song reluctantly ended, as though it wanted to perpetuate itself and enhance the miracle on its own. With the guitar on his lap, Gage tried to breathe deep enough to steady himself. Dad had no idea. Would he make Gage take the thread off the guitar? Having achieved the pinnacle of its potential, would the guitar crumble into dust after the breath of God departed?

And good grief—Dad had said Gage could play as long as he wasn't working sorcery. Did an accidental miracle count? Had he disobeyed even while trying not to?

Jeff hadn't returned. As Dad passed out photocopied pages, Gage reluctantly set aside his guitar and made his way into the staircase to look for him.

Around a bend, Jeff huddled on a step, arms wrapped around his knees, gasping.

"What's wrong?" Gage rushed up, forgetting for a minute everything Grandpa Rivers had said about possession. "Do you need help?"

As Gage's right arm contacted him, Jeff shoved Gage away, knocking him down two steps before Gage caught himself on the banister. Jeff stared with eyes gone wild. He gripped his left arm as though burned.

The guitar had hurt him. The holy music had burned his ears. Gage's hands, in contact with the guitar, were painful to him.

Gage swallowed. "We're done playing songs. If you don't come back, Dad's going to want to know what happened."

Jeff looked like a forest animal with a flashlight trained on its face. "Please, come down," Gage urged. "Dad knows we went to Rutland. He's mad enough. We'll play one more song at the end, but I'll make sure you're out of the room first. I promise. But we've got to go back."

Gage extended his right hand, the one that had held the pick rather than the one that had contacted the thread.

Although Jeff didn't take it, he struggled to his feet. Back in the room, Dad had engaged the kids in a conversation about a typical school day. Gage sat with Jeff in the very back, his eyes returning to the guitar in its open case across the room.

It looked normal. Jeff looked normal. Gage supposed he looked normal, too, but he imagined how the scene must appear to God: twenty bright young souls paying attention to Dad's mellower glow; Gage's dirty soul glittering with the residue of a miracle; a holy object across the room gracing a man-made construction of wood and steel; and a tortured soul burdened with a mute spirit, unable even to ask for the help God would provide if he did.

Gage followed a bit of what the others were talking about. Just a bit because his mind kept returning to the guitar like a compass needle focusing on true north. He heard every number tick on the hall clock, overcome by the thought that at 7:55 he'd lift that guitar again.

When the time came, Gage nudged Jeff with his foot. Jeff waited until Gage had reached the guitar and all heads had turned toward the front, then slipped out the back door. Gage fumbled with his guitar strap and the sheet music to give Jeff time before he finally played a few notes on the lower strings. Warmth flooded his arms even at that little contact.

"One, two, three..." It had been long enough for Jeff to escape earshot. Gage played, focusing fully on the instrument to let it sweep him along with the song. His fingers remembered where they needed to be. The guitar nestled against his chest, and the heady dizziness buoyed his spirit. Freed of worries about Jeff and Dad, Gage let the instrument do as it would and sing praise to the Lord. That was why a guitar was made. For a few short minutes, Gage experienced the singular joy of a guitar fulfilling its entire purpose.

As the kids got their coats and met their parents, Gage laid the guitar in its case. It was a cheap case. A guitar as amazing as this deserved a harder one, lined with soft fabric. When he'd bought the guitar for a hundred dollars, it hadn't seemed like it was worth more than a the cheapest the store had to offer. Surrounded by Gibsons and Martins, Gage had been filled with a sense of "Why bother?" Now he regretted it.

Even as the feeling came over him, a second feeling followed: the instrument didn't matter. What mattered was the player.

Gage closed his eyes. *I wish I were that guitar, then. Play me.*

Jeff helped break down the chairs and tables. When the last of the youth group members had met up with parents and departed, Dad turned down the thermostat, shut the lights, and ushered the boys up the steps.

In the parking lot, the frigid air stung tears from Gage's eyes. Jeff had his hands in his pockets, and Dad hurried toward the car so they could escape the cold all the faster.

Movement in the bushes caught Gage's attention. Jeff stopped at his side and looked at the same spot.

A pair of jinn stared with gleaming eyes. In total darkness, they seemed so solid.

One of them pointed to the guitar, and then jinn held one another's hands, watching the boys with love-brilliant eyes. The cousins stood planted in place, looking right back.

The jinn had heard. Every demon in Chittenden County must have heard, too, if not every demon in Vermont.

"Boys! Come!"

Jeff strode quickly toward Dad's car. Gage took a moment longer before following. Behind him, the jinn giggled.

⸻❧⸻

CHAPTER EIGHT

⸻❧⸻

Dad had quite a few things to say about Gage skipping school. Jeff had inserted himself onto the couch in the family room downstairs and turned on the television, giving Dad the entire upstairs to find places to harangue his son.

"So much about your behavior bothers me." Dad had settled on the kitchen as the best place for the lecture. Gage supposed it was a neutral spot, a 'family' spot. Too often the living room felt like a parlor they kept tidy just in case someone from church dropped by, becoming for that reason a place that wasn't really theirs.

"I'm sorry."

"Are you?" Dad looked stung. "You knew I want no contact with your grandfather. Why didn't you tell me what you were going to do?"

Gage traced a finger on the tabletop. "You'd have said no."

Dad took a deep breath. "Just because I never specifically

told you something was forbidden doesn't mean you can go do it. Good grief, can you imagine the havoc if we read the Bible the same way?" Dad paused for a moment, then raised his eyes. "Now that I think of it, some people do read the Bible that way. But that's another story." He returned to studying Gage. "The fact is, you knew I wouldn't want you to do it. That's enough to make what you did disobedience, even if I never exactly said you were forbidden to tell me you were going to school and then hop in a cab or a—" A sudden concern had come into Dad's eyes. "You didn't hitchhike, did you?"

"We brought my bike and Taylor's to school and took buses out to Rutland, then biked to Grandpa's from the bus station."

"It's bad enough you disobeyed. You shouldn't involve Taylor, too."

Great. Now he'd gotten Taylor in trouble. "Taylor didn't know why I wanted her bike."

"I'm sure she didn't believe you were totally on the level. You compromise her integrity when you involve her." Dad shook his head. "Despite what you think, it's not in everyone's best interests to keep us ignorant, although you wouldn't be the first in your family to do such a thing."

Gage filed away that statement for future thought.

Dad said, "Tell me why you thought you needed to see your grandfather."

"He's Jeff's grandfather, too." Gage swallowed. "I know you're mad. I should have asked you first, and if you said no, I shouldn't have gone."

Dad didn't look angry as he said, "You're getting adept at the evasive maneuvers."

"Thank you."

"That wasn't a compliment. Why did you go there?"

"I wanted to know what he thought was wrong with Jeff?"

"You say that as though you're not sure yourself." Dad shook his head. "I don't understand why you won't level with me."

The phone rang, but Dad ignored it.

"Because you'll be mad if I do."

"I promise you," and here Dad took a deep breath to level his voice before he continued, "I'll get much madder if you don't."

There was so much at stake no matter how he answered. Dad would forbid contact with the jinn. Of that much Gage was certain, since Dad had already forbidden him to contact his grandfather. Dad might make him take the thread off the guitar and burn it or bury it—maybe the thread and the guitar together.

The answering machine had activated. Always the same. Gage could have recited the message on his own by now: *Pastor Jordan, I'd like to talk to you. Call me at—*

Gage looked at his lap. "I wanted something to help Jeff. Taylor and I think Jeff is under a spell that stops him from communicating. But Jeff did ask me for help once. I don't want to say how."

Dad nodded. "I understand."

Gage raised his eyes. "It's hard when the enemy is invisible."

"The good guys are invisible, too, and that doesn't make it any easier. In this instance, you're right to avoid talking about things that may get people in trouble."

Gage nodded.

"And your grandfather's diagnosis was—?"

"A mute spirit."

"What did he suggest?"

Gage said, "Prayer and fasting."

Dad let out a long breath. "Thank you. That's what I would suggest too."

"I didn't have my dessert tonight."

Dad had a sly expression. "Don't worry about hiding it from me if you skip breakfast. I know you aren't supposed to walk around with a long face, but that's one thing you don't need to keep secret from me."

Gage said, "What else can I do, though?"

Dad said, "I'm going to tell you this because you'll find out eventually, but I don't want you involved. Your grandfather may be right that Jeff is in possession by a mute spirit. He's also right that Jesus says in the Bible that these spirits can only be dispatched by prayer and fasting. I've spoken to some of the church elders, including Taylor's father, to consider an exorcism. They're not sure, and neither am I. Jeff could be suffering from post-traumatic stress disorder. He did see his father killed, and we don't know for certain that Zack summoned a demon. I want the complete results of Jeff's psychological evaluation before we make a decision."

Gage said, "Can I be there?"

"Absolutely not. I wish even I weren't going to be there. You'll stay at Taylor's if we have to go through with it, and you'll stay there for as long as it takes. Sometimes demons resist for days."

Gage drew into himself, arching his eyebrows. "Have you conducted one before?"

Dad shook his head. "I've been to one, but I didn't lead it. It wasn't pretty. Possession isn't common—true possession, that is. Most of the time, you've just got someone who needs therapy. Every once in a while, you get the real thing." Dad looked so drawn that Gage fought the urge to move closer. "I can't have you nearby if it is, Gage. Because you're right, and I am afraid you're in danger, too."

"Why?"

"I don't know why. I don't like the explanation your grandfather has, but I don't have one of my own." He looked up. "If we're lucky, Jeff is obsessed and not possessed. Obsession is the stage when the demons hang around without having control, and it's easier to shake. I doubt it's that easy, though. If he's muted, it's because the thing's inside."

Gage said, "Does that mean Jeff's soul is evil?"

Dad said, "God is the judge of that."

"But wouldn't the demon...I don't know, wear him down? Make him cruel?"

"It's hard to say. Usually the victim was cruel to start with."

Gage frowned. "Who was the exorcism you attended at?"

Dad shook his head. "It was a while ago, and who it was doesn't matter." He warded off Gage's next question. "All this gets us away from the topic of your cutting school and your punishment." When Gage flinched, Dad stood from the table. "I'll let you know tomorrow. For now, maybe you need to get ready for bed and get your things ready to go to school tomorrow. For real, this time."

Gage dropped his head. "I'm sorry."

"I'm sorry, too. I wish you trusted me more when I say something is for your own good. Luckily this didn't turn out as badly as it could have."

Dad went downstairs to tell Jeff to get ready for bed. Gage went into his bedroom and touched his guitar case standing tall by his bookshelf.

⸻❖⸻

Gage awoke abruptly. His body tingled all over, and he had no idea why.

A rapid banging struck at the front door. Gage scrambled out of bed and flew down the hallway. It came louder, but now he realized he wasn't exactly hearing it. It sounded far too hollow, as if he were listening underwater.

Jeff ran into the hallway, right hand clutched to his chest, and he followed Gage down the half-flight of steps to the front door.

Gage opened the door, and in rushed a jinn, screaming, "Close it! Close it!"

Jeff flew down the stairs and slammed the door with his

shoulder. It rattled the windows.

Gage looked up at the landing, but Dad didn't come.

The jinn huddled behind Gage in a fetal position. Gage crouched so they were at eye level. "What's wrong?" He thought it was Mek, although it was hard to tell. "Where's Mir?'

The jinn sobbed. With his back to the door, Jeff refused to move. Gage touched the jinn. It looked up with child-eyes, tears flowing freely.

Gage whispered, "What's out there?"

"They were so scary. They came. They threatened us. I didn't know what to do."

Gage whispered, "What happened to Mir?"

"They got Mir. They ripped Mir apart. They came after us, and I went one way, and Mir went the other way. I hid, and they didn't find me. I found some squirrels. They told me where the nuts were buried. But I don't know what happened to Mir."

The jinn looked so solid. When Gage had seen the pair on his front steps after sunset, they'd seemed ephemeral. After midnight, Mek looked as flesh-and-blood as on the night behind Taylor's house. Gage sat on the steps. "You think Mir is dead?"

Mek held out Mir's belt-pack at arm's length.

Gage said, "Were they chasing you?"

Mek whispered, "I didn't stop to see."

Jeff moved closer. Gage glared over his shoulder. "Give some space, okay?"

A strange comprehension lit up Jeff's eyes. Jeff had seen the jinn duo out by the church, and now he heard Mek and could see Mek. Seeing Jeff, so intent and yet so dark and silent, Gage shivered, so he turned his attention back to the jinn. "What did they want from you?"

"Music." The jinn swallowed. "They wanted music. But we didn't have any."

Now Gage had rows of goose-bumps. "You mean the guitar music?"

The jinn blinked. Gage sighed. "Are you safe in here?"

The jinn nodded, then stared for the first time at Jeff.

The moonlight from the doorside window illuminated Jeff just enough to emphasize how gaunt he'd become. His eyes gleamed black, and his expressionless face seemed cast in granite, like a gravestone. The jinn shrunk alongside Gage.

"He's okay. That's my cousin Jeff. I'm Gage. You probably won't remember that, but that's okay, too. You should stay in my room, and Jeff will stay in his. Come on."

Mek looked too scared even to speak, and because the creature wouldn't walk past Jeff, Gage gestured that Jeff go up first. Only then did Mek trail Gage into his room.

"Hey!" Mek laughed and rushed forward. "You found the music!" Mek turned and beamed. "We heard it. But they heard it too."

"They were looking for me. You two got in the way." Gage took a deep breath. "I'm sorry."

Too many apologies for the same day. Too many open wounds.

Mek curled on one side near the guitar and closed both eyes, letting the worry slide away. "I'll stay with the music."

"I want you to hide. Dad's going to freak out when he sees you." Helping a jinn hide from demonic pursuers would make taking a bus to Rutland look like an Eagle Scout project.

Mek said, "He can't see me. When it's day, I can't do anything."

"What?"

The jinn knocked on the floor. "It's night. I'm solid. When the sun comes up, I'm not. But even at night, he won't see me."

"You thought I wouldn't be able to see you. Jeff can see you."

Mek whispered, "He's scary."

Gage flinched.

Jeff had reacted so quickly to the jinn's presence. He'd slammed the door without hesitation, but as he'd done it, there'd been a look of remorse. Jeff must have realized the demons' motives: they'd killed Mir in order to drive Mek to find Gage. Mek had flown like an arrow straight to him.

Gage grabbed his Bible and rushed under the covers. *God, what do I do now?*

Paul had written about God sending an angel of Satan to beat him. Gage had never taken that sentence literally. He'd always considered angels and demons as disembodied entities that showed up to debate when it was time to make a decision. Sure, he knew about a sword-wielding Michael the Archangel throwing Satan and his minions out of heaven. He'd read about demons casting people into fires or forcing them to have convulsions. He'd heard about possession, and he'd been told the demons must hate their bodily hosts because they'd forced an entire herd of swine to plunge to their deaths rather than stay in those bodies.

All that theoretical knowledge lacked the reality of this one frightened moment. Demons could be clustered outside this house, right now. After shredding an innocent jinn like toilet tissue, they could be forging plans to attack him and Jeff. Worse, Jeff was already in their grip and might invite them inside.

Deep breaths. Whatever happened, God was stronger.

Will God protect us, though? God wouldn't always avert the natural consequences of human evil, not when so much of their current problem was happening at their own hands. Because of Uncle Zack summoning something, because of Jeff participating or at the very least watching, because of Dad frightened by what he knew and Grandpa unwilling to break silence, and because of Gage himself manipulating the situations he came across when maybe he ought to have fled from them.

When Gage saw the jinn that first night, he could have about-faced and dived back into bed.

Looking at Mek, though, he wondered if the jinn really could harm anyone. Mek seemed guileless. Even now, the jinn sat in breathless radiance, reverencing the guitar that had pained Jeff. Without knowing any better, the jinn might have worshipped it.

Last night, Mek or Mir had said that if God wanted Gage to use the thread, God would send someone to show him how. It had been a mistake to think Gage needed to do God's work for Him by seeking out Grandpa Rivers. Instead, the answer had come by responding to the quiet call to attend youth group. Brandon had shown him what to do by restringing the guitar.

Playing it got Mir killed.

Momentarily, the thought came to Gage that God owned both death and life, therefore Mir was in good hands.

Where did Mir's soul go? If Mir is untried, unjudged, then is heaven really the right place for a jinn?

Gage got the sense he was asking too many questions about things that didn't matter to him.

Okay, then, how about this? How do I keep the demons from devouring me? Gage found it hard to look around his room, expecting shining eyes in every corner. Whenever the radiator ticked or the house creaked, his stomach tightened. *They've already got Jeff.*

Had they?

All Gage really knew was that something prevented Jeff from speaking. Grandpa said it was a mute spirit. But before saying that, he'd called it a geas, a demonic command not to speak. Why would a demon command something it could control? Or was Grandpa all bluster?

On the other hand, if Jeff were only under orders, why would the guitar music hurt him?

Mek scrambled up and hid behind the guitar. "They're coming! They're coming inside!"

Jeff rushed into the room, thrusting Gage's Grooz Capture game into his hands. Gage stared open-mouthed, but Jeff hooked the two games together, and he started up his. Gage clicked through the splash screen and entered the code for a two-player game. Jeff had used this to communicate before, so maybe he'd use it again, even at risk of demonic wrath.

No message came. Mek stayed behind the guitar, camouflaged in darkness. A frown creased Jeff's forehead as he dispatched his hunter into the digital underbrush to flush out as many Groozes as possible. Gage sent his hunter into a frenzied run to capture them all. He watched for his message light, but when none came, he let himself get pulled into the game, pursuing a particularly elusive Grooz that he'd never been able to trap before. The pursuit music increased in tempo. Jeff's hunter participated but didn't help much. It was up to Gage's higher-level hunter to bag the electronic creatures, and he set about finding them, keeping an eye on his power level, his score, and his weapons readings.

Mek said, "They're gone."

Gage sat up, blinking.

"They're gone," Mek repeated. "Where were you?"

Jeff shut off his game. The clock said half an hour had passed.

Mek said, "How did you go away?"

"I've been right here the whole time." Gage looked at Jeff. "What did you do?"

Jeff coiled his patch cable and returned to his room. Gage got back under his blankets while the jinn kept a hand on the guitar.

Chapter Nine

Gage awoke with a jinn cuddled at his back. His blankets had settled through the misty form, and when Gage passed his hand through the sleeper, he felt nothing at all. He piled up his pillow and blankets just in case Dad might be able to see a jinn-like indentation in the bedding. Gage skipped breakfast and offered up his hungry stomach as a prayer.

At school, he found Taylor. Heads close between two desks at homeroom, they caught up on everything from the Rutland trip to the demonic siege.

Taylor shivered. "I don't even know where to start."

"We're no closer to helping Jeff," Gage rubbed his finger over a scratch on his desk. "I may be in trouble, too. In trouble with more than my father, and this time, I'm expressly forbidden to talk to the one person who might be able to help."

"He didn't help you all that much to begin with." Taylor

huffed. "I looked in some fairy tale books. Jinn are also known as djinn with a silent D, and they're also called genies. A single jinn is called a genius."

Thinking of Mek unable to remember anything for longer than two minutes, Gage snorted.

"I didn't invent the word." Taylor grinned. "Some of the books say jinn are angels that got degraded from their angel status and cast out of heaven with the demons. In Islam, they're good. One person said they give suffering to good people and justice to the evil."

Gage hummed. "So maybe it's really like Grandpa said. They're not good or evil, just untried, so everyone sees what they want to. It's like if Salty walks over the keyboard, I'd get letters and numbers, but if you try to read it as a sentence, you'll be really confused."

Taylor shrugged. "Oh, and in case you find this enlightening, a jinniyeh is the feminine form of jinn."

The bell rang, and Gage quipped, "I'll remember that for French class."

By lunchtime, Gage moved from class to class four times without offering more than his bodily presence. He might as well have stayed home.

Taylor met him at the cafeteria door. "Are we skipping lunch?"

"You don't have to."

"I'll pitch in. I had an idea, too. They're collecting downstairs for victims of that blizzard in Michigan. I read in a book that 'charity covers a multitude of sins,' so why don't we give them our lunch money?"

After they pushed their crumpled-up cash into the plastic jar at the front entrance, Gage and Taylor sat on the inside steps. With one finger, Gage traced the webs of dust clustered at the junction of the step with the wall. There were black strips of something like sandpaper right at the edge of each, but in some spots they'd been worn off by decades of student feet. The gritty floor matched the dusty recessed light fixtures positioned every six feet up the center of the ceiling.

Gage pulled out his Grooz Capture unit. "What's the deal with this game? I wish I understood any of what was happening."

"It doesn't make sense. Maybe just getting your mind off the demons took away their invitation into your house."

"Demons aren't material. They should be able to go right through walls."

Taylor took the game from his hands, turning it over. "Your Dad said your uncle had invited them in. That means there's got to be some kind of everyday barrier. I don't know how angels look at houses. Are the walls just not there, and all our stuff is hanging in midair on the second floor, or do they see the houses as little strongholds they could easily overwhelm?"

"Maybe it's a territory thing. Jeff slammed the door against them." Gage took back the game. "They were coming after me. Me. Not him."

"Or your guitar." Taylor shrugged. "I don't mean to say you're not important, but if it's the guitar they want, you should let them have it."

"How could they want just a guitar? It's a physical object." Gage's shoulders slumped. "I don't believe in magical objects, and any idiot can learn to play the guitar."

"You were the one who managed to get the thread to work. That makes you an above-average idiot." Taylor used her backpack as a shield while Gage whacked her with his notebook. "Wow. That's how you thank me for trying to help."

Gage made a face. "I still need more of this inspired help."

Taylor took a deep breath, then got up from the steps. "I'll pretend to study in the library. Don't tell the principal, but I'll pray there where it's quiet. You should maybe play that game and see if Jeff did something to the settings. Hopefully one of us will get an idea."

Gage listened to Taylor's footsteps retreat up the stairwell.

He laid the game on his lap, but he didn't start it. Instead, he closed his eyes in the dirty yellow lighting, and he prayed, too.

"Hey, Jordan!" Two of his classmates bounded up the stairwell. One was eating a chocolate bar. "Nice place to spend your lunch."

Gage shrugged. "It's a school. How nice can it get?"

Mike, the one with the chocolate bar, broke off a piece. "Here, man, have some."

Gage's mouth watered, and he reached forward but then remembered he was fasting. "No, thanks."

The other one said, "What's the matter?"

Mike said, "He's the preacher's kid. I bet he's fasting."

The first laughed out loud. Gage reddened. "I just don't want any."

"You know," Mike said in a curious tone, "when you fast, no one's supposed to know about it."

Gage's skin crawled.

"It has no effect anymore. When people know, you've already gotten the honor."

The hairs stood at attention on Gage's neck. Mike's tone was all wrong. He'd never shown the slightest interest in religion. Why would Mike even know that Gospel passage?

Evil permeated the stairwell. Gage started getting dizzy.

"Just a bite," Mike said. "Just one."

Gage felt rooted to the gritty steps.

"Get over it, man!" The other kid gave Mike a shove. "Forget your stupid chocolate. I need to stop at my locker before the bell rings."

All of a sudden, Mike's eyes cleared. "Oh, and I need to copy that homework from you. How much time we got?"

They ran up the stairs, their footsteps in time with Gage's pounding heart.

Okay, God, that was freaky.

A minute later, he added, *But if Satan's trying that hard to stop me, then we're on the right track.*

Chapter Ten

Gage opened his front door to find a worried jinn on the top step, elbows on knees. Salty and Pepper sat on either side.

Gage smiled. "I see you've met the cats."

Both cats wore the proper expression of feline disdain, as if to say, *We can stop sitting next to you whenever we want. We just don't want to right now.* Mek seemed surprised by their presence. "Where's Mir?"

Gage's heart bottomed out.

The jinn's eyes went huge. "They got Mir, didn't they? It was so dark, and we ran so fast, and all that's left is the pack. Where's Mir?"

Gage whispered, "I don't know."

"There's someone scary in the house." Mek didn't move as Gage climbed the steps to the upper floor. After a moment's thought, Gage directed his steps between the cats and through the jinn's immaterial form. Pepper bolted, having stayed put as long as he could tolerate. Mek didn't protest, but Mek also didn't follow to Gage's room.

Jeff sat on Gage's bed. "Exciting day?" Gage muttered. His stomach had gone beyond grumbly. Now he just felt crabby.

What could Jeff have meant by sitting in his room like this? Generally he spent his time with the TV. The guitar remained exactly where Gage had left it.

Gage had a mountain of homework to catch up on—no, make that a mountain range. If he wasn't going to start, then he ought to get out his Bible and have a little quiet time. Jesus had said this kind of demon only goes out by prayer and fasting, and so far today he'd done only one.

Gage turned at random to Mark's gospel, then read very slowly until he found a sentence that called out to him. Like a dieter savoring a single M&M, he let the line dissolve in his mind for a long time before continuing to the next. One week, the youth group had discussed this type of prayer, and on trying it Gage had found it fascinating and fulfilling. If he could manage to get his brain totally quiet, after a while he would find himself listening, the words of the Gospel passage gone but their imprint remaining in his heart. Slowly he could be drawn into what he thought of as the purest part of himself, the center of his soul at which the core was God's own image.

Today it took a long time to reach that spot, and Gage kept getting distracted by thoughts of Jeff in the same room, and if Jeff would think it odd to see him sitting so quiet for so long. After all that had gone on in the past week, Jeff couldn't possibly still mock his faith. If all God needed to do was prove he existed, he'd done it. But Gage had been teased so often for being the preacher's kid, and the memories of that stuck like wet bubble gum on canvas sneakers.

"He's the preacher's kid. I bet he's fasting."

Gage's useful prayer time was up. He'd learned long since to recognize the point at which he'd lost the center and wouldn't regain it.

Jeff was gone.

Gage's cheeks burned. *Sorry.* All that embarrassment and distraction, and Jeff wasn't even watching. He reached for his backpack and pulled out his assignment sheets.

A breath-like motion caught Gage's attention as he opened his math textbook. Mek had come into the room.

Mek walked to the corner of the room and took a pinch of the God-thread from Mir's belt pack. The jinn crumbled it between the tips of thumb and forefinger, and then sprinkled it in the far corner of the room.

Gage squinted. "What are you doing?"

Mek jumped, then backed into the corner holding the thread like a shield. It looked more like a strand of hair than a weapon. Then Mek said, "Oh. You." With Gage dismissed, Mek replaced the remaining thread in the belt-pack. "Mir's not here."

A woman from the church had developed Alzheimer's, and when Dad visited the nursing home, Gage also went. Sometimes they had good visits because if they had good news, they got to tell her about it several times. Every time she would react with the same jubilation. But once they had bad news, and Dad had felt compelled not to lie to her when she'd said, "How is my sister?" After the third time, Dad finally answered, "Doing well."

Gage bit his lip. "Mir's not here."

Sadness contorted the childlike face. Gage waited. Momentarily, Mek said, "Do you belong to the cats?"

Gage nodded.

"They have pretty cat-eyes. I have a marble like that." Mek smiled. "The music is in here. I thought now I could come in. I couldn't before."

While Jeff was in the room? Interesting.

Gage said, "Why did you want to get in?"

Mek blinked.

No, not again. Gage said slowly, "What did you just do with the thread?"

Mek smiled a blank smile, one Gage had learned to recognize as a jinn mentally clearing the cache. A computer would have said, "Waiting for data."

"You sprinkled a bit of thread in the corner."

Mek nodded, still smiling.

"What does it do?"

"You can seal a place against demons."

"Really?"

Mek nodded. "That's why walls are useful. God says, this far and no further."

The door. That was why Mek had begged them to close the door. The way Jeff had slammed it last night, he must have known, too.

"Can't demons move through walls?"

"If you don't seal them." Mek stretched. "Do you belong to those cats?"

Gage said, "They have pretty eyes."

"Yeah! Just like my marble!"

Gage leaned against the wall and began his homework.

⸺◦⸺

After dinner, Gage played his guitar. A touch of the instrument still made the blood rush to his head. The thread warmed beneath his fingers as he played.

Mek's unadulterated devotion broadsided Gage. Sitting at Gage's feet, Mek was beholding God's perfection in sound, with a purity Gage could never hope to attain.

Mek had been right that Dad noticed nothing, several times walking right through a jinn who always contrived to get underfoot. The only comment Dad made was to the effect that Salty had been more friendly than usual this afternoon. Pepper remained scarce.

Dad knocked on Gage's door, though it was already open, and then walked inside. Gage set the guitar on its stand.

"Keep playing. I've turned off the phone, so we'll have some quiet." Dad studied Gage's hands on the guitar. "I hadn't realized how proficient you'd gotten."

"I love this guitar."

Dad sat on the foot of the bed. "If you're sounding this good on a starter guitar, imagine what you could do if we upgraded."

"It's a great guitar. I don't want anything else." Gage closed his hand protectively over the neck, as though Dad were about to sell the instrument that very moment. "Have you thought about my punishment? You're not planning on taking the guitar, are you?"

Dad shook his head. "I've ruled out banning TV on the grounds that you don't watch enough of it to register, although Jeff seems to live and breathe it."

"But—"

"I'm not worried. If he's still watching as much in six months, I'll have a talk with him." Dad folded his hands on his knee. "I've toyed with a few different ideas, but I haven't reached a decision."

This was always the worst kind of punishment.

"I thought I'd ask for your input."

Yep, the very worst.

"Your intentions were basically good, which is why you haven't been grounded until graduation." Dad looked right into Gage's eyes, but Gage turned aside. "I thought of asking you to do some research on the occult, but since I'd rather know what it is you're reading, I'd tell you exactly which books were safe."

Safe enough that Gage would learn exactly nothing. He looked at his feet, where Mek sat cloaked in contentment. "You think that will show me none of what Grandpa believes is true?"

"A lot of what your grandfather believes *is* true, which is why he's dangerous. Satan was a liar from the beginning, but he'll tell the truth when it makes the lie easier to believe."

"What else were you thinking of?"

"Give me some ideas."

"You could make me work at the nursing home for a few days next week, since I turned school-time into free-time and went to visit my grandfather?"

Dad nodded. "That's a good one. What else?"

Gage frowned. "You could make me pray an extra hour a day for Jeff."

"Do you think that coerced prayer benefits anyone?" Dad paused. "Me neither. Nice try."

Gage looked right at Mek, though it must have seemed to Dad that he stared at the carpet. "Back at the church, Grandpa told Jeff he'd get him out of danger, but then you never listened. I wanted to know what he planned to do."

"You could have asked me, or you could have picked up the phone. Your grandfather talks big, but he doesn't have any inside knowledge. I'd have said the same about Uncle Zack. And then your grandfather didn't tell you anything, anyhow."

"He gave Jeff a hug."

Dad sighed. "I wish he could give Jeff his love without the rest. Jeff needs as many strong, stable adults around him now as he can get, and instead he has only me. Maybe Dr. Dasson counts, too, but you can't fill that role. Don't think I haven't noticed how grown-up you are, but you're younger than he is."

"I'm doing my best."

Dad said finally, "I want you to hand over your handheld game unit."

"No!" Gage recoiled into the wall. "I can't explain, but I can't give it to you." A week ago he'd have handed the unit over with just a grumble, but after all this?

Dad did a double take. "If you're that attached to the game, maybe you really do need to give it up."

"It's not that. Jeff sent me a message through the game." As soon as he'd blurted the words, Gage went cold. *Please, God, let the thread-protection work on sound as well.* "Jeff used the game to send 'Help me,' and he used it one other time when I was scared of demons. He's doing something to my game. Don't take that away."

In that blizzard of words, the thing Dad picked up on was, "Why were you scared of demons?"

Great. Gage ought to just seal his mouth with duct tape. He stammered, "Everything going on, and you know, and Grandpa talking about possession and mute spirits, and—"

Dad's eyes narrowed. "—and you're not telling me something extremely important."

Gage clenched his hands. His eyes burned.

Dad wasn't Dad anymore. Now he was an incensed preacher talking to someone whose soul was his responsibility. "Talk to me, Gage."

Gage stared at his lap. It was too much. All too much. "I think it's safe to talk."

At least, Mek thought they were safe. Mek sat watching with an expression that indicated the jinn would forget this entire conversation the next time Gage did something interesting, like tying his shoes.

Dad lowered his voice. "What did Jeff do to the game?"

Now Dad was really going to take it.

Gage's voice wobbled. "I don't know."

Dad walked to the window, then paced back to Gage. He fixed an unnamable look on him and then left the room.

Help me! God, what do I do? Gage closed his eyes and tried to reach for the calm, but there was none, none at all.

Chapter Eleven

After five minutes, Dad returned to Gage's room to find him with his arms around the guitar.

"Level with me." Dad's voice was barely audible. "Are you engaging in witchcraft?"

"No." Gage answered with complete assurance, but then he had second thoughts.

"You don't look sure"

Gage said, "I've never tried to work any magic."

Dad decided to accept that. "Do you think Jeff worked any witchcraft on your game?"

"No. I think he used the game to ask for help because our enemies can't get into it. And to work witchcraft, wouldn't he need their help?"

"Yes, but he might not realize that."

"You said demons wouldn't protect us from demons."

"And you're sure you were protected?"

Gage nodded.

"Not that Jeff made you scared, and then nothing bad happened because nothing bad was going to happen in the first place?"

Gage glanced at Mek. "I would know the difference."

"I don't like this at all. There's something very big you're leaving out, and you're not going to mention it unless I ask you directly, are you?" Dad folded his arms. "Aren't you worried about your own soul? Even if you would be callous enough to cast aside Jeff's—and I know you're not—why would you risk your own salvation?"

"I want to help him." Gage rubbed his eyes. "Why is what Grandpa believes so bad, anyway?"

"I can't tell you in this state. You'll embrace every bit of it and go looking for more. You obviously want to believe in something other than the power of the Almighty. God most emphatically does not need our help to straighten things out. Let the angels handle the demons. Let Jesus save the souls. The most we can do is pray and fast and wait and be open to God when the call arrives."

"What if God calls you to do something?" Gage ran his hand along the thread-string of his guitar. It felt warm like skin. "Being open to God means being willing to do what He asks. He told Peter to follow him, and Peter never looked back. Just like that."

"I find it difficult to believe God would call anyone to necromancy."

"What if God called me out of the house in the middle of the night? 'Get out of bed.' That was all. And if I went outside, and if I stood on a snowbank and...saw something?" Gage swallowed. "You said that yourself at church—that we can't just say yes to God once. God wants all our hearts and minds and strength, right? But—"

Dad said, "What did you see?"

Gage was looking right at Mek, and his pulse howled

through his head.

"What did you see?"

"I saw a pair of jinn."

"Oh, for crying out loud." To Gage it sounded as if someone else were the object of the anger.

Mek beamed and jumped to a stand. "That was us, right? Right? Let me tell Mir!"

"I didn't know they were jinn." Gage kept his voice measured as Mek bolted from the room. "I learned that later. I only know God woke me up when I was at Taylor's house, and I saw two jinn. They were scared and said demons were looking for something. That was the night Uncle Zachary died."

Dad said, "Who told you they were jinn?"

Gage skipped a chapter because it was easier for the moment. "Grandpa says they were jinn."

"When you looked up jinn in the Bible, what did you find?"

Gage said softly, "Cats aren't in the Bible either."

"Don't get smart with me." Dad shook his head. "Did the jinn say anything else?"

Gage watched his hands. "Jinn are silly. They were like children. They kept forgetting things."

"Tell me more."

"I don't know what else to say. They collect junk, but they call it treasure. They had a quarter and a bobby pin and a soda bottle cap." Gage found himself smiling. "They're cute, like wild children. They love God, but they act like animals. It's hard to explain."

Dad said, "Do you know who else saw jinn?"

"Jeff does."

Dad recoiled. "Are you certain?"

Gage nodded.

Dad sighed. "The one I was thinking of was your mother."

✦

Downstairs, Jeff sat with the television on and his school books spread around him. Sometimes he glanced from one book to the next, and other times he stared at the television. Right now he was focused on an endless series of commercials. Toothpaste, sport utility vehicles, personal injury attorneys, microwavable snack foods... They paraded past his eyes and cast a flickering glare on the room.

Jeff's eyes returned to the corner of the couch at his back. One of the house's ubiquitous Bibles had been left on the arm of the sofa, open to somewhere at the front. Like a man traversing the streets after midnight, he watched it cautiously, then watched the TV, then watched the Bible again. This scenario had continued for the past hour, since Jeff had first discovered the Bible there.

Uncle Matt probably left it there by accident, looking up something for a sermon and meaning to return later. So far, no one had demanded Jeff accept Jesus as his lord and savior, and nobody had berated him for not doing so. When he'd gone to youth group, no one had told him he didn't belong with the saved kids. The Bible wouldn't have been planted to make him look. Regardless, he kept glancing at it lying on the couch.

When the weather report came on, Jeff swiveled onto his knees and reached for the leather-bound volume. Cautiously he turned a few onion-skin pages. Showers of light didn't erupt from the exposed words, and voices didn't wrack the house. He pressed the text with his fingertips, and the page crinkled. He closed the book to study the spots where the gold leaf had worn off the edges. The burgundy cover, leather, was embossed with *Matthew Jordan*. Jeff weighed the book in his hands. He could flex the entire volume between his hands, and when he did, it made a creaky sound.

Jeff opened the book again, this time thumbing through the hundreds of pages and listening to the steady clicking as they returned to closure. He found a bookmark sewn into the binding and traced his index finger along the satiny ribbon. Others led to different pages, like a fabric interstate system. Jeff left the marker where it was, then flipped through until he found maps. He looked at some of the chapter headings. The line numbers matched the numbers at the upper outside corners of each page. Turning to the front, he found a table of contents listing all the books of the Old and New Testaments by their authors (but didn't Uncle Matt insist God had done it all?) There was a mini-concordance and a thematic index. Jeff frowned. He traced his fingers over the list of books, then raised his head suddenly.

He clapped the Bible shut and tossed it onto the sofa, then glared at the staircase.

The jinn halted at the bottom step, staring at Jeff on the floor with his back to the couch. Salty trotted past Mek's slender ankles.

Mek retreated up one step. Jeff edged forward, and Mek scrambled up two more.

When the standoff continued for another minute, Jeff fished in his pocket for a nickel to toss at the shady figure on the staircase. It passed right through Mek's form, and Mek regarded it narrowly. Squatting, the jinn nudged the coin with fingers that passed right through it.

The jinn turned back to study him. "Will you leave it there? For another hour?"

Jeff didn't respond.

The jinn said, "I can't pick it up now. It's daylight."

Jeff remained still.

The jinn said, "You're mean. Leave the treasure there. I'll get it later." Then Mek scampered back up the steps. After a moment, Salty followed.

Three commercials later, Jeff pocketed his nickel. He didn't return to the book on the couch.

<hr>

Gage's brain couldn't get in gear. "Mom could see them?"

Dad sounded defeated. "You have to understand, I never entirely comprehended what she meant. She called them jinn, too, and I assume she got that name from the same source you did." Gage didn't correct him. "She also said the same thing you did, that cats aren't in the Bible. It's nice to know some excuses will always remain the same."

"What did she do with them?"

Dad glanced out the window. "This is where you're getting into trouble. Your mother was a lot older than you when she saw them for the first time. She didn't *do* anything with them. They came to her, they played, and then they departed. She described them the same way you did, like wild baby animals, and like yours, hers came in pairs. She was rightly cautious and never asked them for favors or information. She certainly didn't think of them as a protective force against evil."

Gage thought for a long time. Finally, "So she treated them like stray cats?"

"In effect, yes."

"I don't understand why God would give someone a useless gift like that."

"Why must everything in the world be useful?" Dad opened his hands. "God likes to play with nature. Why else would there be more species of beetles than every other species combined? In the Book of Job, God created Leviathan for the joy of watching him swim. Is that useless? Maybe the jinn are one of God's ways of showing off the creativity and beauty and innocence of creation."

Gage wrinkled his nose. "There's got to be more to their species than that."

"Maybe there is, but only God would know their ultimate

role in the spiritual ecology."

Mek skittered back into the room and hid behind Gage's guitar.

"So there's nothing wrong about associating with the jinn?"

Dad flinched. "That's a question of discernment. I was never comfortable with your mother's stories, and consequently, she stopped telling me. I know from something she said that Uncle Zachary could see them. I also know she disapproved of how he interacted with them, but she wouldn't say why."

Gage wove his fingers together. "When you asked before, about why I was scared of demons, a jinn said they were coming. It wasn't something Jeff did to me. But something Jeff did made them go away—or at least, the jinn said the demons hadn't come." Gage frowned. "I don't think a demon could force a jinn to lie about something for very long. The ones I've seen forget too fast, and if they faced a demon, they'd be too terrified to bribe."

"Are you sure they're really jinn?"

Gage watched Mek huddling beside the guitar.

"Think about it. You could recognize a cat or a woodchuck, but you've never seen a jinn before."

"And Satan can pretend to be an angel of light." Gage felt a smile beginning, and he quashed it. "I just can't imagine him pretending to be *that*. They're silly. Don't devils take themselves too seriously?"

Robbing the jinn of a stronghold, Gage picked up his guitar and hammered his fingers on the strings. The God-thread felt warm, almost harmonious. When he looked at his father, the thread hummed with sympathetic vibration from the other strings. It wanted him to be talking to his father—or at least, it approved. He wondered what would happen if he doused himself with bits of the thread and started this conversation over again: how much did God want him to tell? If treated with the same medicine, what would his father answer?

Gage said, "What does Grandpa believe?"

"I told you, you aren't ready. I've seen the fruits of his ideas, and they tell me the tree isn't worth cultivating. Leave it at that." Dad shook his head. "Promise me you won't go deliberately seeking out any more jinn?"

Gage worked over the semantics of that and decided that a jinn already living in their house wasn't being deliberately sought out. "Okay. I promise."

"And you'll tell me anything else this jinn tells you?"

Gage nodded. "It's mostly things like the cats have pretty eyes." He squinted. "Did you decide on a punishment? Do you still want my handheld?"

Dad stood. "In light of what you've told me, I've undecided it again. We'll talk more tomorrow."

CHAPTER TWELVE

Taylor sat on her sister's bed while she folded a load of thick unbleached six-ply cotton prefold diapers stitched in blue, folded in thirds lengthwise and then folded in half. One dozen, two dozen. Then doublers, flannel wipes, wraps, and the liner for the diaper bucket.

Her friends often "reminded" her that other families used diapers you could throw away. Mom would never go for that, but on the other hand, Taylor could see where they might have an appeal. At least from a laundry perspective.

Behind her was a wall that backed up on the chimney, radiating heat for the entire house. Above her sounded the steady tak-tak-tak of Dad chipping away at the ice dams. Mom came in before Taylor was done and stacked the folded diapers in the beige laundry basket. "Thanks, honey. This is a huge help."

"No problem." It was boring, not challenging. Besides,

there was something homey about fluffy cotton diapers, warm from the dryer. Taylor remembered two other babies using these diapers, and quite possibly all five of them had used this same stack, sun-bleached in the summertime, line-dried on the dry days, toasted in front of the woodstove when Mom forgot to do diapers before the last few. They used them for spills, for liners, napkins, ad-hoc blankets, and everything else. Taylor was pretty sure you couldn't do that with the ones that went in the garbage pail.

Mom said, "How'd you do on the history test?"

"There was only one question that stumped me."

"That's good." Mom took more folded diapers from her. "How's Gage holding up?"

Taylor paused in folding. "I'd be scared out of my mind if I were him."

"I know what you mean." Mom sat on the bed and smoothed her skirt. "It's an awful situation."

Sometimes there were advantages to having parents on the pastoral council. Her father and Pastor Jordan had been friends since before Gage's mom died, although Taylor didn't remember Gage's mother at all. She had only a vague recollection of playing with puzzles in a gold-carpeted waiting room during the wake.

Taylor folded another diaper far more carefully than it needed. "What actually happened to his uncle?"

"Only God himself knows."

"Gage said it might have been demons."

Mom nodded. "It does sound that way."

Taylor laid the diaper on top of the stack and took another from the unfolded pile. "I can't imagine any problem that would get easier to solve by with the addition of a demon."

"Maybe the problem of life being too boring and safe," Mom murmured dryly. "It wasn't Zachary's best move."

"Why would he do that?'

"He mustn't have thought he was summoning a demon."

Mom leaned back against the warm wall. "He might have believed he was calling on angels or natural forces."

"How would you know if you saw an angel?"

Mom paused. "I'm not certain you could know for sure, which is good reason not to go looking for one."

Taylor laid the last diaper in the laundry basket. "What if one shows up? They do that in the Bible."

"You do your best. You pray." Mom shrugged. "I would look at the collateral evidence."

Taylor squinted. "What evidence?"

"The other things that are going on. If the advice is good, it's more likely to be an angel. If you're trying to escape what your conscience tells you, and the angel shows up to say you're home free, I'd wager that was not an angel."

"I don't know."

Mom sat straight. "Listen. What's that sound?"

Taylor held still. *Tak-tak-tak.* "That's only Dad chipping the ice dams off the roof."

Mom seemed puzzled. "Why do you say that? Do you see him?"

"No, but—"

"Did you see him go up? Did he tell you he was going up? Even if that is him on the roof, what makes you think he's chipping off the ice dams?"

Taylor frowned. "Because it's just Dad."

"And?"

Taylor gasped. "Oh! I can't see him, but I know it's him because he's done it before. Because it's cold. Because when we have ice dams, he usually chips them down. And because when he's done, there won't be ice on the roof."

"One more reason. Think."

Taylor said, "Because I know Dad. I know what he does, and I know what he realizes needs to be done."

"Bingo." Mom laid a hand on Taylor's arm and gave a squeeze. Then she lifted the basket of folded diapers. "Angels show up in the Bible to tell people things they had no way of knowing on their own, things that would otherwise have been so unbelievable that no one would ever have figured them out. If an angel shows up, it's unusual enough to expect the news should also be unusual." Mom settled the basket against her hip. "Probably we don't have to worry, though, and we won't see angels until Jesus is there to introduce us."

If we're lucky, Taylor thought as her mom left the room.

———

Dad had texted, "Gone to Jeff's house; we'll be back a little before 4:00."

Gage got off the bus at 3:40, so Dad had given him very few minutes solo. He couldn't figure out whether this meant that Dad did trust him, or that Dad didn't trust him. It didn't matter. Whatever Dad decided for punishment, it would mean not helping Jeff any further.

Gage dropped his backpack at the front door and rushed to his room, flipped open his guitar case, and pulled out the severed end of the thread. Relief rushed through him as he grasped it, but only momentarily. Mek was pushing in futility at a die-cast car on Gage's desk, and for sure that car would be rolled away somewhere else tomorrow morning—assuming Gage ever found it again. Five guitar picks had already vanished into the jinn's belt-pack.

Still, it meant Mek was occupied enough not to bother him.

"Pepper?" Gage opened the kitchen cabinet where they kept the cat food. "Want a treat?"

Salty appeared. Momentarily, Pepper also entered the kitchen, clinging to the far wall. Gage put two treats on the floor so the cats would approach, but only Salty did. With a sigh, Gage tossed a third, and Pepper darted away, only to peek around the corner and sneak up on it, always keeping his eyes on Gage.

Muttering, "I'm not going to eat you, even if I am higher up the food chain," Gage tossed another treat halfway between himself and Pepper.

Pepper crept up to it. Salty meowed, so Gage dropped another one, then extended his arm and set one where Pepper had to come very close. As Gage clicked his tongue, Pepper came the final distance.

"Good kitties." He pinched off the edge of the thread. "Stay here, guys."

Rubbing the severed end between his fingers, he scratched Salty with one hand and sprinkled the thread over Pepper with the other, then rubbed his thread-dusted fingertips behind Pepper's ears.

Salty purred with a rumbling thrum, not displeased with the attention. Gage slipped the remainder of the thread, coiled again, into his jeans pocket. It burned against his thigh, but he didn't rise. Too often when he moved unexpectedly, Pepper responded by bolting.

Gage reached again for Pepper, and Pepper growled.

Gage yanked back, and Salty skittered away. Pepper never growled—not at the vet, nor at Dad, nor at Gage. Hissed, yes, but cats hissed when they were frightened. Pepper's ears flattened, and he curled his lips to reveal his teeth.

What had the thread done to him?

A moment later, Gage thought, *No, what did* I *do to him?*

Pepper growled again. Salty bolted, and Pepper followed. Gage charged down the hallway after them.

This isn't right. That's not what I wanted! "Mek," he called. "Mek, are you around?"

Mek dropped through the ceiling from the attic. "I found a whole room full of the best stuff!"

"Not now. Something's wrong with one of the cats."

Mek gave a sharp gasp. "Wow! Look at that!"

The jinn was staring right through the wall toward Dad's room. Gage rushed in and flipped on the light. A growl rumbled from beneath the bed, so Gage dropped to his stomach and pressed his cheek against the carpet. Peering between the shoes, he saw green eyes.

He murmured, "Pepper, come here. I won't hurt you."

His own words knifed through him. *I did hurt him. I experimented on him.*

"Is he okay?" Gage asked softly.

"God's all over him!" The jinn jumped in place. "Oh, wow! I gotta tell Mir!" and the jinn dashed out of the room.

Why would a cat growl at God? That made no sense—but then again, this verdict had come from a jinn, so why should Gage assume any response would make sense?

Gage extended his hand, and Pepper backed away.

The front door slammed, and Gage cringed as his father and Jeff climbed the stairs. He retreated to the hallway.

"Good. You're home." Dad was taking off his jacket. "On the way back from Dr. Dasson, we stopped off to get Jeff's bike." He paused. "Are you okay?"

Gage swallowed hard. "I've got some nightmare homework."

"I can imagine." Dad watched Jeff retreat to his bedroom. "I've got a couple of calls to make, so I'll be downstairs if you need me."

Salty and Pepper remained locked in a staring contest beneath the bed, but at least there was no more growling. Gage left them alone to see what Jeff was doing...and bumped into Jeff in the hallway.

"Oh, I'm sorry." Gage looked over his shoulder into Dad's bedroom, then back at Jeff, who was standing way too close. Gage edged off to the side, but Jeff moved closer.

Could Jeff sense what he'd done? That look might be anger, or sadness, or questioning. It was too easy to project whatever Gage feared onto Jeff's blank features.

"What do you want?" Gage snapped. And then, when Jeff didn't react, he pushed past. "Leave me alone, okay?"

Gage's Bible lay open on the bed. He didn't remember leaving it there, and Mek couldn't have because it was daytime. About to close it and put it away, he noticed it was open to the Psalms. He definitely hadn't been reading those.

It would be cool if Jeff was experimenting, but it wasn't anything special. The end of Psalm 37, Psalms 38 and 39, and the beginning of Psalm 40. Gage sat back on his bed. Jeff remained in the doorway.

"You're being a pain." He squirmed, then looked back into Dad's bedroom for Pepper and Salty. When Jeff didn't budge, Gage returned to the kitchen to get a snack. A Bible was lying open on the counter.

Chilled, Gage moved closer. Again, Psalms: part of 38, 39, 40, and part of 41.

The apple in his hand forgotten, Gage looked at the kitchen doorway. Jeff.

Gage went into to the living room. On the couch he found two of Dad's reference Bibles, both open to the same spread of psalms. Downstairs he found one more.

They broke at different points on the page, but every one of them included Psalm 39.

＊＊＊

Chapter Thirteen

＊＊＊

Gage paced, rereading Psalm 39, while Mek caressed the neck of the guitar like a child stroking a sleeping kitten. His thoughts cavorted like leaves in a whirlwind.

I'm too young for this, God.

But hadn't God called David despite his youth? Hadn't God called Amos despite his not being a prophet? Jesus had gone up a mountain and called whomever He wanted without asking for resumes and three letters of recommendation.

But it was easier for them.

Was it? Was it really easy for Samuel, hearing his name in the middle of the night? What strength did it take to respond, "Speak, Lord, for your servant is listening" when you didn't know what would be asked of you? God was God and might ask anything at all. Somehow, you'd end up doing it.

Maybe answering yes the first time made it easier to answer yes the second. What if you said yes to God ten times but the eleventh time you misunderstood what God wanted? Would the whole plan come tumbling down around you?

When Gage had been little, one of his storybooks had a nursery rhyme that began, "for want of a nail, a horse was lost," and because of the missing horse, a knight, and then a battle was lost; and because of the battle, the kingdom fell— and all because of a missing nail. What was the detail in this scenario that could cause disaster? Was it even smaller than a nail, like a needle?

Gage felt in his heart that the God who had created the universe and everything in it could figure out how to give him a needle. Or perhaps the grace to say yes.

But if the grace to say yes comes from You, where's free will?

Gage rolled his eyes at himself. Right now, he should leave the theology to God. All he needed was to be the disciple that God wanted him to be.

Okay. Gage took a deep breath. *Let's see how this works.*

In the center of his room, Gage read out loud.

> *I said, "I will guard my ways,*
> *that I may not sin with my tongue;*
> *I will guard my mouth with a muzzle,*
> *so long as the wicked are in my presence."*
> *I was mute and silent;*
> *I held my peace to no avail,*
> *and my distress grew worse.*
> *My heart became hot within me.*
> *As I mused, the fire burned;*
> *then I spoke with my tongue:*
> *O Lord, make me know my end*
> *and what is the measure of my days;*
> *let me know how fleeting I am!*
> *Behold, you have made my days a few handbreadths,*
> *and my lifetime is as nothing before you.*
> *Surely all mankind stands as a mere breath! Selah*

> *Surely a man goes about as a shadow!*
> *Surely for nothing they are in turmoil;*
> *man heaps up wealth and does not know who will*
> *gather!*
> *And now, O Lord, for what do I wait?*
> *My hope is in you.*
> *Deliver me from all my transgressions.*
> *Do not make me the scorn of the fool!*
> *I am mute; I do not open my mouth,*
> *for it is you who have done it.*
> *Remove your stroke from me;*
> *I am spent by the hostility of your hand.*
> *When you discipline a man*
> *with rebukes for sin,*
> *you consume like a moth what is dear to him;*
> *surely all mankind is a mere breath! Selah*
> *Hear my prayer, O Lord,*
> *and give ear to my cry;*
> *hold not your peace at my tears!*
> *For I am a sojourner with you,*
> *a guest, like all my fathers.*
> *Look away from me, that I may smile again,*
> *before I depart and am no more!"*

Gage let the words descend around him the way he had learned to pray a Bible passage. This time, although he had begun agitated, calm settled over him. Closing his eyes, he rocked in place as the phrases moved through his head with awkward familiarity. *I am mute; I do not open my mouth.*

Gage reached for the guitar. The thread resonated beneath his fingers.

Some psalms began with a mention that they were set to a tune like "The Death of the Son," or "The Dove of the Morning." It would be neat to play the psalm to the original melody. The translation provided no clues. He would need to hear the Biblical Hebrew text even to know the number of beats per line, and that still told him nothing of the melody, nor of the instrument on which it was played. That wasn't a necessity, though. The word of God could be sung to the tune of "Row, Row, Row Your Boat" and still have its strength and resonance. Just not necessarily its majesty.

Gage burst out laughing, remembering a night when the youth group had gotten a little side-tracked and sung the Lord's Prayer to the tune of "Yankee Doodle," and followed up with "Amazing Grace" sung to "The Yellow Rose of Texas."

His thoughts had strayed from prayer. *I'm sorry, God.*

His heart lightened: God enjoyed his ruminations and his laughter. Joy was part of having life to the fullest. And sometimes, God could leverage human distraction to His own advantage.

You mean... Gage pulled the strap over his head. He fingered a chord, struck each string separately. The guitar sang. Gage spoke in a soft voice, "I am a—" (and here he did three chord changes in a row) "*sojourner*—with—you." He strummed again and allowed the sound to settle. "A foreigner as my fathers were."

It was an odd sensation. His ears heard the chord he was playing, and at the same time his inner ears heard the chords as he wanted them played. Trying not to analyze his actions, he adjusted the tuning. Usually he kept it in the traditional tuning of E-A-D-G-B-E, but sometimes he played with the low E dropped to a D, also called drop-D tuning. He tried not to logic through what his hands and ears were doing. With his eyes closed, he adjusted the strings, strummed a chord, then adjusted the strings again. Both E strings dropped to Ds, and soon after he lost track of all the other adjustments. When he was done, he strummed the open strings ,and they resonated the way his heart wanted. One by one he picked through and thought he recognized what Brandon called DADGAD tuning. Gage had never played anything like that. He had lost track of which notes were where, and he didn't figure them out. Instead, he settled cross-legged on his bed with the Bible open.

Okay, guitar. Let's hear what you have to say.

Gage's fingers made their own way. He hit some devastating clunkers, but he was able to pick through a couple of familiar tunes with a little success.

I'm thinking too much. He realized it at once, that he was trying to find the same chords he always used in this new configuration.

For a moment he felt two pulls on his heart: one that he had done enough for today so now wasn't the right time to go further. The other, that God had a job for Gage to do and that it must be done now, quickly, immediately; if so much depended on Gage, how could Gage make it wait? What devastation would result from his delay?

Gage opened his eyes and set the guitar back on its stand. He slid a bookmark into the Bible and closed the cover. *Wait on the Lord. It's in His time, not ours.* He swallowed, hoping he was listening to the right impulse. *It all depends on Him. I'm just trying to help things along. But anyone could do it.*

He walked out of his room feeling convinced he'd said yes when it mattered.

Dad came upstairs at dinnertime looking drawn. Gage avoided him as much as possible without seeming to avoid him. He wanted to tell him about Psalm 39. He wanted to tell him about tuning the guitar with his heart. His father's exhausted pallor stopped his words. Gage instead sat at the table doing homework and fighting the urge to check on the cats while his father read the mail, took a phone call from a member of the congregation, and worked on the weekend's sermon.

Pepper wandered into the kitchen. Gage tried not to stare at the cat as he walked to his food dish and snacked, then drank some water.

In the silence broken only by shuffling papers and the cat's lapping, Dad said, "We'll have the wake on Monday. The funeral will be Tuesday."

Gage said, "Why'd it take so long?"

"The autopsy. They've now released...the body to your grandfather." Dad had hesitated while speaking, as if not sure what to call Uncle Zack, juggling words to sound clinical and familial and authoritative all at the same time. "I'm sorry. I never wanted to have a conversation like this with you. Anyhow, I'm going to have to reach out to a lot of people tonight to make sure everyone knows what's happening. Your grandfather will contact his relatives, but I'm going to reach Jenna's family and Uncle Zack's friends."

Gage said, "Should I get started on dinner?"

"We'll order a pizza." His father ran a hand through his hair. "Zack didn't belong to a church, so your grandfather and I agreed we'd hold the funeral at ours." He met Gage's eyes. "Don't look so surprised. He and I can talk like rational human beings when there's business."

Gage nodded.

"Your job will be to tell Jeff's school friends." He squinted. "You do know who Jeff hangs out with, don't you?"

"I know enough to get the word out."

Pepper was looking around the kitchen without keeping his ears cocked toward them or awaiting the first sudden movement. Gage was replacing his books in his school bag when he realized what he'd missed, and his bag hit the floor with a bang.

Pepper didn't run from the sound. And he hadn't dipped his paw into the water when he'd started to drink, something he'd done every time he'd had any water at all for ten years.

Dad sat back. "Have you thought more about our conversation?"

Gage couldn't take his eyes off the cat, struggling to simultaneously process both his father's question and the cat's transformation. The thread coil had grown hot, and he rubbed it, unable to do anything else.

Dad sounded irritated. "Is that 'No'?"

"It's, 'I haven't thought about anything else.'" Gage closed his eyes. "I really messed up, didn't I?"

He had, but then he thought about Pepper, and maybe he hadn't messed up everything.

He wrenched his attention back to Dad. "You're never going to trust me again."

"I admit, I've been leery of letting you out of my sight. I'm still wracking my mind about what it is you've been hiding from me." Gage stepped back. "I know you didn't tell me everything," Dad muttered. "Give me that much credit."

There passed a long silence between Gage and his father. Finally Gage posed himself a question, a test. "Can you come to my room with me?"

In his room, he fought the urge to spread out a blanket on the floor or light a candle to make a small space for them. God made it sacred enough where two or three were gathered. Mek watched with opalescent eyes as Gage picked up the guitar and idly strummed. The new tuning sang, but Dad didn't notice the difference.

What should I tell my dad? he prayed. *How much is enough? Should it be everything?*

As he played, his mouth grew hot, and a slow fire built in his chest. The sound of the guitar thrummed outside as he strummed chords slowly and meditatively.

Looking at Mek, he said, "Are we safe?"

Dad said "What?" even as Mek said, "Why wouldn't we be?"

With Mek that relaxed, demons weren't around. Every time Gage touched the E string, it felt warm to his fingers, almost like a live electrical wire, and the words churned inside. He thought about Jeremiah the prophet, enduring torment until he spoke the Lord's words.

The thread enacted the will of God. God must want him to

entrust everything to his father.

Still playing, he began to speak. "The night that Uncle Zack died was when I found the jinn."

Five minutes later, still strumming, Gage finished his story: the thread, the visitor at the bush, the trip to see Grandpa, even the cat. Everything. Exhausted, he struggled to keep the guitar singing. If demons hated the thread, they'd hate the sound of it, too. They'd be unable to hear anything that was said softer than the strings.

Dad looked stern, looked worried. It was all going to come down on Gage's head. He'd be grounded for a lifetime, his guitar seized, his game crushed beneath the car's tires. Although, he should face facts. The thread would enact the will of God, and if God wanted Gage to trust his father, then God would likewise guide the man to be a trustworthy parent. Maybe God wanted Gage punished, and if so, that was the best outcome.

Dad eventually said, "This is way too big for you."

"I'm trying my best, but I didn't know what else to do."

"How could you? You're thirteen." Dad folded his hands in his lap, flexed his fingers, and shook his head. "What can a thirteen-year-old do in the presence of angels and demons?"

"Jesus was twelve asking questions in the Temple."

"But that was his Father's business, and I'm certainly not sending you to the mouth of hell on my business, let alone your uncle's." Dad closed his eyes. "You've tried to head in the right direction. It's surprising but gratifying to know how well you've managed to stay on the straight path despite all sorts of snares."

"I disobeyed you to visit Grandpa."

Dad nodded. "Now I'm understanding more of why you made such a bad choice." Focusing on the guitar, he leaned closer. "It's the top string?"

Gage angled it for Dad to see. He'd already gotten used to the new configuration, and his chord changes had begun feeling natural.

"I don't want to touch it and stop it from sounding, but I'd like to look at it more closely later. Where is the jinn?"

"Right under my window." Mek was running a child-sized finger over the carpet fibers. "Can you see anything?"

"Not a thing." Dad took a deep breath. "I don't want it to stay."

"How would we even evict a jinn" Gage frowned. "Besides, what if there's still danger?"

"That's a concern." Dad smoothed his mustache and gave Gage a sudden quirky smile. "Why couldn't you bring home a puppy like every other boy?"

It took Gage a half second to realize his father was joking. Dad rested a hand on Gage's knee. "Let the jinn stay for now. If its memory is as poor as you say, it will wander off on its own without any encouragement."

Dad waited a moment before taking a very deep breath and getting to his feet. "Now for the most serious part: what was it you saw in the garden?"

Playing the guitar meant Gage couldn't knit his fingers or bite his nails. "I was hoping you'd tell me."

"People train for years to discern something of this complexity." Dad paced. "You don't get that luxury. Either way, you're dealing with something smarter than the smartest human that ever lived. It's going to be difficult to catch it in a lie and impossible to trick it."

"Except for the grace of God," Gage said.

"Which we mustn't presume on." Dad frowned. "I dislike that it came when you tried to use the thread. It implied that you can use the thread, once you know how. If using that thread is working magic, that's exactly what a demon would want you to think—that you can do it, if only you do it the right way. But by the same token, ostensibly it came to caution you to use the thread judiciously, maybe to protect you from yourself."

Gage was frowning. "You mean I might not have the grace to discern this spirit because I invited it in by trying to use the thread?"

"Unfortunately. All I know is that God doesn't appreciate demands and presumptions. Prayers, requests, praises, questions—those God seems to honor. Doing something foolhardy while presuming that God will act just because He can—that's an attempt to make God less than God." Dad sighed. "If God is nothing more to us than a force we can manipulate by just having the right amount of faith and saying precisely the correct words the right number of times, then we might as well be working magic ourselves."

Gage whispered, "I really messed things up."

"I still think you're navigating remarkably. Better than your uncle did."

"And Mom?"

"Your mother didn't face anything of this severity." Dad's mouth twitched. "Nothing even close. To her, the jinn were stray animals. They showed her the humor of God. They taught her about trust and about living in the present."

"Mek can wander away in the middle of a sentence. Their treasure is what interests them at the moment. They really like small things." Gage watched his fingers picking through chords. "They'd rather collect marbles than talk to angels."

"They're not equipped for that kind of interaction." Dad sighed. "Neither are we."

He sat again on the edge of Gage's bed. "What I'd say to anyone from the church with such a visitation is to pray over it and not to do anything inconsistent with revealed truth in scripture." Dad raised his eyes and bit his lower lip. "If an angel appears and urges you to pray for Jeff, do it. It's unlikely that having you praying could thwart the will of God. If you receive a heavenly message urging you to kill Jeff in order to save his soul, don't do it."

Gage frowned. "But this—"

"—sounds ambiguous enough to go either way. Exactly." Dad shook his head. "Did you find the thread against God's will so that you mustn't use it? Did you find it because God wanted you to use it? Is it a tool to be used only when the time is right? Or, and this thought frightens me, is it an ordinary steel string, and the demons are making an ordinary object seem invested with power?"

Chapter Fourteen

"Yikes," whispered Taylor. "I never even thought of that."

"Me neither." Gage clenched his hands. "I thought Dad could help, and now I'm more confused than before."

They were in the church before Sunday services. The Greymore family took up a lot of space before being seated, and most of a row afterward. Even then, one or the other parent was often taking a noisy baby or a preschooler out to the foyer or escorting one of the older children downstairs to use the restroom. Gage sat with them to play shepherd to the younger ones. (Youth-herd?) The jovial chaos seemed like how a "real" family ought to feel, rather than Dad at the pulpit and Gage sitting alone.

Gage said, "How would I know if the thread is making things conform to God's will, or if it's demons making it seem as if the thread is doing those things?"

Taylor pulled a hymnal from her three-year-old sister's

hands and replaced it in the rack attached to the row in front of them. The Greymore family always sat in the back of the church so as to disturb as few families as possible. Even so, once every few Sundays someone would sit next to this family, fully seeing their five children, then give irritated sighs when the baby fussed or the toddler whispered to herself while fitting together a cardboard jigsaw puzzle.

Pulling a stuffed toy from her mother's diaper bag, Taylor said, "I'd look at the collateral evidence."

Someone said hello to Gage as she walked up the aisle. Gage usually tried to sit in the middle to avoid this kind of thing. He turned back to Taylor. "You're losing me."

Taylor made the stuffed animal into kind of a puppet. Every time she jabbed at the three-year-old and pretended to bite, the little girl giggled. "*Roar!* You know, what it seems to have done—*roar!*—and what it hasn't done—*roar!*—and what everything else does around it."

"That won't work." Gage watched the puppet show. "They're smarter than we are. Anything I can think of to test for consistency, they'll have too."

"What else do we have to go on?" Taylor stopped playing for a moment, and the three-year-old protested. "At some point you'll get to something that's either true or it's not true. *Roar!*"

Gage said, "You should be able to tell a tree by its fruit. But to tell the fruit of this tree, I'd have to use the thread first, and that's what I'm not sure about."

Taylor huffed and rolled her eyes. "You have so already used it. Didn't you consult it about whether to talk to your dad?"

"But I also disobeyed and went to Rutland to find out more about it."

Taylor grinned. "That's the fruit of you being dumb."

Gage made a face at her. "Gee, thanks."

Taylor said, "Anytime," and then the service began.

Jeff remained in the church parlor, so Gage concentrated on the service without worrying about what his cousin might think of him, or if his cousin might feel pain when he heard Dad preaching. Gage listened to the readings with hunger for reassurance. Since it was Dad giving the sermon, Gage knew it might not necessarily be inspiration or divine coincidence that guided his father's words. That was the problem with having your own father as your pastor. It must be easy to hear a regular pastor—a guy you only saw on Sundays—as inspired and authoritative. But Gage looked up and saw the guy who sometimes forgot to buy milk or ran the washing machine on hot with one red sock among the whites.

During the period of reflection, Gage first saw the man. Tall, dressed in a suit, he stood in the center aisle about ten feet in front of Gage. Gage glanced around, but no one else was reacting.

Gage blinked, but the guy remained right there, staring at him.

"The Lord has said this," the man said in a dusky tone. "You have disobeyed and experimented with powers reserved for the angels. The Lord says to you, 'This far and no further,' for you have worshipped my angels and played the lord to my jinn."

Gage began to reply, then stopped himself. Everyone else sat in silent reflection, and they'd hear him. The man cast no shadow. His voice made no sound. Like the previous visitor, he had no body language.

Who are you?, Gage mouthed.

"I am the messenger of the Lord," the man said. "Defy my words at your own peril. Destroy the thread. Leave the boy to those charged with his safety. You are foolish, and you will only jeopardize your own soul."

The man was no longer there. Gage turned his head to scan the other worshippers, but no one had reacted. The time for reflection ended, the music began.

Was it light or darkness he had seen mirrored in the center aisle?

At the end of the service, Gage separated himself from the Greymore family and sat in one of the front rows to wait. He might as well go get Jeff. Sometimes it took an hour for Dad to extract himself from his congregation. Today, Gage fidgeted while remembering everything about the tall man. The people of the church were nice, and ministering to them was his father's job, but it always seemed like the last person had departed when suddenly one more would show up with a life-changing crisis.

Come on, Dad. Jeff was waiting, and Gage needed advice. Pastors were allowed to have problems too—weren't they?

Dad looked as if he hadn't slept well, but Gage had gotten a full night's worth, comforted by the slight weight of the jinn at his back. Once during the night he'd awakened to feel it pushing something small into his hands—a gift of treasure. It sang a simple phrase, like a preschooler chanting a nursery rhyme. It could have been ancient Hebrew or Mayan or the tongues of the angels or maybe just gibberish.

sha-la-ma-ren-a-det-ma-doe,

a-ver-a-mer-ka-la-sa-noe.

Hey-diddle-diddle. Georgie porgie pudding-in-pie. Anna banana plays the piano...

Taylor darted over to Gage. "I looked at Psalm 39, and it hit me that *God* shut his mouth, not demons. Maybe it's not a mute spirit."

Gage straightened. "Why would God stop Jeff from speaking?"

"You'd have to ask God." Taylor glanced up. "Mom and Dad are leaving, so I've got to run. But we already talked about how John the Baptist's father couldn't speak either, and that was something the archangel Gabriel did."

Gage looked at his hands as Taylor left. Dad was still speaking to Mrs. Isaacs about her son's unemployment, and

Gage seethed. She was the grandmother of one of his classmates, and the kid's parents were getting a divorce, so Mrs. Isaacs could be talking forever. No one cared about the pastor's kid. They only cared about themselves. It wasn't fair.

Gage closed his eyes and tried to find God. It was hard to get calm. Instead, he opened the nearest Bible and thumbed through it.

Son of David, he read, *have pity on me.*

And Jesus asked the man, what do you want of me?

Lord, I want to see.

Gage held that scripture in his mind. *Lord, I want to see.* His eyes burned with unshed tears. *I just want to understand what's going on, what I should do, who I should listen to. I'm afraid and I'm stupid and I'm just me. Everyone's hurting all around me, and I don't know what I can do, or what I should do. Lord, I want to see!*

As he prayed those last words, his father called, "Hey, Gage?"

He turned toward his father and opened his eyes—

—to find the world in sepia tones. Gage shot out his arms to steady himself, but the benches were an almond-hued haze. The church sanctuary wavered like an image projected onto a classroom wall.

The people, though! The people glowed like the glass-tinted flames of votive candles. He couldn't make out anyone's facial features or their clothes or their hair. Instead he recognized everyone by the "selfness" streaming from their souls. Without any ability to interpret what he perceived, he absorbed from his father's heart all the characteristics that made Dad himself. Everything Gage admired or found annoying about his father had expression in that radiance of soul—a composite of everything his father had ever done or experienced, all his dreams and sorrows and hopes, but Gage couldn't remember his own father's name. A name was sound. This beholding was the fullest expression of his father's identity.

Gage recognized all this just in time to register the current rippling through the room—the grace of God surrounding them like a stream. As Gage focused on each person, he saw the sinuous wavelets either passing through the bright lights or breaking around them like a rivulet around rocks. Not all the souls glowed the same way. Some were shot through with colors, and some cast their light further than the rest.

Still gripping the semi-transparent bench, Gage now recognized the presence of the more powerful beings, the angels, each transcending language exponentially more than a soul transcends its human name. Like a man gazing into a canyon, Gage found himself dizzied by the hot holiness of the creatures—and at the same time terrified by the patient hatred of the empty spaces in the room, patient like a cougar waiting.

One of the empty spaces turned toward Gage, and its gaze bore right into him.

Gage screamed. He bolted, forgetting that although he could see through the bench, he couldn't run through it. The back of the next row knocked the wind from him even as he dropped to the floor. Nowhere could he hide—not from this thing that saw through walls that had no more substance than imagination.

Dad rushed toward him, but Gage backed away so the thing wouldn't come after Dad, too. *God—God—help me!*

The dark thing halted. Dad's hands rested on Gage, who curled around himself like an egg. *Please, God, protect us from that! Please, please, please...*

Gradually Gage realized the thing wasn't there any longer, that the room felt lighter. He looked up to find himself enveloped by the glow of one of the angels. The liquid light took the shape of a face, then coalesced into a boy his size wearing armor and a helmet. The evanescent figure thrust his sword into the floor to resemble a cross.

The boy squatted face to face with Gage, between him and the sword. *You prayed to see.* The boy looked friendly, although he wasn't smiling. *Don't be afraid of me. God knew you were ready to see. But for now, stop seeing, and find peace.*

The angel traced his fingers down Gage's face from forehead to cheekbones. Gage found himself utterly focused only on the angel's eyes, which then diffused once more so he could see the design on the handle of the weapon—three triangles inscribed by spirals and surrounded by four stars.

The world snapped back to itself, solid walls and benches and his father embracing Gage on the floor of the church. Gage's breath caught as he looked into his father's ashen face. Dad was repeating, "Gage, what happened?"

Gage started crying, burying his face in his father's neck and shoulder, glad for the solidity and the scent of his father's aftershave.

⸺◦⸺

Dad paced his office for five minutes by the clock.

"I really don't know what to say," Dad finally admitted, "except that this is all-out spiritual warfare."

Gage knit his fingers. What would his father's desk look like in see-through sepia? How did the African violets on the windowsill seem to an angel, and what would the jinn have looked like had one been present?

The phone rang. Dad ignored it.

"We both think what you saw was 'real'," Dad added. "But I have no idea why God's will would be to show that to you."

Gage heard a plaintive note, almost jealousy...but not quite. There was awe, but also confusion. God called the people God wanted—not the ones most qualified. If Gage could hear his father's sermon and see only the man who squeezed the toothpaste from the middle, then how much harder was it for

135

his father to see his awkward, scatterbrained son as the recipient of such a spiritual gift? They both knew how little Gage deserved it.

Rubbing his leg where he'd banged into the bench, Gage said, "The thread wasn't anywhere near when this happened."

"What?" The pure surprise in Dad's voice brought Gage up short. "I figured you were carrying it."

The phone rang again.

"I'd probably lose it." Gage forced a smile. "That'd be me: give me the True Cross of Christ, and I'd leave it somewhere."

"Maybe it left residue on you?" Dad didn't sound entirely convinced as he said it.

The thread had broken cleanly the two times he'd pinched it off. "The first time I saw jinn, I didn't have a thread."

Dad paced the office again. Another phone call. If enough people called, maybe the phone itself would begin to worry about Gage. He rested his chin in his hands and let his mind return to the world in sepia tones, the susurrations of grace streaming about him, and finally that young face which dismissed the famished emptiness of the demon. The experience came back to him with the same clarity, replayable in his mind as if indelibly inked.

"Earth to Gage." Dad rested a hand on Gage's shoulder. "You've now had two visitors and something that seems to be a vision. The two visitors had different messages. The question is, which to believe, if either."

Gage said, "The first said not to play with it or experiment. The second said not to use it at all."

Dad folded his arms. Gage recognized from the furrows in his father's brow that he was praying.

"We're so small," Gage murmured.

"That's why I wanted you out of this." Dad shook his head. "Zack said he'd protect Jeff, and Jeff got hurt—hurt twice, because first he lost his father and then he lost his voice. I don't know what Zack agreed to, only what he was asking."

Dad glanced at Gage. "He wanted me to send you to be protected as well. They turned on him when I refused."

Gage's voice wobbled. "You mean, if I'd gone, he wouldn't have died?"

Dad rubbed his chin. "If you'd been there, you'd have died too."

Late that night, Gage flopped in bed and couldn't find a comfortable position.

The vision was real. Of that Gage felt convinced. It had come in response to prayer—to a specific prayer—and it felt as vivid to him now as it had at the time. He could still recreate in his mind's eye the face of the angel.

Gage hadn't thought to ask for instructions from the vision when it happened. He wasn't eager to pray again for the same experience, and even if he did, he wouldn't have the presence of mind to ask questions this time, either.

"God's mad at him."

Gage propped open one eye. Sitting on Gage's ankles, Mek had substance now. Even though Mek obviously meant Jeff, Gage said, "God's mad at every human, Mek. We're all sinful."

How much did you have to water down theology for a jinn? Regardless, Mek seemed less intent on human-divine relations than on Jeff. "I'm going to tell God what he did, and God will get madder." Mek paused. "Do you think God will hurt him?"

"God isn't mean."

Mek's lips pursed. "Jeff makes the world unhappy. The world doesn't like being sad. It will try to send him away."

Gage's agitated mind toyed with the image of the Earth forming a personal-sized volcano beneath Jeff's feet and blasting him—and only him—into space, Jeff all the while with his arms folded and his eyebrows solemnly knit.

Mek said, "Take this."

Mek pressed something into Gage's hand, but he couldn't see it in the darkness.

"It's a pretty stone," Mek said. "I found it between the walls yesterday."

"Thanks." Gage tucked it underneath his pillow. "Treasure for me, huh?"

Mek laid across the foot of the bed, feet waving in the air. Both cats sat on the bed as well, Salty sharing Gage's pillow and Pepper halfway, paws tucked, not quite relaxed but not perpetually ready to bolt.

Gage said, "Do I make the world sad?"

"The world is always sad. You don't make it any sadder."

Maybe the little jinn footprints crisscrossing the earth served to make the earth happier in the places where they alit. Settling deeper beneath his blankets, Gage imagined the sparks of innocence traveling the world's surface in pairs, seeking bits of treasure and encouraging the animals and the trees. Through the jinn, the world could cry for every broken-winged bird and mourn every flower snapped at its stem.

Never tested, and therefore never found wanting. For a moment, Gage envied that freedom. With better long-term memory, Adam and Eve might have behaved like this in the Garden. A life lived moment-to-moment, unneedful of contingency plans or insurance: humanity could have had this. Even more, the human race could have lived with the intimate knowledge of what its home wanted, and it could have known in an instant all the ways human development could hurt or help the land and the sea and the air. Instead, the first pair had rejected the standards God set, and now the earth could only use the jinn to express its pains and its flickering joys.

Mek nudged Gage. "Hey! Come back."

"It's late. Let me sleep."

Maybe jinn didn't sleep at all? Was sleep a need of nature

after the fall?

"No, no, no. Tell me how to make God get back at him."

"Jeff's got enough problems." Gage turned on his pillow, freeing an inch that Salty immediately claimed. "You already told God what he did. Now let it go."

Shortly afterward, the bed shifted as Mek climbed down, and Gage cocked open one eye to watch. The jinn touched the guitar reverently, then settled in the middle of the floor to play with treasure from Mir's bag. He closed his eyes and set his mind free again to wander the problem of the visitor, what the thread had done to Pepper, and what he should do about Jeff.

Gage jumped when a low note sounded. Scrambling to his hands and knees, he continued hearing notes sounding tentatively. Two flowed together, repeated, then replayed with more notes. The effect was more experimental than ominous. A couple of times Gage was sure the player had flubbed a note.

Jeff? That would be interesting, if Jeff were trying to communicate through music. A talented musician could communicate through whatever songs he selected or by the notes themselves, or by the tone and rhythm. Of course, Gage wasn't sure he could do that himself with the guitar, so if Jeff managed with a penny whistle, that would be darn near miraculous.

Presently Gage caught a movement in the center of his carpet, and he identified the child-sized shape of the jinn, still sitting criss-cross. The jinn raised a plastic recorder again and blew a few more notes.

Oh. It was only Mek, playing the recorder they'd used to raise the thread.

Before the jinn on the floor, something shivered. The jinn crouched forward, then played again. The notes were utterly without organization, played in no discernible rhythm or melody. Gage rested his chin on his folded arms.

Mek's head bobbed in time with the song, such as it was. The jinn seemed so much like a little kid that Gage pressed his mouth into his forearm so he wouldn't giggle.

In the dim light of his clock, Gage could make out very little, but the silvery thing on the floor had risen into the air in front of the jinn.

The silly notes picked up speed as the thing in the air sparkled and undulated. Gage came up a little off the mattress, squinting.

What danced before Mek was a segment of thread, either Mek's or Mir's. As the jinn played, the thread spun in spirals, then dipped and wove like a sine curve. It coiled tight and wove around its own body like a very tiny basket, then uncoiled and spun like a galaxy. Rocking side to side while playing, Mek coaxed the thread first one direction, then the other. The thread coiled and uncoiled, twisted and then straightened, dove and rose once more. All the while, the thread threw off a light almost solid in the way a nighttime jinn became semi-solid.

On Gage's guitar in the corner, the E string glowed, and Gage could hear its sympathetic resonance. The wood must be buzzing the way it would after the sound had faded but before the string stopped vibrating.

Mek grinned as the thread did laps around the room. It orbited the jinn, then tightened its rounds until finally forming a circlet, weaving around itself, and dropping on top of the jinn's head like a tiara.

The jinn shrieked with laughter. Gage found himself laughing, too. God was playing with His creation.

The jinn was fooling around with arguably the most powerful object on the planet—or in all the created universe—and it was playing back. And that was good.

Gage nestled deeper under the blankets even as the jinn scampered from the room, spinning the circlet of thread around one finger. It was very good indeed.

Chapter Fifteen

Early Monday morning, Jeff played a two-player game of Grooz Capture with Gage while the latter waited for the school bus.

Jeff was only a few months older than him, but right now it seemed like years. Gage glanced at his own reflection in the window. Did he look older today, too? At the same time, Gage ached as he saw his own face reflected so faintly that if he changed his focus, he saw only the world behind the glass. That was the way he'd seen the material world on Sunday.

Had it been so intoxicating that Gage wanted to do it again? Or was it selfish curiosity? Or, more troubling, did he want to do it again because it made him different? Different, or even powerful?

What a nasty thought. Couldn't that vision be attractive to him just because it was attractive, and nothing else?

Gage wished Jeff would send another message. Gage hadn't

sent much to him, either, not even game-related messages. He didn't speak much to Jeff now, as if being mute made him unable to hear.

For a moment, Gage recalled John the Baptist's father Zachariah, everyone asking him via signs what to name the baby instead of just speaking. Was part of Zachariah's punishment the fact that everyone around him thought him suddenly stupid?

What *do* you say to your cousin on the morning before his father's wake?

"It's not fair," Gage murmured.

Jeff paused the game and rubbed the palm of his right hand. In the background, carnival music played on and on.

⸻ ⬦ ⸻

The guys at school hadn't let up on Gage since the chocolate bar incident, and he flinched every time the bell rang for passing period. At least during class they couldn't call him Pastor Gage or make the sign of the cross or fall on their knees begging forgiveness. Between classes, however, Gage could only hunch his head and hurry to the next class, hoping his teacher was already there.

This also isn't fair, God. Blessed are you when they harass you because of me—that sounded so clean. They assault you, and you're blessed. Voila! But this wasn't clean or easy. Blessed are the poor—but you're still poor. Blessed are the hungry—but the ache still devours your thoughts and leaves you weak and short-tempered.

Gage had eaten a meager breakfast and a spare lunch with nothing sweet. Somehow his classmates always noticed. "Fasting Gage." "Saint Gage of Vermont." "Gage the Evangelist."

It isn't fair.

He wished he could tell them off so they'd leave him alone.

Dad would say that by tomorrow it would all be forgotten. Taylor wasn't getting harassed, but Gage had distanced himself from her to prevent the obvious escalation to "Saint Greymore" and "the Apostle Taylor." The bullying would never end.

Dad said that God chooses the weak things of the world, but why wouldn't God also make a few strong people to rein in the persecutors? If Christians were sheep, shouldn't they have a shepherd?

As Gage listened to his Spanish teacher, he wished he could prove to everyone he was right. He could whip the jinn out of his hat and stand at the front of the classroom with the thread. He could do something wondrous and make them all believe. Then they'd feel remorse for what they'd said because Gage had been right all along. Most of these idiots would probably hide under their covers clutching an old teddy bear if they had to deal with demons and people under real spells.

For that matter, they'd probably be so dumb that they wouldn't know what a demon was if it showed up. Then it would eat them.

Gage grinned, then looked down at his notebook so the teacher wouldn't see.

"Hey, Gage, what's this thing that's swallowing me?"

"It's a demon, Mike. Too bad you never went to church so you'd know what it is."

It couldn't possibly be God's will that everyone walked around all the time wearing blinders and bumping into walls. All that was a result of the fall in the garden.

But you know...Gage could fix it.

A dose of the thread could set straight all the kids who called him Pastor Gage. He could work just enough of a miracle to show them God's glory so they had no choice but to believe. He'd use it to make sure they all heard their consciences and admitted what they'd said to him was wrong.

Why stop there? If he could convince a school, why not

convince a whole town? Why not the state? He could go from school to school. He could send his classmates ahead of him and then follow up. It would require him rationing out the thread, but he could tell Mek the demons were still out there and make Mek dig up another thread. This time, Gage could keep it all.

God's will for Gage at school was to learn, but these bullies were stopping him from learning. God would want Gage to shove this impediment out of the way. Come to think of it, though, it would be much faster to use the thread so he could learn without studying. No matter what God wanted Gage to do with his life, he'd do it better if he knew more, and he'd definitely be better off if he went to a good college. Use the thread to ace the SATs, and he'd be in the money. Ivy League or a terrific Christian college—the sky was the limit. Find a way to apply the thread to his applications, and any admissions board would pass him right through with a full scholarship. It didn't matter at that point if God didn't want him to go to his top choice school. If "the things in the middle" loved the thread, then the people reviewing his application would get a good feeling just from looking at it. Wherever Gage applied, Gage was in.

How many threads were there? Perhaps Gage needed to downscale. He didn't have to bring *everyone* into line with God's wishes. Some people—like Mike—didn't even deserve it. Gage would have to use it sparingly, on only the people who really ought to have it.

Now everything made sense. The true power of the thread lay in using it discriminatingly. That must have been why the figure told him not to play with it. You could use it surgically to make specific things conform to God's will, but not others. The others would continue unchanged in their sinful trajectory, while the things you changed would align with God.

Gage's eyes widened. His Spanish notes looked totally

unfamiliar. He'd have to read them later to find out what the class had even been about. It hardly mattered, because he'd realized something.

God doesn't step right in and intervene. God lets people make their own decisions and lets them suffer the consequences of their own actions.

Therefore once he mastered the thread, he'd mastered God.

Gage could harness God. Then at the end, he could use the thread one final time and get himself into heaven.

Gage dropped his pen. The teacher glanced at him, but Gage got out of his seat and crept under his desk to find it.

God, I'm sorry. I shouldn't even have been thinking that.

"Hey, Saint Gage is praying!"

Gage came out from beneath the desk with his stomach tight. "Shut up, Mike."

"Mr. Jordan, Mr. Hall," the teacher said, "would you please quiet down?"

Gage sat again. The kid behind him passed up a note balled into a paper wad. Without opening it, Gage snapped it off his desk.

His stupid classmates. If they would only do what God wanted them to, they wouldn't be instruments of Satan right now, tormenting him, making him think up things like world domination. But that was why God had given Gage the thread in the first place. He was better at it than these morons, who wouldn't recognize a Godly thought if an angel descended from heaven and chiseled it into their foreheads.

Besides, what was so wrong about thinking of ways to use the abilities God gave him? Since the thread enacted God's will around it, God must want him to use it, otherwise Gage wouldn't even have it.

A smile burned in his throat, and he squinted narrowly at his paper. *Bully me all you want. But enjoy it now, because when I'm done you're going to wish you'd never been born.*

Gage blinked. He raised his hand and asked to be excused

from class. The teacher handed over the hall pass without so much as interrupting his own sentence.

Mike whispered, "Going on a pilgrimage?" and his friends sniggered.

In the bathroom, Gage ran water into his cupped hands and rubbed it on his face. *Please make it stop. I want to do what's right.*

If the enemies couldn't bully him into using the thread wrong, they were going to frighten him into not using it at all.

But what if I use it and things snowball?

Gage felt his heart stirring: trust.

I don't want to presume. They're telling me to presume.

Trust.

He closed his eyes. *They're all over me like cockroaches on a sewer.* Another deep breath. And another. *I'm trying to do the right thing by fasting to help Jeff.*

You have fasted enough.

Gage immediately denied he'd heard that, wrote it off as another temptation, and then found himself insisting he could fast Jeff into the kingdom of God if only he persisted long enough, prayed hard enough, and denied himself enough.

Discernment was...well, tough. These were two good things, but which of two apparent goods was from God?

Will you obey? came the question. *Will you try to force God's hand?*

Forcing God's hand?, Gage thought. *Isn't that working magic?*

Then, *Oh.*

Continuing to fast after he knew God had considered his prayer was like working magic. Do *this* and *this,* and God had to obey. Do *that* and these other things five times, and it insured God's compliance.

But Jesus said to be persistent. What about the widow and the crooked judge?

God was asking him to stop fasting.

But then why did Jesus say this kind of demon only went out with prayer and fasting?

God wasn't asking him to understand. God was asking him to obey.

Gage looked at himself in the mirror.

Magician.

Servant.

Gage took a deep breath and knew which title he had to choose. With that, he sacrificed his desire to fast the demons out of his cousin.

<hr>

Mek watched from the stairs. Every now and again, the jinn peeked up above the level of the carpet like a periscope, and always those eyes trained on the same threat.

The silenced one sat at the kitchen table, sometimes turning pages, sometimes only making sounds that resembled tiny bites. Fzt. Pause. Fzt. Pause.

An aftertaste of power surrounded the silenced one. Up poked Mek's head, and shining eyes regarded the back of the boy's head for a minute or longer. Hunched shoulders. Fzt.

Like a cat drawn to a twitching string, Mek neared the silenced one, then inched up the railing to get enough height to peer over Jeff's shoulder. In Jeff's hand was a green booklet, and also something that made Mek's fingers itch for its sweetness. It was silvery, pointy, less than a finger's length and with a tiny hole at the blunt end. It was wonderful—splendid—magnificent! God made so many wonders, and this was one. So pointy and smooth, it would slide into fabric without snagging. So pretty!

The silenced one opened to a new page, one with a picture. It looked like a boy and a man sitting on a bench. A butterfly hovered between them. Butterflies adorned the air like floating jewels. Mir once found a dead one and kissed it.

Mir. Dead butterfly. Mir. God, please. Mir.

Jeff picked up the shiny object and pushed it through the picture, through the face of the man, through his chest, through his heart. Fzt. Fzt. Through the boy. Through the butterfly. Dead butterfly. Dead Mir. The flat aftertaste of power. That beautiful, straight, powerful metal treasure.

Jeff turned toward Mek, who jumped off the banister and darted down the hall.

Mek now remembered another shiny thing, something the silenced one had taken, a treasure that he'd given to the jinn but then taken away during daylight. Mek's eyes glittered, and with no more impact than a shadow, Mek drifted into Jeff's room.

This wasn't comfortable like the place where Gage slept. Mek remembered the tall one had even said that, how the room needed to be different if the silenced one would stay in it. The bed was bigger than Gage's, but the desk and drawers were mostly empty. There wasn't a lot of furniture, just a clock on a small stand. The closet had boxes on the floor, not the riot of wonder at the bottom of Gage's or even the useful fun things like shoes and a fallen belt in the tall one's. Even the walls looked different, with tiny pictures behind glass, not big colorful ones affixed to the wall with plastic-topped wires. (Mek would have to get those out of the wall once nighttime brought solidity.)

The cats settled by Mek's feet, and Mek got down low to look into their entrancing eyes. They glared but remained.

Oh, right, the treasure. Mek moved for the drawers, head poked through the wood at eye level to search each of them for the circular bit of metal, smooth on the edges, just a bit of green in the grooves.

Not here, not here... Mek moved to the pile of clothes. Clothing had funny folds to hold things, and they were a thrill to explore. Mek dove through the pile and found some interesting bits, but not the purloined treasure.

Terrible silenced one. "God, he's so mean."

Try the backpack.

Mek turned toward the red backpack with black straps and silvery zippers. (Those made such a wonderful noise.) Mek inserted a hand through the fabric, and at the bottom encountered round metal flat bits.

Treasure!

Five, six, seven, so many! So many treasures, and didn't the silenced one deserve to lose all of them for being so nasty?

No.

Mek pulled back. "But that's my treasure."

Only the one. Not the rest.

Mek pouted. "They're all pretty. He doesn't deserve them."

Only the one.

"Fine."

It was only a few hours until nightfall, and then solidity meant a chance to take back the treasure.

A long time ago, that one time, Mir and Mek had been solid during the sunshine. They'd gone solid all at once, not gradually like when the sun went down, and it was a couple of hours before sunset anyhow. Both had felt a call, the irresistible thought of treasure in a bowl. No, not a bowl. Treasure in a circle. They'd run through the street, hiding when they had to, and then when they'd gotten close to the treasure, they'd heard demons. They'd heard a man dying, so they abandoned the treasure and ran like crazy. They had become insubstantial again, and that made it easier to hide because they could dive into a tree trunk and wait. That night, they'd asked God for help, and then Mir thought of finding a thread.

Mek rested against the backpack. After dark, that was the time to reclaim the treasure. Only one, God had said. But maybe Mir could take one, too. Something about Mir...? Oh, well, no matter. God had said Mek could take one, but doubtless Mir would take the rest.

Giggling, Mek darted downstairs past the silent one to look at the wires in the walls. The jinn gave no further thought to the hazy aftertaste of power as Jeff pushed a needle through line drawings on small papers.

Chapter Sixteen

Jeff's steps creaked as he walked over an inch of fresh snow. New snowflakes accumulated in his hair with a featheriness he couldn't feel and wouldn't care about until there had gotten to be too many of them. He kept his coat zipped all the way to the neck, and he wore a pair of Gage's gloves instead of his own.

He wandered from landmark to landmark in the front yard, took a snow shovel out of the garage and cleared a quarter of the driveway before abandoning the shovel against a snowbank. He walked around the side of the house.

Every so often he held himself motionless, a deer scenting the air with attentiveness for the steps of a hunter. The sounds of the main road traveled only faintly through the snow-laden air. Half an hour ago, a train whistle had sounded from the railroad crossing. Nothing more sinister gave evidence of itself. Jeff scanned the sky, but the only motion to catch his eye was smoke from a chimney over the hill.

Presently he continued toward the back. This time, he headed for the shed with the puny rosebush. At the heap of snow covering the roses, he pivoted. He could see the kitchen window where he'd watched Gage having a midnight conversation. How long ago had it been? Time felt telescoped, either too close or too far.

Jeff brushed the snow off the thorny stems with care, then studied the exposed plant to note every turn, every irregularity of color, every thorn, every bump where a leaf had sprouted this past summer. However many nights ago, Gage had used that thread on this bush, and the visitor had shown up in response.

Jeff stayed still long enough for new snowflakes to accumulate on his sleeves. There were plenty of thorns, but not all of them useful. That one, though? That one was sharp and exposed.

Jeff removed the glove from his right hand and jammed his palm onto the thorn, holding it there for nearly a minute. Red dots spread on the snow.

Eventually, Jeff returned to the house. Inside, he microwaved a mug of water to make hot chocolate, then applied pressure to the heel of his right hand while the water heated.

Just as the timer beeped, the front door creaked open. Momentarily came the sound of slow footsteps on the stairs. Jeff turned, then tensed as he saw who it was.

⚬

Gage's father met him at the door. "Put your backpack in your room. We have to talk."

"About what?"

"Just get a snack and then come downstairs."

In the kitchen, Gage grabbed a granola bar and poured

himself a glass of milk. In the family room, he found his father, Jeff, and—

"Grandpa?"

Dad was sitting on the recliner. "You laid all your cards on the table. I think you deserve the same respect. Your grandfather will tell you what he thinks is going on, and I'll tell you why he's wrong." Here Gage caught his grandfather chuckling. "And then you'll understand why your uncle did something I'm sure he regrets."

This had to be killing Dad. Gage settled himself with his snack on the carpet. On the couch, Grandpa sat with Jeff.

Despite that beginning, no one seemed to want to speak. Gage shifted his weight. Jeff was no help: he sat with his knees to his chest, staring only at his feet.

Dad met Grandpa's eyes, but instead of opening with a prayer, he said, "Well, this is your show."

Grandpa said, "I'm interested first in what Gage wants to know."

Dad hadn't shot Gage a warning glance, and this was, most likely, his only chance to get answers. So which was the better tactic—to go right for the tough ones and hope Dad didn't stop the conversation cold, or to lob a few easy questions to get a better sense of what his father would allow?

Curiosity won out over caution. "What kind of danger are Jeff and I in?"

Rubbing the heel of his right hand, Jeff showed every sign of paying attention. Gage was getting answers for them both, only Jeff would have never heard Dad's side before, just as Gage had never heard his grandfather's.

"The demons want to kill you," his grandfather said, "It's a physical danger, not spiritual. Only the things you do to yourself can harm your soul."

It's not often good news that someone only wants you dead. Gage followed up with the logical, "Why do they want us dead?"

Grandpa Rivers looked at Dad. Dad only folded his arms and sat back. "Go on. This was your story from the start."

"It's my wife's mother's story," Grandpa said, looking at Gage, "told to her by her father, and to him by who-knows-who." Grandpa pursed his lips. "I'm not really a part of it, other than I lost Vera, and then Jeannine and Zachary."

"If you're superstitious," Dad added.

Grandpa snapped, "After enough things happen to you, you take a second listen to that superstition."

Gage prompted, "So—?"

Grandpa said, "The two of you are the newest generation in a family line blessed by God."

Gage's eyebrows shot up. "What?"

"The Bible says the sins of the fathers will be visited on the children. It's even built into the Ten Commandments: *I the LORD your God am a jealous God, visiting the iniquity of the fathers on the children to the third and the fourth generation of those who hate me—*"

"But—" Gage scrambled to his feet, knocking over his glass of milk. "You said *blessed!*"

Grandpa said, "You didn't let me finish."

Dad went to get a towel. Grandpa went on, "It continues, *but showing steadfast love to the thousandth generation of those who love me and keep my commandments.*" Grandpa nodded as Gage stood open-mouthed. "It's also in Deuteronomy. *Know therefore that the LORD your God is God, the faithful God who keeps covenant and steadfast love with those who love him and keep his commandments, to a thousand generations.*"

Gage said, "Jeff and I—? We're one of those generations?"

Dad returned with a towel. "If you believe this story, which I don't necessarily. In Ezekiel, God did away with the notion of children being punished for the father's sins. *The son shall not suffer for the iniquity of the father, nor the father suffer for the iniquity of the son.*"

Grandpa Rivers said, "God did away with the curse but didn't do away with the blessing. God looks for every excuse to shower good things on His people."

Gage sat again while his father sopped up the milk. "If we're blessed, why would we be in danger? Shouldn't that make us safer?"

"Much has been given, and much is expected. The danger seems to increase with each generation." As Grandpa folded his hands, Gage noticed how worn they were, how spotted by hard work. "Your mother died because of it. Your grandmother died young as well—only forty years old. Her father died young, and I remember it mentioned that his father also died before his time." Grandpa sighed. "What they believed was there's a time of attack. The devil gets a chance to harm you, and you get a chance to choose sides. The ones who didn't die early lived extremely long lives—into their nineties and hundreds."

Gage's brow furrowed. "What about second cousins, or any other family lines?"

Dad said, "Your mother compiled a genealogy while she was a college student. There should be quite a few more of you out there, assuming everyone survived to have children, and assuming no one turned away from God. Especially if this line goes back as far as they say."

Before Gage got a chance to ask, Grandpa Rivers answered, "Back to the man whose death started the conversion process in Paul, whose words converted the known world at the time. You're a descendant of Stephen, the first martyr."

Gage looked at his lap and blinked hard. "And for a thousand generations, we'll keep being martyred."

Dad returned again without the towel. "Don't take it all unfiltered." He sat back in the recliner. "It's easy to believe any explanation in a time of crisis when we're desperate for answers."

Gage rocked back on his heels. Where was Mek? Also, Dad was holding this conference in the room farthest away from the guitar and the thread. Gage couldn't consult it to find out which man to believe.

Maybe Dad was saying Gage didn't need to rely on it—or rather, that he *mustn't* rely on it. God could speak to a person's heart any way God wanted to. The thread was—well, pardon the pun, but just an instrument. Everyone else discerned without using a thread. God had used it to help Gage make a tricky decision, but if God could reach Gage in a middle school boy's bathroom, God could reach him pretty much anywhere.

Gage turned to his dad. "Since you're saying Grandpa's story isn't true, then why have all these problems happened?"

Dad opened his hands. "As a pastor, I know *every* family has this kind of tragedy from time to time. The Stonehams had four funerals last year, remember? Are they cursed, or are they human? I've counseled too many families who are hip-deep in crisis, to the point where they wonder whether God exists at all. It may seem as if there's a trend, but it also may just be coincidence, or God may be testing our family right now, or challenging us to grow closer as a community." He folded his arms. "While it's true that your mother and aunt both died young, keep in mind that your aunt isn't in the family line—she's your aunt by marriage. In your uncle's case, it was a self-fulfilling prophecy. He thought demons were going to kill him, so he worked the kind of sorcery that enabled demons to kill him. He might as well have painted a target on you and Jeff."

Gage said, "What about seeing the jinn?"

As he asked, Gage had a sense of just how deeply he had betrayed his father by traveling to Rutland. His grandfather had learned about Gage's jinn and Gage's thread before his father had. His grandfather had heard about the rosebush before his father had. Thank heaven he'd listened to the voice of inspiration and told his father about that. He couldn't imagine how stung his father would have felt now if the first he'd heard of the visitor was through his estranged father-in-law.

Dad said, "Are you okay?"

"Yeah." Gage swallowed against the queasiness. "But the jinn—why can we?"

Dad's shoulders sagged. "Seeing jinn does seem genetic. But just because you've seen jinn, and your mother and uncle saw jinn, doesn't mean a generational blessing or curse is true. It's been coincidental so far that the ones who've seen jinn have died young. But again, Aunt Jenna couldn't see jinn."

Gage turned to Grandpa Rivers. "Could Grandma see jinn?"

He nodded. "She left them food on cold nights. They used to take our spoons, and one night she waited by the milk and demanded to have them back."

Gage said, slower, and in a quieter voice, "What about angels—or demons?"

Grandpa fell silent. Dad said, "You appear to be the first."

Gage looked at Jeff. "You saw the angel, too, right? That night in the garden?"

Jeff didn't look up.

Gage hungered to stop time for a few hours and think about what Grandpa had already disclosed. In a few hours he would come up with all the logical questions. Right now he could barely comprehend it all.

Well, this next one was for Dad. "Why did you change your mind about telling me?"

"There are too many temptations and trials being hurled in your direction. You were bound to become curious again. I'm letting him tell you in a controlled fashion."

"If I'm in this line of descendants," Gage said, "what can

Jeff and I do about it to save ourselves?"

"That was precisely my point in not telling you." Dad rubbed his temples. "I didn't want you to hear this rubbish because I didn't want you to feel impelled to take matters into your own hands like Zack did. I convinced your mother not to do anything, but both she and your grandmother lived their whole lives with a sword suspended over their heads. Tension, fear, anxiety—when would the blade drop? They acted as if they had no faith that God would protect them from the fruit of His own blessing."

Grandpa Rivers said, "Your grandmother died early because she gave up. She was resigned to the idea it was just around the corner, and it would be terrible when it came. She withered away."

Gage frowned. "And Mom—?"

Dad said. "Your mother tried to trust, but the fear was too ingrained." He didn't add, "by her parents," but it was clear from Grandpa Rivers' huff that Dad might as well have. "She envied the jinn their ignorance of the evil to come."

Grandpa said, "There are two big mistakes about the devil. The first mistake is thinking he's not good at what he does. The second is thinking him as strong as God, to the point that you can't resist when he comes for you. They're equally bad mistakes."

Dad said, "Your mom needed to let God manage Satan, and she needed to trust God would take care of her."

Gage got to his feet. "You can't tell me this and expect me to not react. I want to find out if it's true. And I want to know what to do if it is!"

Dad said, "There's no way to test if it's true. That's the first thing."

"Even if it is," Gage protested, "why would demons want me dead? So what if my family is blessed? Big deal!"

"So that you don't survive to make the next generation," Grandpa said. "Let's say you grow to adulthood carrying this blessing. What might you be able to achieve?"

Gage's heart grew momentarily cold. The hair had risen all along his neck and arms. He was barely aware of what he was saying when he whispered, "Each generation gets more powerful, closer to something. Each succeeding generation walks more closely in line with the will of God. Who do you then become? The next Apostle Paul? The next Elijah? The witnesses who pave the way in the Book of Revelation?"

Dad blinked. "Gage, I don't even think it's true."

"It makes sense, Dad." Gage dropped to sit on his ankles. "There's something we're working toward, isn't there? Genealogy is important, otherwise two of the Gospels wouldn't start with Jesus's lineage. Every generation that doesn't turn aside from God gets closer to that something. We must be a hundred generations in by now. No other line has lasted this long. The enemy's running scared."

The words felt correct as he said them, even if Dad wanted them to be wrong. At the same time, Grandpa's version didn't feel entirely right, either. Taken the wrong way, it did sound like a curse. You get blessed, and then you die. But that was wrong. Something bigger would be at play. As Dad had said, Satan could tell you part of the truth if it led you to swallow the more frightening lie. His grandfather had swallowed the biggest lie of all, that God's blessing meant suffering. Instead, Gage had to listen beyond the edges of the truth they knew, and he had to hear the truths that hadn't yet come to light.

CHAPTER SEVENTEEN

Uncle Zack had an open-casket wake. When Gage arrived in a room oddly hushed for having so many people, he went up close to pay his respects.

Uncle Zack didn't look like a man murdered by demons. Gage had never verbalized his fears, but now he realized he'd interpreted his father's reticence as a statement of dismemberment, a body pulverized and then stitched together like Frankenstein's monster. Instead, here lay Uncle Zack, all of him. All the damage was inside. That made it both better and worse.

Even so, Uncle Zack wore the ghosts of his fear in the tightness of his lips and eyes. Gage had attended quite a few wakes, but never before had he noticed tension on the deceased. Of course, never before had he looked for it, either.

Behind him, Gage felt the presence of his grandfather. He stepped aside to give the man a bit more space.

"Don't go." The thick carpeting and burgundy drapes swallowed the sounds in the room. Grandpa's voice barely penetrated the silence. "You just stay near me for a few minutes."

Grandpa draped an arm over Gage's shoulders and pulled him against his side. The air was sick with the scent of lilies and formaldehyde. Gage let the man's grip surround him like a stronghold. Grandpa had buried his wife, his daughter, and now his son. He had no more children to bury, but he might have to bury his grandsons. Dad had done Grandpa one mercy: at least he could keep them near.

When Grandpa released his grasp, Gage searched for Jeff. It made him queasy to see Jeff sitting on a velvet chair in the second row, unfazed. He might as well have been waiting for history class to begin.

Grandpa Rivers sat heavily at the opposite end of the front row, and he rested his face in his fingers. Uncertain, Gage put his hand on the man's arm, then leaned close again.

Dad came through later and rubbed the top of Gage's head. He wasn't the bereaved brother-in-law now. At the moment, he was the pastor, and he had to take care of details. Had everyone made him take care of all the details when his wife died? Being a pastor ate your every waking moment, leaving you little for being a husband, a son, a father. If you let it, the calling could devour all your energy. You had to tell it no. *No, although the cause is worthy and the need real, no, I cannot do this and that and at the same time that thing, too. Paul was all things to all men, but now I will just be sad.* Dad had always done his best for Gage, but he was never really off-duty. From the time Gage was little, he'd always run the risk of awakening to find a babysitter because someone had died during the night. Then Dad would return to make breakfast, barely awake enough to eat his corn flakes. He'd put Gage on the school bus before heading out to begin his day, five hours after it had already begun. Dad did set limits, but he tried to do as much as he could. Had he swallowed the unvoiced injunction that he could be his wife's pastor and bury her before being his wife's husband and grieving for her?

Gage slipped out of his seat and approached Jeff. His cousin hadn't reacted to any of the friends who spoke to him, and he also didn't react when Gage put a hand on his shoulder.

It was a page from his father's instruction book. His dad had squeezed him on the shoulder ever since Gage could remember to tell him "Good job" or a dozen other things he didn't put into words.

Gage went on to the back to join a bunch of kids from school. "Hey, Jordan." One of the guys got closer to Gage, and the others clustered around. "Doesn't he even care? He hasn't said a word."

Gage said, "Cut him a break. Let's see if you're making speeches when your father dies."

"What happened to him?" one of the other kids whispered. "No one will give us a straight answer."

"Because no one knows. There was an autopsy, but it's inconclusive."

That left everyone awkward until someone started complaining about the English test. Gage let them change the subject so he could approach Taylor, who was signing the guest book.

"Jeff doesn't even look sad," Taylor whispered as he joined her. "Whatever silenced him didn't take just his voice. It took every means of communicating."

Gage nodded in his grandfather's direction, and Taylor followed his gaze until she saw the man. He was talking with two other mourners.

As Taylor's eyes widened, Gage whispered, "Dad invited him over before dinner so he could tell me all the things Dad didn't want me to know." Gage's hands clenched. "Now I'm not sure what to believe."

"Can you tell me?"

Gage hadn't taken his eyes from his grandfather. "I probably shouldn't."

"It figures." Taylor's shoulders dropped. "I knew it had to be something big if your dad didn't even let you visit him."

Gage chuckled as he stared at his hands. "It's not as if Grandpa is the tree of knowledge of good and evil."

Across the room, Jeff sat as if waiting for a bus.

Taylor said, "So your dad was wrong? Your grandpa did know what was going on?"

Gage turned his gaze back to Grandpa, who looked so much older now than he had before. "I have all the information he has, but I think he's missing some of it. And now, it's up to me not to make all the same mistakes as Uncle Zack."

<hr>

Vermont winters came with a crystalline quality, sharp clean air, clearly defined clouds, and frothy breaths rising like chimney smoke. Icicles glinted along the house eaves in the strong sunlight, and the Tuesday morning shadows went from long to short while they buried Uncle Zack.

In the back seat heading home, Jeff sat as though waiting through a commercial break. Gage thought, *He just said goodbye to his father. Or maybe he didn't. Maybe he can't think the words.*

Gage said, "Dad, what was it that happened to Mrs. Fieldman?"

Dad's voice came thin to the back seat as he drove. "Lots of things happened to Mrs. Fieldman."

"I mean when she had a stroke."

The blue-grey shadowing beneath Dad's eyes had seemed to grow darker every day this week. Running a hand through his greying hair, Dad said, "She had temporary partial aphasia. When she had the stroke, a bit of the blood clot went to her brain and hit the part that allows us to speak."

"But she can talk now."

"The clot dissolved in a few months. It took work and a lot of time for her language to come back. It's still not perfect."

Gage said, "Maybe that's what happened to Jeff?"

"I don't know, Gage."

"Did she want to talk?"

"She tried constantly. It was as if she had lost her words."

Gage looked at his lap. Jeff simply stared out the windows at the snowy fields. It would have been bitter for Gage even wearing his jacket, but cows stood there, ordinary cows, and didn't seem chilly.

Whatever had stopped Jeff from speaking, it also seemed to have frozen Jeff's will to speak. Cows didn't have a "life of the mind" or an awareness of the world outside themselves. There's hunger and food, thirst and water, cold and shelter. Beyond that—satisfy the needs, and was there any thought?

Jeff had successfully communicated twice. Once through the game. Once by leaving the Bible open. Other than that, he went where told, ate and drank, and absorbed himself in the television.

They needed more information. Uncle Zack had worked magic to protect Jeff—maybe even protect him from God. Whatever Uncle Zack's technique, the demons had responded by killing him. They'd wanted both Jeff and Gage in the same place, presumably to slaughter them both.

Except that made no sense. Could the demons attack Gage before they got permission?

Gage closed his eyes. They were pulling into the driveway. They'd held the funeral at ten o'clock, followed by the burial and then a buffet meal back at the church hall—and although it was only three, he felt as if he should head for bed, as if the morning's funeral had tipped over and poured out the rest of the day.

Instead, he heard Dad say, "Taylor's here."

She had pulled up her bicycle onto the front walk and waited near the door. She probably hadn't been there long, or else she'd have been frozen.

When they got inside, she had a glow in her eyes, and based on how she watched Dad, she wanted him not to hear whatever she had to say. Gage brought her to the kitchen for a glass of milk. She trilled, "Ooh! Non-organic. Don't tell my mom!"

"What's the deal?"

"The deal is, I think I know how you can talk to Jeff again, or how you can get him to talk to you."

Gage blinked. "Should you be saying this?"

"I've been praying for protection nonstop since school ended." Taylor raked her hair back over her ear. "God's going to protect us from them. You know how Jeff talked to you last time?"

"Through the game?"

"Through another world. That's what we keep missing. When you get involved in something, you go away as if you tune out this world and go into another one in your own head."

Gage backed up a step. "What are you talking about?"

"You know how angels and demons are all around us all the time, only we can't see them? Or jinn—they're around, except you can see them, and I can't? You're able to see a world I can't, but maybe it's not just seeing." Taylor took a deep breath. "Maybe sometimes you're really going."

About to reply that this was bonkers, Gage stopped. "Mek says that sometimes. 'Where did you go?'"

Taylor bounced up on her toes. "The night the demons attacked the house, didn't Jeff play the game with you?"

"Yeah." Gage folded his arms. "It's just— That's so weird."

"It's bizarre, but this explanation explains a bunch of things."

"You're saying I'm 'going away' by being absorbed in what

I'm doing or by praying?"

"Prayer absorbs you that much?" When Gage nodded, Taylor said, "You're better at it than I am, then. I always get distracted."

Gage kept his arms crossed. "You're implying that when I go away, *they* can't find me. That doesn't make sense."

"Could it be you're moving closer to God, and they can't pursue you?" Taylor shrugged. "Or maybe they don't know where to look."

"That implies our enemies aren't very smart, and we know they are."

Taylor looked out the window. "You can't deny that whatever you're doing does seem to offer you protection. Either they won't go there, or else they can't. When you're missing a pen, you don't look on the ceiling. Maybe it never occurred to them to check somewhere you shouldn't by rights be able to go." Taylor finished her milk and set the glass in the sink. "Something else to consider. They never tried to come back to the house after that one night. Why not?" She cocked her eyebrows. "I don't know either, but whatever it was, you eluded them."

"Or the defenses got stronger." Gage sighed. "Or they wouldn't have done anything in the first place and they just wanted to scare me." He paused. "Jeff was the one who gave me the game to do this. For your theory to work, he'd have to be able to do it too."

Taylor looked at the floor. "I guess that's true. So it's not a good explanation after all."

"No." Gage lowered his voice as he moved closer. "Because of things I didn't tell you before, it means you're probably right."

⸺⸺◆⸺⸺

The logical step was testing Taylor's theory by attempting to "go" somewhere. Gage suspected he ought to tell his dad, but after thinking about it, he didn't, since even if it worked, he wouldn't be "leaving" the house, and he didn't need permission to stay inside.

Gage and Taylor moved to his room with snacks and their school bags. Gage had his loose-leaf binder open on his legs, and he ought to be writing the answers to his essay questions about the start of World War I. He ought to, but his brain churned too much on the problem of "traveling." Should he play the game? Should he try praying?

Hadn't Dr. Dasson said Heaven was equivalent to doing something a person loved and immersed them fully? What had she called it...? "Flow." She said flow was a little bit of heaven on earth, being matched up against an activity that's just a little too tough to do, so every part of the brain and body got marshaled to complete the task. That blocked every other thought, and the person became fully engaged.

Taylor finished reading her literature and picked up her math. Gage still had nothing but his name on a sheet of paper. With his ball-point pen, he sketched the design he'd seen on the figure in the church. Three triangles surrounded by stars and spirals.

Trying to achieve "flow" was impossible, as far as Gage was concerned, or rather, recognizing flow once he achieved it. He never did anything while "away," just whatever he'd been doing to "go" there in the first place. How would he detach from himself and his own consciousness enough to recognize it, let alone act, once he flowed away?

Moreover, Gage knew before starting that if the point of the exercise was to go outside himself, the act of monitoring himself to see if he'd accomplished it would drag him back. Hadn't exactly that happened when he'd try to pray with Jeff in the same room? Unable to concentrate, he hadn't prayed at all.

So what do I do, God? He really ought to be working on

different answers—his history essay, for example. He'd already drawn the insignia twice. He pulled out another piece of paper and re-printed his name at the top.

Taylor set down her math problems and went to Gage's guitar in its stand. She ran her fingers over the strings, letting them make random notes. She had a smile as she fingered it. Hers was a total awe of the miracle that was the thread, even though she had to take on faith that it was happening. Unseen by her, Mek sat at the guitar's other side.

Gage had been avoiding using the thread for so long that he hadn't considered it now. But if it was God's will that he be able to "go" places, maybe the thread could do the moving. That way he could stay in control of himself and what was happening.

Gage looked back at the paper with the insignia. The sound of Taylor messing with his guitar soothed him. Without regard for his unwritten essay questions, he drew the insignia a third time.

Mek looked at the paper and said, accentuating each word, "God is our only protection."

Gage dropped his pen. "What?"

Even as Taylor stopped playing, Mek said, "What?"

Gage stared right at the jinn. "What did you just say?"

Mek took a step backward. "Pictures mean things. I said what you wrote."

"Jinn can read?"

Mek blinked repeatedly. Gage groaned as he watched a jinn in the act of forgetting.

Taylor had never been a third party to this kind of discussion. She whispered, "What's going on?"

Very slowly, Gage raised the paper. "This. It's what I saw on the angel's sword."

Taylor nodded. "Okay."

Gage flashed the page in Mek's direction. "Mek, tell me again what this says."

Mek's face rounded into a smile. "God is our only protection."

Gage repeated it to Taylor.

She said, "The first figure. You asked his name, and that's what he said."

Wide-eyed, Gage nodded.

Taylor swallowed. "That means the angel who protected you was the same as the figure by the rosebush."

"And that was the one," Gage added, "who said I could use the thread."

⸻ ❧ ⸻

CHAPTER EIGHTEEN

⸻ ❧ ⸻

Gage sat with the loose piece of thread between his fingers, rolling it until it warmed to his touch.

"This is freaky," Taylor whispered.

Gage took a deep breath. "You're my lifeline. You'll be praying for me the whole time."

Taylor clenched her hands, but she forced a grin. "Be sure to come back because I'm not sitting here and praying forever."

Enoch had walked with God and was no more. Gage wouldn't dwell on that.

Taylor strummed the guitar. Gage had taught her three simple chords, but in reality any noise from the guitar would serve. He prayed for her protection. He prayed that whatever the jinn had done to the room would hold fast.

Taylor strummed from E minor to A to E minor to A minor. The guitar still held its odd tuning from when it had "spoken" to him about how it wanted the strings, so Taylor's fingers looked like a mismatch for the sound. The guitar rang with the richness for an extremely long time after every strum, and Gage felt the thread loving the instrument, the instrument loving the thread, and both loving their God.

With the loose segment of thread between his thumb and first finger, Gage prayed, *Lord, let me come to you. If it is your will, please let me come to you.*

Gage opened his eyes and was disappointed to see he was right where he started. Here he was, listening to the drone of Taylor's strumming, breathing, watching a jinn pushing in futility at a toy car.

Before Gage could gather himself to try again, he had the sensation of coming up from underwater and emerging into a lighter, gentler world. As he fought vertigo, he felt drawn to think deeply, to go inside himself where he could focus with single purpose. Although he could see the room, for all practical purposes he didn't because it was unimportant.

The sound of Taylor's playing may have continued, but why stop to notice that, either? Instead, Gage recognized the boy he had seen in the church, the one whose sword bore the insignia and whose presence had driven off the demon.

"Recognized" wasn't in the way the boy looked because Gage couldn't truly be said to be "seeing" him. Recognition lay more in the way the individual felt in his memory, his feelings combined with his experiences. Whenever he remembered his mother, Gage never remembered what she looked like, but he had a general sense of what it felt like to be near her. The same way, Gage knew the boy was with him.

He realized a number of things in immediate succession, feeling them like his own realizations but understood as "inspirations" from the boy.

The boy hadn't thought Gage would make it this far.

He was, however, pleased that Gage had done so.

Gage mustn't think of "going somewhere" as a place. He

could only move this way if he had a specific goal and a task that would absorb him.

Gage thrilled at it all. Was this Heaven?

The boy laughed, and happiness brimmed over the boy's heart. This was not heaven. Gage thought of an apple, of his human life as the skin of the apple, and God as the seeds at the core. Right now he lay on the underside of the apple peel.

He relaxed then. The boy let him know it was good to be here, that he enjoyed being with Gage, and that it was good for them to be together.

Gage wondered what the boy's name was. Oh, but he'd missed the obvious—it was the name written on his sword. "God is our only protection."

Gage tried to think of the words to tell the boy that he liked him and enjoyed being with him, too, and even though the words never formed, the boy was glad to hear this. A moment later, it came to Gage that God had made him and the boy so their souls fit together like two spoons. The boy had been made to protect him. The boy and he had been simultaneously made in the image of God and one another.

Gage smiled. *You're my guardian angel?*

God is our only protection, the boy sent back.

After a moment, Gage tried to shake off the marvel of the angel's presence. Focusing, he resolved to bring Jeff with him next time, if he could. Surely an angel could lift a geas left behind by a demon.

No!

Gage's heart raced. The angel had pulled closer to him. Didn't he understand?

I don't, Gage thought. *Help me to understand.*

It all blossomed then in his mind. Jeff wasn't mute because of a demon. Jeff had been muted by God—by a prayer Gage himself had made.

The angel had drawn so close that if he'd been fully in his own skin, Gage would have shoved him back. Instead, it felt more urgent, more as if they were united.

Gage had asked God to intervene to protect Jeff, to protect him before he asked. Instead of protection, though, Jeff had been about to ask for a terrible thing. In answer to Gage's prayer, God had muted Jeff so that Jeff couldn't trade his soul in exchange for protection. The demons had retaliated, but Jeff was safe.

Safe until the moment he could speak.

Gage went cold.

God had effectively paralyzed Jeff's will, stopped the words before Jeff could even form them, in order to protect him from blasphemy. From worse.

Gage thought, *But after all he's seen—*

If he won't believe the Bible, the words arose unbidden, then even for miracles, he won't believe.

Gage covered his face with his hands.

The world thickened around him. Slowly Gage looked around at his room, at Taylor strumming the only three chords she knew. He watched her—minute by minute by minute—until she looked up and met his eyes.

She seemed worn and relieved both. "It didn't work."

"Praise God," Gage breathed, "it did."

⸺◦⸺

At Dad's office door, Gage waited while Pastor Jordan explained to a member of the congregation how to flip a circuit breaker. He and dad had a system for warning Gage off if the call were sensitive. Dad had a look in his eyes that said he wished the caller, not his son, would leave him alone.

As he disconnected the call, Pastor Jordan turned back into Dad, muttering, "Just because God said *Let there be light* doesn't make me an electrician." Then he saw Gage's face. "What happened? Are you all right?"

It was no longer "What's wrong?" because he and Dad were

on the same page. That was a relief.

The phone rang, and Dad silenced it. "Give it to me."

Gage related the story while someone across town talked to a recording device. Gage finished up with, "How do I make Jeff believe?"

Dad's face read a mixture of pride and resignation. *"You don't. God does."*

Maybe Jesus had also felt "powerless" in the face of free will. Even if Gage could someday work miracles, the one thing he couldn't do was force Jeff to accept the gift of faith. Fists clenched, Gage said, "After all he's seen, how can he not believe?"

"Just as the angel said. An attitude of unbelief colors all one's perceptions. You'll interpret ambiguous events exactly the way you want to. Signs look like coincidences. Miracles like regular unexplained phenomena, or else you convince yourself they're delusions."

Gage bit his lip. "How do you move someone past that?"

Dad leaned his chin on his folded hands. *"You don't.* I'm telling you this as a pastor who's seen hundreds of people wrestle with questions of faith. I used to roll up my sleeves and leap into the fight, defending God and providing proofs and theories and arguments. Sometimes it worked, but over time I've learned to provide the information and then back off."

Gage took a step backward. "We're supposed to preach to all nations."

Dad's brows raised. "Agreed, but we're not the ones who do the saving. God can soften a hardened heart. We're not making converts any more than we died on the cross. Don't forget, Jesus said it's a wicked generation that asks for a sign."

Gage folded his arms. "Peter converted because of a sign. All those fish." A moment later he added, "So did Philip."

Dad opened his hands. "God gave it freely, and they recognized it. They didn't hold their own souls hostage to magic. If you tell God, *Do this and I'll believe*, what do you value? A relationship with God? Or are you seeking thrills?"

Gage wrinkled his nose. "It's hard to win an argument with you."

"The object isn't to win. Let's get back to Jeff." Dad collected his thoughts. "Your uncle and grandfather—and for a while your mother—thought of God as a watchmaker. They'd tell you God set up the mechanics of the universe and then left them alone. To them, once God bestowed a blessing, it rolled downhill like a boulder, and He never paid it any attention as it crushed whatever lay in its path. In their scenario, God was a force."

"That makes sense." Gage pursed his lips. "Grandpa asked if I thought God's blessing was a curse."

Dad drew a sharp breath. "God doesn't set into motion scenarios He can't control. That's something I had to convince your mother of. If God gives us a gift or a trial, He's there with us. Becoming a man and dying with us was the ultimate way of expressing His presence."

Gage folded his arms. "But with my relatives dying young —"

Dad raised a finger. "Let me finish. God's greatest blessing is being with us every moment and loving us. In that sense, we don't need any of this thousand generations nonsense. We're all blessed."

Dad rested his hand on the Bible that lived on his desk. "Jeff will be blaming God for all this, since Uncle Zack certainly did. And now you're telling me that the reason Jeff can't communicate is God after all."

"But the reason—"

"Angels and demons are talking to you. We have to assume they're talking to him too." Dad met Gage's wide-eyed horror with weariness. "That occurred to me the instant you told me they'd approached you. Not everyone has the ability to discern spirits. Not everyone knows what questions to ask and how to sift the answers. Especially in someone already convinced that God's not merciful... Well, God's enemies would have a willing audience."

Gage worked his fingers into one another. *God, won't he let you touch him?* Running his fingertips in light circles, he prayed, *If today he hears your voice, don't let his heart be hardened.*

They tempted me, came the words into Gage's mind. They tested me although they had seen my works.

Be his God, Gage prayed, *and let us both be your people.*

Dad ignored the message indicator as it flashed at his elbow. "Theoretically, do you think that now you know enough of what you're doing to give him back his speech?"

Gage stared at the woodgrain on Dad's desk. "The angel seemed to think I could."

"I admit I'm in over my head." Dad shook his head. "I didn't take a seminary class covering what to do if your son receives a divine calling to free people from preternatural punishment."

"I got the sense," Gage said slowly, "that it's not a punishment. More like God put a protective shield around Jeff to prevent him from making the words that would have given the enemy power over him." Gage looked up. "It's a harsh mercy."

"That's the part of being a pastor I find the most difficult, and that's where only faith can keep the tires on the pavement." Dad met Gage's eyes without flinching. "All things work together for the glory of God, even things that hurt to the bone." Dad put his hands flat on the desk, then stood. "You and I—both of us—should pray over this. Pray for Jeff before you do anything, keeping in mind that I'd rather you not do anything at all. Also, I need to speak to your grandfather once more."

As Gage was leaving, Dad said, "By the way, even though you don't wear ties, would you happen to know where all my tie tacks went?"

"No, I—" Gage paused, then dissolved into laughter. "They're probably great treasure."

Chapter Nineteen

Mek had discovered a kitchen drawer full of nothing but treasure.

Off to the side of the other drawers, it was a marvel. There were buttons, batteries, strings, and a pair of chopsticks. Clothespins, a spool of thread, tweezers, instruction manuals, and a thumbtack that Mek touched over and over with one immaterial finger.

It was only noon. Mek didn't have enough substance to scoop the treasures into his bag, but in only nine hours, it could all go in. Just to see the treasures, Mek had to sit amidst the pots and pans and poke an immaterial head into the drawers. Oh, to lie on it, chin resting on his arms, eyes half-closed in content mastery.

The jinn traced incorporeal fingers over the rough strip on a book of matches. Only nine hours.

A bigger bag. That would be better. The belt pack would

never hold it all.

Mek paused, wondering.

Something about the belt pack. Where had it come from?

Like autumn leaves swirling in the wind, multicolored memories tumbled. Long hair, bracelets, and a beautiful laugh.

Mir.

Oh, Mir.

Mek huddled down among the pots and pans, knees embraced, mouth trembling. Those dark eyes, those hungry spaces and sharp edges. Swallowing and gulping so a jinn could only cling to any handhold. Sucking like a tornado. Like quicksand.

"God—I miss Mir. I miss Mir so much."

I know. I know. God was all around Mek, inside and outside, gentling the spirit and soothing the ache. Cuddled by divine grasp, Mek stayed absorbed in light for a very long time.

After a while, the limbs uncurled. The embrace eased. Mek looked up, then once again poked an incorporeal head into the drawer above the pot and pan cabinet.

Mek breathed, "Have you ever seen so much treasure?"

Yes, said God, making Mek feel very looked-at. *I have.*

Grandpa arrived in time for dinner, which left Gage startled and nervous. Jeff followed Grandpa around the house, avoiding Gage and Dad as much as possible.

What have the demons said to him? Is Grandpa his only ally?

As Gage set the table, he said, "Grandpa? What do you believe about God?"

"I believe in God," he replied.

"But what do you believe?"

Dad and Grandpa exchanged curiously blank glances. Oh, that again—he was afraid his views would be inappropriate to Gage's father. "Do you pray?" Gage asked. Maybe some yeses and nos would loosen things up.

"I read the Bible and pray," Grandpa said.

Gage said, "But who is God to you?"

Grandpa glanced at Dad, who said, "Go on."

Grandpa chuckled. "You've changed, Matthew."

Dad laid the hamburger patties on the frying pan. They sizzled. "I trust Gage to weigh his experiences against yours."

That was quite a compliment. Gage said, "Does God love you?"

Grandpa said, "I suppose."

Gage hid his inner flinch. "Do you love God?"

"I do my best," Grandpa said. "I don't think it's all about emotion and feeling. Those kinds of things are too changeable, too easy to misunderstand. You break up with a girl and think the world is ending, and the next day you meet another girl and thank God the first one dumped you. Clever people can manufacture feelings with lights and dramatic music, but that's not God. God gives us a job to do in this world, and our duty is to buckle down and do it. No feelings required."

"You're saying God is like a teacher," Gage said, "and we get graded on how well we do our homework."

Dad snickered. Grandpa grinned. "I like that image. God gives us assignments and report cards."

"But—"

"Gage," Dad said, "don't reward his honesty by being critical."

Gage pursed his lips. "Aren't we supposed to make disciples of all the nations?"

"Absolutely." Dad flipped the burgers. "But as I told you yesterday, dialogue is better than ranting, and your grandfather does have a point. How many times have you heard people saying God asked them to do this or God laid something on their heart? God does give us assignments, and at the end, I suppose we get a report card, only it's pass/fail."

Jeff still sat very close to Grandpa's side.

Dad said to Grandpa, "You've seen God acting in Gage's life to keep him protected. You've seen the kinds of decisions Gage makes when it's his own doing versus the kinds he makes when it's God guiding him. Plus, I know you're smart and your heart is open. That makes you a good debate partner for him." Dad turned back to the stove. "And you, Gage, remember what I said. The purpose isn't to win the argument. It's to understand."

Grandpa said, "Would God send Zachary to hell?"

Dad said, "Zachary might have sent Zachary to hell."

Grandpa looked devastated. "I don't like to think about that."

"I don't like to think about anyone making that choice." Dad snapped off the burner. "It's worse to think it might be my brother-in-law who made it. But God is merciful. We don't know what was in Zack's heart when he died, or what happens in the seconds between a human soul's death and its final judgment."

Grandpa said, "I thought you were one of the kind who thought, 'Out of the body, present with the Lord.'"

Dad said, "What are the mechanics of the soul leaving the body?" and Grandpa snorted. "Well, if I said I'm going home and making dinner, does that mean I didn't walk up the stairs or take off my coat? There could be time between bodily death and spiritual judgment, and for God, time is on His side."

Gage pulled dishes from the dishwasher and set the table. "Why didn't you ever preach the word to Uncle Zack?"

"Why do you think I didn't? Of course I did." Dad drained the corn. "I also tried to live a Christian life, and I prayed that God would open Zack's heart as well as Jeff's."

"Not me, though." Grandpa had a stern smile. "I'm just a

superstitious idolater."

Dad's shoulders slumped. "Please forgive me. I was too furious at you for too long."

Gage stopped setting the table and faced his father with confusion.

Grandpa nodded. "What's past is past."

Dad said to Gage, "God had to work on me for a while even to get me to the point where I could want good things for your grandfather."

Gage returned to setting the table. "So if we're not allowed to argue with people and we're not supposed to work wonders and signs, how did Jesus expect us to go out and make disciples of all the nations?"

"That's a worthwhile question." Dad brought the hamburgers and corn to the table. "Go get the buns and the pickles."

Go get the buns and pickles. Go make disciples of the nations. Go live a life so full of Jesus that at your own funeral, the preacher won't say "Turn to Jesus" because he can say, "Look at what Jesus did in this man's life." Oh, and while you're there, grab the serving forks.

God did give assignments. Sometimes your assignment was to set the table.

Dad's brow furrowed. "Why do you think Uncle Zack conjured up what he did?"

Gage said, "Because he didn't have faith in God."

Dad made a *go on* gesture. "Think. Lots of people don't have faith in God, but they don't walk around working incantations. What did Uncle Zack want to accomplish?"

Gage glanced at his cousin. "Protecting Jeff."

Dad leaned across the table toward Gage. "And why did he want to protect Jeff?"

Gage shrugged. "Because he loved him."

Jeff and Grandpa were both watching with intent. Dad said, "Zack knew there was a risk, but even if Zack had to die to protect his child, he was going to do it. That may even have been the bargain—take me, but let Jeff go. If you were looking at Uncle Zack as an example of how to be a parent, wouldn't you take away that you have to love your son no matter what the cost? Uncle Zack loved Jeff enough that he gave up his life to save him. *That's* what I mean by preaching with actions. But it presumes an open spirit in your audience, and you can never guarantee that. Only God can."

A moment later, after Dad put the ketchup on the table and pulled out his chair, he paused. "Now push it further, and that's what Jesus did, too. *Don't take them. Take me.*" Dad drew a deep breath. "Sacrificing yourself to save your child, if I may put on my preacher cap, is Christ-like behavior. I'm not convinced that anyone who acted like Jesus did is automatically condemned. That's how I still have hope for Zachary's soul."

⸻◦⸻

For what it was worth, after a very long conversation with Dad, Grandpa agreed that Gage should not try to end Jeff's silence. Gage wandered through the next two days, wondering then what good he even was.

"Where do you think it's all headed?" Gage asked Taylor as they sat in his family room. Dad was out at the church until dinner, and this being wintertime in Vermont, it was already dark at four o'clock. Jeff sat downstairs, watching a popular cartoon.

Curled on the edge of the couch, Taylor looked up from her short story assignment. "How do you mean?"

"I mean, what happens at the end of a thousand generations?"

"That's what, twenty thousand years? I'd hope Jesus would return sooner than that."

"If the enemy wants to disrupt the line, we've got to be

heading somewhere." Gage ought to have been doing math, but instead he twirled his pencil on his fingers.

"Maybe you get more able to do things, so your kids are able to see jinn and they're always able to see angels?" Taylor shrugged. "Or maybe they heal people with their hands? God doesn't always continue things the way we assume. Dad says grace is sometimes a surprise."

About to respond, Gage stopped when he heard a weird thumping. It happened again. Gage sat forward. "What is that?"

Both cats ran into the living room and stared at the fireplace.

"Oh, no," Gage whispered. "Are they attacking? We need to get you out of here. Maybe if you hold the thread—"

"Get a grip." Taylor snorted. "That's a bird in your chimney."

Gage's cheeks burned. Normal explanations seemed the furthest from his mind after all that happened. Except now that she said it, the random banging did sound like a bird thrashing its wings.

Taylor went over to the chimney. "Is your damper open?"

"Damper?"

"The thing that lets the smoke go bye-bye?"

Gage recoiled. "Why wouldn't you want the smoke to go up the chimney?"

Taylor sighed in exasperation. "When there's no fire you keep it closed so the heat doesn't go up the chimney and out of the house. How can you live in Vermont and not know what a damper is?"

Defensive, Gage muttered, "I'm sure lots of Vermonters don't know what a damper is."

Taylor chuckled. "When was the last time you made a fire?"

"Never."

"Then it's closed. We're going to open the damper and then get the bird to fly out of the house."

Gage bit his lip. "How do you do that?"

"I've seen my mom do it." She had a glint in her eye. "The time-honored technique is you chase it toward an open door while screaming, 'Sweet Jesus, get this bird out of my house!'"

Gage covered his mouth with his hands. "I'm sorry. Did your mom really—"

Abruptly Gage broke off. Mek ran up in front of the fireplace, pressing one cheek against the chimney wall, face wrinkled up in a frown. "The bird is scared. Let it out."

This was convenient. "Can you go inside the chimney and get it?"

The jinn's fingertips tapped the chimney bricks. "It's dark. I'm too solid."

Gage said, "Why can't the bird fly out?"

Taylor said, "Inside the chimney, they can't open their wings. The only way out is down."

Gage shifted uneasily. "We should wait until Dad gets home."

Pastor, there's a bird in my chimney. Can you get it out?

Mek pressed against the chimney. "So scared. The bird doesn't understand."

Gage clenched his fists. "Fine."

Taylor opened the glass doors, stuck in her head in the fireplace, and declared the damper shut. With a groan from the metal and a push from her hand, it clanked open.

Nothing happened. Taylor backed off.

Gage wrinkled his nose. "Why isn't it leaving?"

Taylor said, "I'll go look it up in my bird psychology textbook."

Mek whistled, a sweet trilling song—and with that, the bird burst from the fireplace. It careened around the walls of the room, banging into the windows and ceiling, and Gage yelped before ducking down on the couch.

Jeff ran up from the family room, then dodged as the brown missile swooped at his head. Mek stood on the arm of the couch, arms spread and laughing.

"I'm willing to try it your mom's way!" Gage called.

"Grab a broom." Taylor ran for the windows. "You'll need to shoo it toward the front door. I'll make it dark in here. Jeff, turn on the porch light and hold open the door so it has a clear path."

Taylor shut the curtains and lowered the lights while Jeff made the exit look as attractive as possible. With everyone at their stations, Gage approached with the broom. Clinging to the bricks, the bird kept adjusting the angle of its head. The bird had a round body with brown feathers. It was amazing something so small could create so much chaos.

"Mek," Gage said, voice shaking, "tell the bird to go to the door. Tell the bird we want to help."

As Mek got close to the bird, it exploded into flight. Gage ducked, and as the bird landed on the arm of the couch, a second dark shape launched.

"Pepper!" Gage shouted as the cat struck the bird.

The cats—he'd completely forgotten the cats.

Gage swatted the cat, but with the bird in his jaws, Pepper sprinted for the hallway and then Gage's bedroom. Gage dove to the carpet alongside the bed, lying flat to swipe through the under-bed with the broom. "Pepper, get out!"

Gage shoved the broom, bristle-first, at the cat, and finally the cat let go. Gage shoved the broom in between the bird and the cat, and then pushed. The cat backed off, eyes glittering.

Taylor dashed in with a towel as Jeff chased Pepper from the room. "I'm so sorry," Taylor gasped "Pepper doesn't usually even come near us. I didn't think."

Gage pulled back from the bed. "It's under there."

Taylor reached under the bed and came back holding the bird upside-down, her hand around its shoulders to keep its wings shut. Her eyes were glistening. "It's hurt."

She laid it out on the towel, and the bird extended then closed its wings.

Gage said, "We can't put it outside like this. Get your dad. He'll know what to do."

While Taylor texted her father, Gage laid the bird in a shoebox, piling up the edges like a nest.

Mek crouched at his side, lip trembling, enwrapped in the pain of tiny feathers, claws, and a little beak. One mistake in judgment, down a chimney, fear, and then death because the helpers hadn't been fast enough to avert it.

This was Gage's fault. Pepper wouldn't have been around if not for the thread, and Pepper wouldn't have dared attack the bird if he hadn't become more like a cat and less like a wounded creature himself. It wasn't fair. This shouldn't have happened.

Mek faced right up to the bird, crooning like a car engine. The bird flexed its wings again. It was bleeding. It probably had broken bones.

Could they use the thread now? But wasn't it God's will that cats hunt birds?

Mek crouched on the carpet with one knee on either side of the box. "Be still," the jinn whispered. "I'm near. Be still. Be God's." Slender immaterial fingers traced the bird's tight feathers. "I'm with you. Don't be sad."

Gage said, "Mek, can you do anything for the bird?"

"I'm being like God." Mek looked up. "God cuddled Mir. God will cuddle the bird, so I'll cuddle the bird, too." Mek shrank around the bird. "God did this for Mir. I'm going to stay, just like God."

Gage and Jeff stared, both transfixed.

Taylor set down her phone. "Dad says birds with broken bones don't heal, and the cat bite will likely kill it anyway." Her eyes glistened. "He said to either break its neck or suffocate it in a plastic bag."

Mek was still crooning. Gage choked, "I can't do that."

Taylor took a deep breath. "Dad could come here to take care of it, or I could bike it up to the vet and have them do it."

Gage had never been good at figuring out what types of birds were which. Blue jays he could identify, and cardinals. But beyond those, he was at a loss. This was one of the palm-sized brown birds he considered as ubiquitous as field mice. It was either a finch or a wren, or maybe the kind sparrow the Father grieves over when it falls.

Gage shuddered. "Tell your dad to come."

The jinn remained beside the bird, breathing onto it. "Small little one. I won't leave."

Jeff picked up Gage's guitar. His thumb brushed the the thread, but he didn't drop the guitar when he flinched.

Gage shook his head. "I won't use the thread."

Taylor recoiled. "Why not?"

"What Mek was saying—" Wait, Taylor hadn't heard that. "What if God's will is already happening?"

But Gage noticed something at that moment, something he wouldn't have understood if not for the angel's warning, his father's guidance, and his own experiences. Jeff's eyes were moist.

Jeff hadn't cried at his father's funeral nor blinked during his father's burial, but in a room with a dying bird, now he had tears.

Taylor sat back on her heels. "I think you should do whatever God tells you."

"You're right." Gage's throat tightened. "It's time."

Chapter Twenty

Jeff must think they were going to manipulate the thread to heal the bird, and as far as Gage was concerned, that much passive deception was acceptable. No, he wasn't elaborating his intentions, but he shouldn't telegraph to their enemies what he was doing—nor to Jeff. Jeff would resist.

Using the thread to force God's hand would be working magic. This looked like magic in a good cause, of course, but what temptation ever looked like evil? None. The lure had to stink of goodness, all the while prying the jaws of hell wide enough that Gage could dance right over the incisors.

Their enemies might have pushed that bird into the chimney. Or maybe they were capitalizing on a random accident. They wanted Gage dead, and they wouldn't hesitate to hurt a bird in the process. Maybe they'd provoked Pepper, too, hating God's merciful gift of amnesia and thinking it funny when one of God's creatures attacked another. By making Gage inadvertently responsible for the bird's pain, they had fine-tuned a situation where Gage could either work magic or feel guilt about watching an innocent creature suffer.

But for all their intelligence, the demons hadn't counted on the inherent goodness of the jinn. They didn't anticipate the way the jinn would mirror God's love, and in so doing, would touch Jeff's heart.

Are you ready? Gage prayed.

God had better be ready. God, who waited entire lifetimes for that one clumsy grasp from a muddy hand, poised to yank a soul out of the swamp where it was mired. Yes, God would be ready.

Gage set up Jeff with their Grooz Capture games connected via the pass cable. Next, he wound his length of thread around the cable and fastened each end to the units' belt clips. Although puzzled, Jeff didn't remove it. Taylor had her fingers resting lightly on the guitar. When he frowned at her, she whispered into his ear, "It's buzzing."

Gage hated involving her, but he had no choice. "Can you strum again?"

Lips tight, she settled the guitar on her lap.

Mek remained with the bird. Gage sat cross-legged in front of Jeff, then turned on both their units.

God, please bring us to you. Help us flow toward you.

The carnival music began, and Gage initiated the hunt. His little man set off in pursuit of electronic quarry, letting Jeff lead. Gage reached for God with his heart, waiting, caring, hearing Taylor's chords and Mek's assurances. Jeff's brow furrowed as he concentrated. Gage poured himself into the game, focusing only on the routine of pursuit and capture and the struggle to collect every last one of the Grooz figures without leaving even one behind.

Feeling a wave wash over him, Gage "came up for air," and he blinked. He could see the room, but more importantly, he could see Jeff. They were still playing. But at the same time, they were paying attention to one another. The thread burned against Gage's forefinger, but without discomfort. He sensed presences all around, one sensation familiar with its conviction that God was their only protection. Gage could trust that one to lead him only toward God.

Gage hadn't planned what to say, but he the angel at his side prompted him. "Do you choose these?"

That was when Gage recognized that the multitude around them weren't all angels. They were vacant spaces. They had hollow jaws and emptier eyes, sharp edges and a desolate yearning. They endlessly wanted—wanted not to *have*, but instead to consume.

Before he could recoil, Gage felt the angel's reassurance: they were not there for him. They could not touch him now.

But Jeff—

Jeff alone had the power to choose for himself.

You can speak now, Gage thought urgently. He didn't want to pronounce the words aloud. *God, tell him. Help him.*

Jeff had put himself beyond God's help unless he spoke up. Staring at the maelstrom encircling his cousin like a tornado, Gage forced himself to repeat, "Do you choose these?"

Jeff whispered, "No."

The empty spaces howled with the sharpness of sand in the wind. Gage grasped desperately for the angel, who reminded him that God was the one protecting them both.

I am a son of the Most High. They don't dare touch me. They cannot.

Gage felt the angel's prompt again, and he said to Jeff, "Do you reject them?"

Jeff's voice was broken. "Yes."

Okay, next step. "Do you choose the Lord?"

Jeff reached for Gage from the cyclone of empty spaces, and Gage felt the strong warmth of his cousin's hand clasping his. Jeff closed his eyes. "Just leave me alone."

"You have to choose." Gage gripped him hard. "The God

who held Mir, or the ones that lied to and devoured your father?"

Jeff's head whipped up. "God lied to and devoured my mother! They're both awful!"

"That wasn't God!" Gage was pulling Jeff as if to haul him out of the maelstrom, but Jeff was tugging back. "They lied to you! God's love isn't a curse. God is with us, just like Mek was with the bird."

Jeff yanked back his hand from Gage. "God stole my voice!"

Gage shot back, "God saved your soul!"

Jeff glared at him.

Gage clenched his hands. "My prayer took your voice, and I'm sorry. But I can't be your voice now. I can't choose for you."

Jeff recoiled. Gage said, "If you don't believe me, believe Mek."

The hungry empty spaces awaited. Patient. Craving.

Jeff reached again for Gage's hand. "I'll choose you. I can't choose God after everything He did, but I'll go with you."

The wild wind dropped to a breeze.

It is enough for now, the angel said. *He needs to grow beyond rejecting evil, but this is enough for now.*

The world solidified around them, and as even the breeze vanished, Gage blinked to find himself in his bedroom with Jeff still gripping his hand.

Jeff exploded into sobs, and Gage held him while Taylor wrapped her arms around them both.

<hr>

Jeff cried forever. All the pain and the terror of watching his father die while he'd stood helpless, all the anger at being misunderstood, all those times he'd wanted to speak, and the raw need for anyone to be with him... It came out all at once. Cheeks flaming, Jeff would pull away and try to backpedal, and then he'd lose the fight. When he didn't want Gage touching him, Taylor was still able to hold him, and he cried onto her shoulder.

Where was Dad? They needed Dad.

Jeff finally settled enough that it stopped, maybe because the grief had broken him, or maybe because he was too exhausted to keep going. He curled on his side, and Taylor sat with one hand on his head, the other on his arm. She met Gage's eyes, prompting him.

Gage flailed for whatever it was she wanted him to do. "I should text Dad."

His voice was wispy. Uncertain.

"Call Grandpa," Jeff rasped. "Please."

Mek was still focused on the bird, as though Jeff's tears and voice and soul hadn't all rushed back at the same time.

Gage went into the kitchen and texted Dad. "We need you home now."

What would Jeff be saying to Taylor? And was he really safe? Was the fight truly over?

Dad's reply came immediately. "What's the matter?"

"Jeff's talking."

Dad replied, "Give me fifteen minutes."

Gage sent, "I think it's going to be okay."

And from Dad, "Stay with him."

Gage moved toward the entrance, then remembered he was supposed to call Grandpa, too. He texted, instead. He may have won the world record for typos, but Grandpa agreed to come as soon as he could. That would be almost an hour.

"You did it," Grandpa sent at the end of the conversation.

"God did it." Gage's hands shook on the phone. "I was just there to help."

The doorbell rang, and Gage flung open the door to find not his father, but Taylor's. Oh, right. The bird.

While he'd been texting, Jeff had moved to the couch. Seeing Jeff's tear-streaked face and red-eyes, Taylor's father did a double-take.

"He's better," Taylor said in a whisper that broadcast her awe. "He can talk."

Mr. Greymore's tone was a match for hers. "Praise God."

Jeff stared at his lap.

Taylor had the bird in the box, and Mek remained at her side, stroking the tiny feathers.

Gage told the jinn, "It's time to give the bird back to God. Taylor's father is going to stop it from hurting."

Taylor's father would wonder who he was talking to, but who cared any longer? They were dealing with angels and demons and witchcraft and exorcisms—so why not add invisible nature-loving entities to the mix?

Mek looked only at the bird. "Say goodbye," Gage prompted.

Jeff sat taller. "Wait." It was so unusual to hear his voice that Gage jumped. Jeff said, "You were going to heal the bird."

Gage felt cold. "That's working magic."

Jeff's eyes darkened. "The bird is suffering because you're afraid to use something powerful enough to heal it. You're effectively killing it, but you're all like, 'Oh, I'm a good little Christian who doesn't work magic.' Are you proud of yourself?"

Gage recoiled. Taylor said, "After everything that's happened, yes, I'm proud he's not making things worse."

Jeff leaned forward. "Use the thread. Do you really think God's happy with people who torture sparrows? Why would God even give us that thing if we're not supposed to use it?" Jeff's eyes were brilliant against his flushed cheeks. "Why put the bird out of its misery at all if you're so concerned with letting God do His own thing in His own time? Maybe 'God's will' is to let it suffer until it dies in agony from a massive infection."

Terrified, Mek covered the bird with trembling hands. Gage lowered his voice. "I'm not going to work magic."

Jeff's mouth tightened. "How brave of you to say that when you're not the one who's suffering."

Taylor looked from one to the other. "Maybe if you just prayed, though? It's not working magic to pray. It's up to God if He answers or not." Taylor looked at her father. "Am I wrong? It's the difference between asking and telling."

As if Mr. Greymore were a spiritual warfare expert...? But at the moment, he really was the only authority they had.

Then beneath their feet came the rumble of the garage door. Good. Dad was home.

Jeff sat like a dark statue on the couch. "You can use the thread and make it happen."

Gage said, "I won't tell God to do anything."

Taylor said, "We *can't* force God to do anything. But we have every right to ask."

Gage glanced at Mr. Greymore, who said nothing.

Is it okay, God?

The bit of thread spread warmth through his hip, and Gage reflexively put his hand into his pocket. *Whatsoever you ask,* came into Gage's mind. *Whatsoever.*

Dad came upstairs, and Mr. Greymore stepped aside. Did the man look relieved? All he said was, "These kids need a pastor."

Gage pointed to the bird. "It's hurt. Jeff wants us to heal it. Taylor says we could pray. Can we?"

Looking from Jeff to Gage, back to Jeff, then back to the bird in the box, Dad's eyes were wide. "How would you do it?"

Gage said, "I would hold the thread. And I would pray."

Dad looked at Taylor's father. "Did you examine the bird?"

Mr. Greymore folded his arms. "I'm here to put it down. You can't help after a cat gets them."

Dad met Gage's eyes. It was a moment, a long, long moment. He was probably praying, too. Praying for guidance. Praying to be the father his son needed. Praying to give spiritual direction to someone whom it seemed God was already directing.

Finally, seeming uncertain, he nodded.

Taylor transferred the box onto Gage's lap, and Gage held the thread in one hand while he laid the other on the towel over the bird. The bird was still now. "Dear God," he said softly, "please breathe your healing spirit into this bird."

Jeff didn't hide his snort. Gage could almost hear him thinking, *"Lame."*

The thread warmed to Gage's skin.

"Please, God." Now the thread buzzed as if it were attached to his guitar. "If it's your will, please restore the bird." Gage closed his eyes. It felt like the right thing, and he pulled deeper inside himself. No one else needed to hear—only God, and God would hear this. *Lord, you are the master of life and death. You send out your spirit, and we are created. Please, send your spirit into the bird and renew its broken body. Please spare the bird suffering.*

In his heart, Gage felt the question: *Gage Jordan, what have you to offer Me?*

I have nothing, Gage prayed, *except for your love.*

Bright laughter flashed in Gage's heart, and his eyes flew open. Unable to control it, he grinned, and as he did, the bird burst from his hands into flight around the living room.

Taylor shrieked while Mek leaped in place.

Mr. Greymore shook his head. "Ah-yeah. You don't see that every day."

The bird fluttered up to the curtain rod and stood, safely out of reach of everyone except Mek, who climbed the fireplace mantle to reach for it.

Jeff's eyes glinted. "Are you satisfied? You could have done that all along."

Mr. Greymore, with Vermont practicality, drawled, "It would have been better to pray for the bird outside the house."

"Mek?" Gage glanced from the bird to the jinn. "Can you

talk to the bird? Can you ask the bird to go out the front door?"

Beaming with delight, Mek sighed. "Why?"

"It doesn't belong in here."

Mek's eyes shone. "A house is lonely without any birds."

Jeff dropped his head back against the couch, and Gage stared.

Even without hearing the jinn, Taylor could tell what they were dealing with. "Hold out the thread."

Jeff said, "So it can build a nest? That'd be more useful than what Gage does."

Taylor ignored him. "The jinn told you the things in the middle love the thread. If you hold it out like a telephone wire, the bird should stand on it."

"Tell me you're kidding."

Taylor tilted her head and opened her hands.

I don't know how any of this works, God. Gage wrapped the thread around his finger, then approached the bird. It didn't fly away. He climbed onto the couch alongside Jeff, then raised his hand close to the bird's feet. The bird hopped onto his finger.

"Keep the door open," Gage breathed. Dad and Mr. Greymore moved aside. Gage stepped off the couch, then carried the bird into the cold night.

The bird regarded him with a clear eye, its tiny talons clutching the thread.

Of course. It loved the thread, so naturally, it wanted to stay. "Time to go. God's will for you is to be free."

Gage flung out his hand, and the bird burst away from the house's artificial light.

This is crazy. Gage had never imagined actually using the thread—not for real. Not this many times in one night.

Gage turned to Dad, dizzy. "I don't understand this at all."

Dad was pale. "I don't understand it, either."

CHAPTER TWENTY-ONE

Never was anyone as glad to see a menthol green Jeep as Gage, and he pelted down the stairs to meet his grandfather in the driveway.

Grandpa looked past him. "Where's Jeff?"

"In his room with Dad. They've been talking for an hour." Grandpa gave him a huge, warm-coat smelling hug, and Gage pressed his face against the green canvas. "I'm so glad to see you. I can't make sense of anything anymore. Do you want me to get Dad?"

"We'll let them talk a bit longer. I'm not much for pastoring." Grandpa shook his head sadly. "I'm only good at being his grandfather."

Taylor and Mr. Greymore were sitting at the table. Gage caught him up, with a lot of help from Taylor, on everything. Grandpa listened with worry clouding his face, and his mouth a sad curve.

"You're still shaken," Grandpa said. When Gage nodded, Grandpa put a hand on his. "I would be, too."

"At least there won't be an exorcism," Mr. Greymore said. "It wasn't easy on you all, but it could have been far worse. You could have lost both boys."

Jeff's door opened, and as Grandpa got to his feet, Jeff ran right into Grandpa's arms. Jeff had been crying again. Grandpa wouldn't let him go.

Mr. Greymore stood. "Taylor and I have taken enough of your time."

"On the contrary," Dad said, "I'm very glad you were here."

After a blast of cold air from the front door, they were gone. Jeff hadn't let go of Grandpa, and his shoulders shuddered as he sobbed again.

So many tears. Did the sadness ever end? Could it?

And what could Gage do? Nothing. He rummaged around in his head for any ideas, and all that came out was, "Do you want me to make some hot chocolate?"

"Hot chocolate sounds perfect, but just be a kid for now." Dad rested a hand on Gage's head. "You've done so much."

Gage scraped his chair away from the table and sat. The air felt like it weighed a hundred pounds, and he resisted the urge to lay down his head. Dad made hot chocolate for everyone, and after a moment's thought, he put a leftover candy-cane in Jeff's. Gage forced a smile.

Grandpa guided Jeff to the table. Jeff wouldn't look at anyone.

Gage said, "So... Is there anything about tonight that Jeff couldn't explain to you?"

Dad sipped his drink, decided it was too hot, and set it back on the table. "How did you know the right time had come?"

Gage explained about Mek and the bird. Not all, but just enough to catch the light in Dad's eyes when Dad realized. Oh, that amazing moment when Jeff internalized Mek's words about God staying with Mir. If he'd waited, Jeff might have rationalized it away. Gage definitely didn't want to say *they* might have talked to Jeff. But more than anything else, he didn't want to scare Jeff back from the precipice of falling in love with God. The angel had said it was only enough for now.

Dad glanced at Jeff, wonder in his eyes. After years of hearing Dad preach, Gage could almost hear this thought, too: God was so good, so good all the time.

Grandpa said, "Sounds like it was a near thing."

Pepper wandered into the kitchen, and as he rubbed his face against Gage's leg, Gage lowered one hand to scratch just behind the ears. Pepper wove through the chair legs, then jumped onto Gage's lap.

"What you did with the bird is astounding." Dad steepled his fingers and rested his chin against them. "I don't even know what to say. Other than not to spread that information around."

Gage imagined the pastor's phone ringing off the hook for everything from ingrown toenails to cancer. But then he caught a glance from Jeff—hard-eyed, tight-lipped. "We should use this, shouldn't we? Once we figure out what God wants. Something this big feels like a city on a hill."

"I want to protect you," Dad said.

Jeff snapped, "Well, you can't."

Dad and Grandpa and Gage all froze.

Outside, a bird was darting in the cold air, unaware it had been touched by divinity. A battered blue Yukon was crossing the railroad tracks back to a home full of children. The snow was weighing down a rosebush due to awaken next spring. And inside, Jeff glared frostily at the table, eyebrows contracted, hands in fists.

Dad lowered his voice. "Using it is one thing. Advertising that you're willing to work wonders would put you in the way of danger."

"God's got a purpose in mind," said Grandpa. "He doesn't give people talent and not expect something from them."

Dad traced a circle on the tabletop. "Even Jesus grew up first."

Mek came into the kitchen, and both boys (and Pepper) turned toward the jinn. Dad compulsively glanced toward where they were watching, then looked back at Gage, who had already returned his attention to the adults.

"You didn't happen to retrieve my tie tacks, did you?"

"Sorry, I forgot." Gage turned to the door where the jinn gazed up at the light switch. "Mek? I need to see your treasure."

Mek grinned. "Why?"

"You took some of my Dad's treasure, and he wants it back."

Mek shrunk toward the wall, regarding Dad with unease.

Jeff said, "Have some respect. You stole from the man who gave you safe harbor."

Mek's lip trembled.

"He won't hurt you." Gage set Pepper on the floor and stood, gesturing to his seat. "But he'd like his treasure back."

Mek climbed Gage's abandoned chair to clamber onto the table-top. Kneeling between the mugs of cocoa, the jinn unzipped Mir's belt-pack, then upended the bag over the table.

Dad and Grandpa jumped backward as the contents clattered out, scattering across the table before them.

Mek rocked in delight, bouncing and laughing. "So much treasure! Look what God gave me!"

Jeff leaned closer. "Now we get to hunt for tie tacks."

Dad reached forward, recoiled, then slid two tie tacks from the pile. He moved some more stuff, then found three more.

"Buttons, a safety pin, die cast cars, soda pull-tabs." Dad listed Mek's wonders in a soft voice. "A thimble. Is that a petrified brownie?"

Mek pushed it with a fingertip. "This is a rock that God loves."

Gage related this to Dad. Mek picked up each piece of treasure and showed it off, then replaced each in the bag one at a time.

"When an object vanishes off the table," Dad said, "that's when the jinn is picking something up?"

"I guess? I have no idea when you're seeing it vanish." Mek was now singing the praises of a bleeder valve from a carbonation canister. Gage grinned. "I told you, they're compulsive collectors, but harmless."

The jinn picked up a nickel, gave Jeff a nasty look, and dropped it into the belt pack without comment. Jeff smirked.

Mek poked a barrette. "This came from the River Woman."

"My mom?" Gage said, even as Grandpa exclaimed, "That's Vera's!"

Gage extended his hand. Mek, lower lip bitten tight, relinquished the barrette. It was a simple steel style, rusted at the edges, half the length of Gage's forefinger. Its only adornment was four rhinestones and an empty square where the fifth once rested.

Dad looked at it as Gage passed it to Grandpa. "Are you sure?"

"I gave this to her on our first Valentine's Day." Grandpa's voice hushed its way to the core of Gage's heart. "We'd been going steady since Christmas, so I got her a pair. One is still at home. This is the other." He touched the empty socket. "This stone came out when she fell off a tree swing in her mother's front yard."

Pepper jumped onto Gage's chair, and Gage rubbed the cat's head absently. "The River Woman gave this to you?"

Mek sighed. "It's so pretty."

Gage turned to Grandpa. "Mek doesn't remember the circumstances."

Dad said, "Zack might have given it to them, too."

Mek and Mir, when talking about the River Woman, had sounded so certain it came from her. Grandpa handed the barrette back to Gage.

Gage said, "Don't you want to keep it?"

"I have the other." Grandpa looked wistful. "Let your jinn remember her."

Gage returned the barrette to Mek, who beamed.

A moment later, the jinn dropped both the barrette and the belt-pack, bolting from the table and diving into a cabinet. Pepper puffed out, glaring at the doorway, and hissed.

And then—

—like the emptiness of hunger, a ball of tension in the top of the throat, a heaviness of the eyes—

—Gage felt it arrive.

⁂

You owe me a life.

The room tilted at them. Afraid he'd collapse, Gage locked his knees and grasped the table.

Jeff breathed, "Oh, God, oh, God." Grandpa caught him and pulled him closer.

Dad put his arm around Gage, who backed into his father's chest.

A figure shimmered before him with a hatred as patient as stomach acid. The loathing reverberated through Gage, only the man looked normal, totally normal, which made it all the worse.

"What do you see?" Grandpa said. His tone proclaimed he knew. Dad knew. Dad's hands clenched on Gage's shoulders, and Gage knew he'd be praying. The kitchen smelled sulfurous. Gage's stomach lurched.

The man said, "See and believe."

Dad and Grandpa gasped simultaneously. Gage wanted to close his eyes. He couldn't.

The man said, "I have been before the throne of the Lord, and He acknowledges my claim. You owe me a life. I was promised two lives. I was given only one. I will have my second. I have the pledge, and I have the promise."

A tug at his hands. Mek was offering Gage the metal tab from a soda. It must have been in a crevice behind the cabinet, and it was wonderful enough to outweigh a demon's presence.

Dad said, "Leave here. We are servants of God. You have no authority."

"I retain the authority I was given." The man's voice was steady. "God does not interfere in my agreements, and I will be paid. In the next days, I will have the life I am owed." The man looked at Jeff as if appraising a second-hand sedan. He set his eyes next on Gage, then on Dad, and lastly on Grandpa. He ignored the jinn. "One of you can fulfill the pledge now. Or I can take my choice." His hematite eyes shone with a dark fire. He looked at Gage. "Perhaps Taylor. Or her mother. Or her baby brother."

Gage drew breath, but Dad gripped Gage's shoulder so hard that he said nothing.

The man said, "I'll return when it's time. You won't see me again."

He vanished, but the smell lingered.

Jeff staggered into a chair, nearly missing. Grandpa went to the sink and opened the window to the nighttime chill.

Not trusting his voice, Gage handed Mek the pull-tab. His hands were shaking. Dad sat, but Grandpa stayed by the window, staring toward the shed at the back of the property.

Jeff said, "What he said about still owing a life— For real?"

Dad rubbed his temples. "It might be."

Gage shoved his trembling hands under the table on his lap. "What about God's protection? Jesus set us free."

Dad closed his eyes. "Free to make agreements of that nature, apparently."

Gage bit his lip. "What do we do?"

"We pray," Dad said.

Jeff said, "We find a life to offer."

Dad and Gage turned to stare at Jeff.

Jeff opened his hands. "If they're going to take one, it's better we choose whose."

Gage exclaimed, "That's heartless!"

Jeff glowered. "It's strategic."

Dad said, "It's not ours to choose."

Puzzled, Jeff sat back. "He said it was."

From across the kitchen, Grandpa said, "You can take mine."

"No! For Pete's sake, everyone stop and think." Dad drew breath. "I'm not volunteering anyone to die. I don't know what or how Zack promised anything. We don't even have proof that it's true. Jeff, if you know the exact wording of the promise, you have to let me know. But I'm not going to permit anyone to volunteer to die or to pick someone else to be sacrificed on the altar of Zachary's mistake. We have one weapon at our disposal—prayer—and we will use it."

Jeff said, "We have more than one weapon. Gage has the thread. And we have the jinn."

Mek spun the soda tab on one finger. Gage said, "We'd better stick with prayer and the thread."

Grandpa said, "Matthew, I'm old."

"Old is not the same as having no life left to live. If God wants you, God can take you just fine on His own."

Jeff said, "Then who do we pick?"

Dad threw out his hands. "We don't pick. We pray for deliverance, but we haven't even established that thing was telling us the truth. I'd rather end up dead than treat life with so much disregard that I'm ashamed of my own behavior before God Almighty."

Jeff's eyes flared. "The behavior already happened! Whatever Dad promised, we'd just be directing the fallout."

Grandpa said, "I'm ready to go to eternity. We know I'm going to die someday."

"Satan knows we're all going to die, so why would a demon care *when* it happened?" Dad's eyes were wide, his voice urgent. "What matters is how we relate to God in the time before it happens. If it's God's will that any of us dies, then I hope it happens exactly as God wants. But it cannot be God's will that we sacrifice another human being. That's all." Dad laid his hands flat on the table. "We won't act. We'll let God take control."

"Can we do something additionally?" Gage uncoiled the remaining thread and spread it on the table. "I want all of us to keep a bit of this, just in case it can protect us."

Dad glanced at Grandpa from the corners of his eyes. "Don't divide something that powerful."

Gage said, "The jinn didn't worry about dividing it."

Dad remained quiet for a long moment. Then, "No."

Jeff snorted. "You're afraid I'll use it."

"Maybe I am." Dad's face darkened. "You and your grandfather wanted to play into the demon's hands by offering a life. Keep the temptation out of your reach." He looked at Gage. "You, too. I don't want to dictate policy to God, not when the potential losses are this high."

CHAPTER TWENTY-TWO

In the morning, Gage and Jeff got ready for school as if their biggest problem were a math quiz. Gage carefully talked around the important stuff: they talked Grooz Capture and movies and school stuff without ever mentioning demons, jinn, or God.

Gage and Jeff sat together on the bus. Taylor waved from her seat, then returned to talking with the girls nearby.

Dad would be calling the guidance counselor about easing Jeff back into his classes. There would be assignments excused, a timeline for makeup work, and possibly half days until Jeff felt ready to be back full-time. Jeff kept muttering how that was stupid. "What kind of person looks at a kid and thinks, 'He's behind in his classwork, so let's give him half days and make him get more behind'?"

This felt so pointless compared to the preternatural offensive launched in their own kitchen. Although if Gage wanted to be cynical, it sounded as though Satan had needed to file paperwork with God to get permission to claim the second life of his contractual payout.

How do you void someone else's contract with devil?

The morning was a bright winter-spring, warm enough to begin melting the snow piled against the sides of the street. The sunlight lay low enough to sneak in horizontally beneath the cloud cover, then got trapped so it bounced and gave a gold cast wherever it landed. A sheen of water lay over the pavement, reflecting trees, houses and picket fences.

As they pulled away, Dad's car followed. The bus would turn onto a smaller road for more pickups while Dad would continue in a straight line to the church.

Gage glanced out the window and saw a stern face reflected. Even as he gasped, Jeff sat upright. A voice intoned, "You owe me a life."

With a slam, the bus lurched to the left. Students screamed as it rocked, then toppled sideways. Gage slammed against the windows, Jeff crushing down on top of him. Glass, breaking. Screams. The continuous bellow of a car horn.

Gage couldn't see where he was. Jeff struggled off him, gasping, and Gage popped up his head.

Taylor—where was Taylor?

Both boys maneuvered until they were standing on broken glass, and under their feet was pavement where a bus window used to be. Other students were picking themselves up. "Is anyone hurt?" the driver shouted over the din, his arm clamped to his side. "Everyone check your seatmates! Is anyone hurt?"

"Taylor!" Gage's shout was overwhelmed by the melee. "Taylor?"

At the front, finally—finally—Taylor got to her feet, dazed but helping her friend. Gage closed his eyes and fought to catch his breath. *Thank you, God. Thank you.*

The bus lay on its left side, the seats forming waist-high

compartments. Some students climbed onto them. Gage moved into the next seat-cubicle, which was empty, but his foot slipped on prisms of glass. He reached up for the hatch on what should have been the bus ceiling.

Jeff got on an adjacent seat and helped Gage pry it open. Someone else popped the emergency door at the back. Light flooded in, then cold air.

In front of the bus, a man screamed obscenities alternately at the bus driver and into a cell phone.

Through the roof exit, Gage heard, "Gage? Jeff? Where are you?"

It was Dad. "We're fine!" Gage helped one of Taylor's friends over the glass toward the emergency exit. The opposite row of windows was like a long skylight, admitting dirty sunshine. Gage helped another kid move past. At the front of the bus, a second horizontal shaft of light penetrated where the driver had opened the second ceiling exit.

Taylor passed, and Gage grabbed her hand. He met her eyes, and she forced a smile.

The last few students were all making their way out without help, so Gage went to the back as well, bending triple to get through. Jeff caught his arm as he emerged blinking into the brightness. A moment after, Dad had gripped him by the shoulders and looked him over at arm's length.

Gulping, Gage looked at the bus lying sideways like a beached whale. He sought out his father's eyes, but they didn't need to speak.

They owed the enemy a life. He was making sure they understood.

He would collect.

———⸺◆⸺———

The police arrived to sort out the mess, and the sheriff confided in Dad that there would likely be criminal charges against the pickup driver. "How fast was he going, to knock over a school bus? I know this town every inch. There's nothing that important."

Dad waited with the kids while parents were called. Some got retrieved. A few went to the hospital to be checked over. Eventually, one of the church members showed up with a fifteen-passenger van and drove a bunch to the school, including Gage, Jeff, and Taylor. They got intercepted by the guidance counselor, who gave a quick mental health screening, after which they got turned loose to wait in the library for the next period. That was, naturally, lunch. Jeff was getting a half day whether he wanted it or not.

In a hushed voice, Gage told Taylor about the demon. "I wish we could do something about it."

Jeff leaned forward. "Breaking news, genius. We can do something about it."

"We already went over this."

"You already went over it. Don't be a coward. We need to finish the agreement."

Gage said, "I never agreed to anything."

Jeff rubbed the heel of his palm. "I think I did kind of make the agreement, too. I'm not sure." He glanced at Gage. "I didn't understand how all this works, and I still don't. Dad took care of the details. But I think I did something that meant I agreed."

Gage exclaimed, "You agreed to it? And did you tell Dad that part?"

Taylor had even less of a poker face than Gage. "What did you do?"

Jeff glanced at Gage. "See, I always honor agreements. And Uncle Matt made me promise that under no circumstances would I tell Gage how we did it."

"You're not telling Gage," Taylor said lowly. "You're telling me."

Jeff grinned. "I think I like you. But as for the 'how,' I'm not sure. Dad poked my hand with a needle to seal the agreement, and he said that was a pledge." Jeff rubbed the heel of his hand again. "He told me to ask my part, and...abruptly, I couldn't speak. When I couldn't speak, that's when everything went wrong." He swallowed. "I couldn't ask them to take a life, so they took Dad."

Taylor whispered, "Who would you have chosen?"

Jeff shrugged. "That part was easy. We'd offer him two jinn."

Taylor and Gage stared openly.

Jeff said, "That was Dad's plan. He lured the jinn so we'd have a pair of lives to hand over as an offering. No one would miss a couple of creatures they never saw in the first place, and jinn have no souls. It's like sacrificing a goat, only without the mess."

Taylor slumped in her chair. "How could you even think about doing that?"

Jeff cocked his head. "It's not wrong. They sacrificed animals in the Temple."

Taylor looked at Gage. "Tell him it most certainly is wrong!"

Gage just stared.

Jeff sighed. "Look, it's not terrific. I'm as fond of the jinn as you are, but they're not exactly useful. They move your keys so they're not in your backpack when you get to school. They say cute things, but they're pretty much animals."

Gage said, "If you remember, we went to great lengths to save the life of a bird."

Jeff rolled his eyes. "That's so different."

Taylor said, "You were just going to use and discard two jinn because no one would know?"

"Wow, the high queen of judgment speaks. Maybe I *don't* like you anymore." Jeff looked her up and down. "Your dad keeps dairy cows. You drink their milk, and at the end you put their usable parts in your freezer. You're wearing leather sneakers." He picked up his pen. "Try convicting me again when you've gone vegan."

Gage said, "If God wanted us to use the jinn, more people would be able to see them. We're flukes." Jeff waved the words aside, but Gage leaned forward. "Using the jinn to pay your father's debt is beyond wrong. I'm sorry you don't see that. Even if Uncle Zack wanted to do it, I can't."

"Then what do you suggest? Did you forget they threatened Taylor?" Jeff glanced sidelong at her. "The demon mentioned you as one of the lives he might take to pay the claim. You or the baby."

Taylor gasped. Gage said to Taylor, "Grandpa offered his own life."

Taylor's voice quavered. "Do you think your grandfather is ready to face Christ?"

Gage huffed. "He says he is, but I don't *want* him to face Christ."

"You didn't answer me. Is he ready? If he's ready, then even if they take him, they lose. If they took me—of course I don't want to die, but they'd lose any chance at me forever. I think they'd rather have me alive so they can try to corrupt me."

She hadn't addressed the enemy killing the baby, or the pain it would cause to her entire family, or if some of them might even lose their faith over the senseless loss. "What you're saying," Gage said, tracing his finger over the edge of his backpack, "is that they'll try to take someone who isn't ready to go to Heaven."

She nodded. "Or one of you, since their attacks so far have been geared toward stopping you."

"That means you're pretty much off the hook." Gage sighed. "Taking you would waste their ammo. They'll want checkmate in one move."

Jeff grinned at Taylor. "You realize I don't care. It's really only Gage who'd miss you."

"You're such a softie." Taylor balled up a paper and tossed it at Jeff, who batted it aside. "I'll remember that next

Valentine's Day."

One of Taylor's friends joined them. "You were on the bus, right? Was it freaky? How are you even here?"

Taylor launched into the full tale, drawing a crowd that effectively stifled any further conversation and left Gage wrestling with the question of how to protect them.

If they let the demons do whatever they wanted, they'd claim a life in a way calculated to do the maximum damage. On the other hand, choosing someone would in and of itself do damage to the chooser's soul. But already Jeff teetered on the edge of rejecting God. What if the demons claimed Grandpa? Would Jeff be angry enough to slam the door?

The bell rang, and Jeff took off in one direction while Taylor went in the other. Gage went to study hall and prayed for a few minutes, but God revealed no answers.

Drawing stars and swirls in his notebook, Gage realized there was one other he could ask.

He didn't have the thread or the guitar. He did have his video game, but pulling it out during study hall was a very good way not to have it any longer.

That left Gage with only one way of "flowing." He laid his head down on his English textbook, closed his eyes, and reached for God.

Every noise in the library intensified. Pencils scratched; pages turned. Classmates' whispers resounded like a harmonica and bagpipe duet.

Gage concentrated until he slipped deeper into himself. Breaths, deep and regular. Rhythm. Relax. Reach inside, reach upward, extend outward. He thought about Psalm 39 and felt through the phrases he could remember, hoping one of them would resonate enough to take him away.

Dear Lord, he prayed, *I want to talk to him again. Please let me talk to him.*

Last Sunday he had prayed to see and had been gifted with sight. He didn't want something so overwhelming that he couldn't control it. He just needed to ask and hear the answers—without being attacked at the same time. *Please, God.* Desperation prickled in his throat. *Please, God, I need advice.*

Then he knew. With the force of conviction, with the same certainty as when he had actually been with the angel, he knew he would not have a conversation with the angel now. He needed the thread's help to "go" anywhere. When God chose to grant his prayers, he could go. But right now, God said no.

Gage's heart dropped.

A moment later, he "realized" two more things:

The demon had been telling the truth that a life was owed.

And the angel loved Gage.

Head down, Gage smiled.

He opened his eyes and drew more swirls and stars. Prayers were just fine. That much he always trusted, especially if he really prayed and resisted the urge to dictate to God what needed to be done and when and how to do it. More than that, though—choosing a victim for the demons, trying to outmaneuver the enemy—wouldn't help and might hurt.

He drummed his fingers and drew another insignia.

Brandon, the youth group guitar player, leaned toward him. "What's that?"

Gage snickered. "It's my coat of arms."

They both laughed. "Sir Gage of Vermont," Brandon whispered.

Gage said, "On my mighty ten-speed steed."

They put their heads together. "You joust much?" Brandon said.

"Only with my guitar."

"Man, I wish my parents would give back mine." Brandon chuckled. "You have a sword?"

There flared in his mind the sepia image of a sword made of flame, jammed into the ground to stand like a cross. "I do."

"My mom caught me looking up swords online, and I nearly lost the internet too." Brandon laughed. "Make me a coat of arms."

Gage sketched a design similar to the one already on his pages, rearranging the swirls and the circles, then adding a tree at the base. He snapped open the rings of his binder and handed over the page.

Brandon put it into his own binder. "Does that make me your man-at-arms?"

Gage shook his head. "I think knights have to serve a king."

"I'll serve your king," Brandon said, and chills crawled Gage's neck. "How's that sound?"

"Sounds good to me." Gage swallowed. "Thanks."

"No problem." Brandon grinned. "You survived someone jousting your bus, so you've got to be pretty good."

Gage leaned back in his chair.

And then he knew in his heart and his brain and his gut simultaneously: the thread would tarnish.

It was the same force of realization as when talking to the angel, only it had slipped in while he and Brandon were bantering. He hadn't "gone away," had he? But still he knew, and they'd just established that without the thread, he couldn't go to see the angel any longer.

Heart racing, Gage hid his eyes so Brandon wouldn't notice his expression. Not to see the angel ever again? Not unless God allowed it specially. Gage couldn't just "pop over" for a visit. He couldn't rely on the angel for advice or direction or—or just for friendship. Even though the angel loved him, they couldn't talk freely.

Gage kept trying to quantify what he was losing, and he kept returning to the thrill of being alongside a soul the mirror of his own, snug-fitting like puzzle pieces. Being absorbed in someone else who knew Gage so totally and only wanted him to grow as close to God as he was.

God could let him see the angel again whenever God

wanted. But to have to wait on God's timing— *That stinks.*

If the angel really was guarding him, then they were never further apart than a thought. The angel loved him, and the angel could see Gage just fine.

It still stinks. Gage wouldn't be able to sense him, or have a conversation with him, or even feel like they were together.

He wondered if his pouting made God laugh in agreement.

What to do about Uncle Zachary's promise, though? He still had no clue.

Thy will be done, he prayed. *Not the enemy's.*

Gage hoped that was enough.

Dad's car was in the garage and Grandpa's Jeep in the driveway when the bus dropped them off. Gage and Jeff both rushed up the front walk (carefully, in case of ice). Grandpa sat in the kitchen doing a crossword puzzle.

"Get a snack," Grandpa said. "Matthew said he'd be up in a minute."

Gage pulled out the gallon of milk and some glasses. Jeff watched with a strange grin as Gage went into the cupboard and pulled out a jar of mixed nuts.

"No potato chips?" Jeff said. "No Coke?"

"Right after school?"

"I thought Taylor was the nutrition police."

Gage snorted. "She dives into the chips when she's here." He paused. "You could have an apple."

Jeff flinched, a shadow that overtook his whole face. It wasn't his home, wasn't his Dad, wasn't even the right kind of food to scarf down while doing his math problems. The junk mail on the table was all the wrong catalogs and the wrong charity solicitations.

Gage offered, "I guess Dad won't mind if you have the soda," and it was also the wrong Dad.

Grandpa said, "What's a marsupial beginning with K?'

"Kangaroo." Jeff looked over his shoulder. "Oh, that's too long. Try koala."

"Kiwi?"

"That's a fruit, dork."

"It's a bird, too—nerd."

Grandpa said, "Koala fits."

In his room, Gage glanced at his guitar. What would happen to the guitar once its sustainer had gone? Would the glow remain after the spark had dissipated? Or would it just fade back into its former self, a cheap guitar that made only the standard sounds? Either possibility left an ache in Gage's throat, and he moved toward the guitar as if toward a deathbed.

His hands brushed the polished neck, and he lifted the guitar off the stand. Back in the living room, he fetched the Bible from the bookshelf and opened to Psalm 39, Jeff's psalm. He read it through, and as he meandered through each line, he found a fingering and strummed a chord. The guitar still sounded odd with the alternate tuning, but Gage didn't adjust the pegs.

Grandpa came into the living room with his crossword puzzle and settled in the easy chair opposite Gage.

Gage looked up. "You want me to play somewhere else?"

"Nah. The light's better here, and I want to hear you." There were no lamps lit in the living room. "You played guitar long?"

"About two years."

Grandpa made a noncommittal grunt. "Vera played the flute."

Gage returned his attention to the psalm. His heart quieted, and he waited for the center of his heart to dimple in a way that made room for God to rest in the hollow part. Momentarily, he felt enlarged, and then he felt enveloped.

Please, he prayed, *one more time, please play with me.*

Play with your thread before it fades. Sing an old song that was silenced by time.

A note sounded. Gage started, unaware that his fingers had even moved, but more notes flowed. He gathered himself to stay atop the song, knowing the melody that was to come as surely as any song he had practiced for hours. One measure at a time was all that presented itself, but taking each measure as it came, he could play the entire psalm. His inner ears "heard" the Hebrew as it would have come in the time of David. The tune was plaintive, thoughtful, discordant. Words, notes, instrument. Player. God in the sound, God in the creation.

Jeff emerged from the kitchen. Mek perched on the windowsill, half in and half out of the house. A moment later, Dad came to the top of the steps, fingers light on the banister.

Gage spoke the psalm words as he moved through. *My heart became hot within me. While I mused, the fire burned.* A line at a time, the guitar felt more and more solid, pressing against his chest as it vibrated beneath his strum. *Give ear to my cry; hold not your peace at my tears.*

At the end of the psalm, Gage lowered his eyes, his vision blurry. He couldn't remember anymore the melody that had haunted him as it played, only wisps of it. He tried to strum it again, but the lower strings slipped out of tune.

Jeff looked impressed, but Gage only slumped back into the couch.

You're going back to whatever you were, he thought to the thread. *I think that's goodbye.*

<hr>

Before going to bed, Gage found two discarded lengths of thread on the carpet. Mek had jettisoned something that was no longer treasure.

Chapter Twenty-Three

Gage dropped the coiled threads onto the kitchen table so he wouldn't forget to mention it to Dad. Before breakfast, Jeff saw them. "Are you out of your mind? Why are these here?" He picked up one. "Cool, you made decoys."

"Not decoys." Gage got down the cereals, remembering that first morning when he'd had to pick a cereal for Jeff. "They're tarnished. They're done."

Jeff's eyes flared. "*Done*?"

"Expired." Gage sighed. "It turns out threads have a use- or sell-by date."

Jeff was breathing hard. "How can they be done? What kind of protection do we have?"

The world did feel a lot closer right now.

Jeff's eyes were wild. "There's nothing we can do anymore to stop them! They're going to take a life, and we don't even have the thread. Does God want us to die?"

Gage opened his hands.

"Terrific. I should have known." Jeff kicked the nearest kitchen chair and sent it sliding it along the floor. "Any time you think God's going to let you win, he stops you."

Gage raised his hands. "God's not stopping us."

"It's a game to God, and we're the playing pieces." Jeff stalked to the edge of the kitchen, then turned back. "You're not surprised by this at all. You wanted to run out the clock on the threads. If we'd used this as much as we could have, we wouldn't be in this mess. You waited and waited because you're afraid of violating some stupid rule written in a book that's two thousand years old, and you don't care about the people who are standing right in front of you. Maybe Abraham and Moses will keep us from dying, since you don't feel like doing it. Oh, wait, they're both dead, too."

Jeff's bedroom door slammed, and Gage stared at his bowl, unwilling to eat.

By contrast, Dad said, "It's just as well. You don't need to rely on the thread if you're only going to make it a crutch."

Gage and Jeff biked to school instead of riding the bus. It felt safer, and at the very least, they weren't endangering anyone else. They avoided the puddles and tucked their heads against the wind. At school they locked up their bikes side by side, then headed their separate ways.

Gage found Taylor at her locker. He said only, "The thread's gone. Its time is over."

She offered, "Maybe that's the life you owed?"

Wouldn't that be nice?

Gage went through social studies, math, and history classes without incident, praying when it got boring (that was most of social studies) and wondering how you arm yourself against a demon.

Lunch was fourth period, but Gage couldn't find Jeff in the cafeteria. He asked Jeff's friends, but no one knew where he'd gone. Had Jeff opted for those half-day re-entry days after all?

Gage checked in at guidance. "Hey, did you dismiss Jeff early?"

Guidance said, "I'm supposed to meet with him in an hour."

In a way, that was also a relief; Gage had half feared he'd hear Jeff had been loaded onto a stretcher by paramedics.

Walking back to the cafeteria, Gage passed the front entrance. Reflexively he glanced out at his bike in the bike rack.

It was alone. Jeff's wasn't there.

Gage went cold. *God, where is he?*

Jeff had cut class, but why?

God, please, reveal what is hidden.

The rule was no cell phones at school. Sometimes you break the rules. Gage called Dad, but Dad didn't pick up. Grandpa didn't answer, either. He texted Jeff, but naturally Jeff didn't reply.

Had Jeff gone somewhere to offer a life? Was he back at home, offering himself? Had he biked back to his own house?

Taylor rushed up to Gage. "What's going on?"

"I don't know." Gage swallowed. "Jeff's bike's missing."

Taylor pulled out her phone. "I'll ask if Mom can check your house."

"The debt." Gage's voice faltered. "Your mom can't go anywhere near him, not with your baby brother."

Taylor's eyes stood out against the pallor of her cheeks. Gage handed her his backpack. "I'm going to find him. You keep trying to reach my Dad." He took a couple of steps, then turned back and met Taylor's eyes.

"I know." Taylor stood tall. "I will."

Gage bolted for his bike.

Pumping as hard as he could, Gage set his heart like a beacon on God. *Lead me, Lord. Lead me, Lord. Lead me to him.*

It felt wrong. He didn't know why, but it felt wrong to be biking in this direction.

He can't get into his own home. The door's sealed.

His tires crackled over a shell of ice in the road, a lost puddle trapped by the cold into a solid state. A tinkle like broken glass lingered in Gage's mind.

God. God.

Home. Home.

As he pedaled, Gage didn't think about the roads, only about his body and his bicycle. The distance remaining, the pump-pump-pump of his legs in a rhythm carrying him closer every wheel-length to home. There weren't even words to his thoughts, but they would have been set to the rhythm. *I have to get home. I have to find Jeff. I have to get home. I have to find Jeff.*

His street, his house halfway up the hill, his driveway. He skidded off the bike, leaving it lying on its side.

The front door banged open. "Jeff!" Silence. Jeff's bike hadn't been in the driveway, but Jeff's backpack lay just inside the door. His jacket wasn't on the hook. He'd been and gone. "Jeff?"

Then Gage realized what was missing: the preternatural prickle that had greeted him every time he'd entered the house for the past several days. "Mek?" Louder, "Mek!" He shot up the steps, and again and again and again he called without getting a response.

God, where are they? Gage's chest heaved because he couldn't catch his breath.

Jeff had come home and dropped his backpack, then left again, presumably with Mek.

Gage ran back outside, but there were no footprints in the aging snow. He ran around the outside of the house anyhow, looking. Nothing.

Okay, God. Gage triangled himself, hands on his knees as he struggled to regain his breath. *Where are they?*

He took a step, and ice crackled beneath his boot. Looking at the ice, he remembered again the moment biking, how the ice sounded like the breaking of glass. Jeff must have biked back to his father's home, then broken a window to get inside.

Gage lunged for his bike, but he stopped. How long did it take to work a spell? Jeff had too much of a lead. Gage screamed at the sky, "Jeff, you idiot! You jerk!"

I could chase him. I might still be able to stop him.

No, I'll never make it in time. I have to leave this one to God.

It sounded so right. Let Gage wash his own hands of the blood of the jinn. Let God take it all into His own hands now. What Jeff did was on Jeff's soul. If it tainted Jeff and all his descendants, so be it. Gage would remain pure, untouched by whatever Jeff had sacrificed. Gage had done enough. It was time to stop fighting.

Gage stalked back to the front of the house, but he didn't get on his bike.

That was it, then. Dad couldn't even intercept Uncle Zack in the car. The only reason Jeff had survived the first time was because of Gage's prayer.

Gage blinked.

He ran back into the house. Not pausing to slam the door behind him, he streaked to his room. His prayer the first time —of course! Prayer crossed distances with no difficulty. Prayer could even cross time. The enemy had been tempting Gage to despair, but he had one weapon and always would have that one weapon. Leave it in God's hands—so clever. The enemies were getting better at confounding Gage and making it sound absolutely right.

Gage picked up his guitar. It was only a guitar, no longer a miracle in wood and steel, but he didn't need a preternatural tool. He needed God, and God might always respond to a thread, but He wasn't limited to only responding to a thread.

Cross-legged on his bed, Gage strummed. Playing "Be Still My Soul," he let the notes flow. *"Be still my soul, the Lord is on thy side. Bear patiently the cross of grief or pain."* He could play this song without thinking about it. Send his mind away, and he could achieve flow. *Lord, let me flow to you. Let me come to you.*

The angel had said he couldn't do this on his own, couldn't "go away" without the thread to help. He'd never make it.

We are confident, Gage prayed, remembering a line that had once puzzled him. *We are willing rather to be absent from the body, and to be present with the Lord. Lord, let me be present with you and absent from here.*

It felt like enough. *Lord, I want to see,* Gage prayed. *Lord, I want to see.*

Son of David, have pity on me.

Lord, I want to see.

The notes flowed, and Gage lost himself. "*In every change, He faithfully will remain.*" The song cycled from one stanza to the next. "*Be still, my soul, thy God doth undertake to guide the future as He has the past.*"

Over and over. The trembling dissipated from his hands and the heaving from his chest. *Lord, let me see.* Only the one prayer rang in his head. Only one thing. "*All now mysterious shall be bright at last.*"

Gage inhaled like a diver breaking the surface. The room went to sepia. Gage breathed in the Spirit.

Lord, send your angel before me. Gage tried not to rejoice that he'd gotten this far because that would make him conscious of himself. He needed to be only a song playing in the background of his own thoughts.

The angel appeared. Gage prayed, *God is our only protection.*

The angel drew eye to eye, face to face.

The angel understood what he wanted to do, but also, the angel didn't want him to do it. Gage felt the angel urging him no, but with desperation rather than outrage. To pursue Jeff wouldn't be wrong, but the danger was real. That's what was speaking to his heart. The angel was supposed to protect him, but if Gage continued, the angel couldn't.

God is my protection, Gage thought to the angel.

As if dew drops hung on the air moments before a drizzle, the angel surrounded him, coated him. It was a laying of hands by a creature with no hands.

A moment, and like a rainbow, it dispelled. Gage felt alone.

No, Gage protested. He tried to center himself, then prayed, *Though I walk through the valley of the shadow of death, I will fear no evil. For you are at my side. Be at my side. Be my rod and my staff. Be at my side.*

Gage felt his hand close on something. He was holding a staff.

His body must still be in his room, playing guitar. Nevertheless, he'd "gone" somewhere. His spirit was here, just under the apple peel, as the angel had put it.

Dear God, he prayed, *let me put on your whole armor.*

He couldn't remember right now what Paul had written made up the whole armor of God—righteousness, truth, something—but he felt a sheen of armor surrounding him. His chest, his arms. He didn't want to move, but he found his limbs wrapped in a rainbow. He tapped the staff against his leg and felt nothing, only the sense that he should have felt the blow.

I have no body here. They can't hurt me.

Although, of that he wasn't so sure. They couldn't hurt his soul, but maybe they could strand him here in the sepia, or maybe kill his body while he left it unattended.

Nothing for it. He had to go after Jeff. *Lead me in safety, Lord. Lead me to Jeff. May your word be a lamp to my feet and a light to my path.*

Amid the sepia, the world became darker, and gold flowed forward from Gage's feet. He took a step, and the gold continued to pour forth, so he took another. Like playing a song without knowing more than the next measure, Gage was able to walk the path seeing only the next footfall.

Brandishing the rod, he strode away from wherever he'd been and into the swirling wind along the gold-lit road. He took a step to the side, to see if the path changed, but it remained where it had been. Another step in the wrong direction, and the gold pooled before him, then flowed sideways, like a stream unable to be diverted. Down the length of the road, Gage could see no terminus. He prayed, *They will run and not grow weary,* and he broke into a sprint.

Please let me find Jeff. The words were in counterpoint to his steps. *Let me find him, let me find him, help me find him* —

The golden road spilled away beneath him like a waterfall plummeting, and Gage stood over the road's end like a bird hovering over the brink of Niagara Falls.

Where was Jeff?

Gage found himself in a rapidly darkening whirlwind, nothing to grasp, no landmarks. The remains of the golden road showered away to infinity beneath his feet, and here his path ended.

Where am I? He closed his eyes. *Please reveal what is hidden.*

Gage felt as if he were weighing down the rainbow armor, settling closer into the ground that wasn't under his feet. Then the spot beneath his feet felt more solid too, as if his arches were finally pressing against a floor. In the blackness, Gage no longer had the sense of floating, but rather standing in a lightless room. He took a breath, and the air tasted linty.

Whatever was happening?

A swift rasp split the silence, and a glow appeared ten feet from him.

Blinking, Gage leaned forward.

A second glow appeared, then a third. There was a pause, and then another rasp. Mild sulfur tainted the air. A fourth light touched off a fifth, then a sixth. The smallest vanished, and only five lights remained.

The world brightened as if dawning. Gage stood in a basement.

"Come down, Mek," called a voice, distorted like sound underwater. "The treasure is down here."

A shade soundlessly descended the staircase across the basement. It was a white glow surrounding a clear figure, an embryo inside a sac. It was cold sunlight glinting off icicles. It was a jinn, seen the way an angel sees.

The world coalesced around Gage, and abruptly he was in Uncle Zack's basement, next to the washer and dryer, near the hot water heater, surrounded by shelving and old boxes and extra supplies. Gage's voice returned. "Mek, run! Don't come down!"

Jeff whipped around within the circle of light, eyes wild. "Gage? Get out of here!"

The armor vanished as Gage saw the flames for what they were—five candles set in the points of a star. Jeff stood in the center, the final line chalked into place.

Gage exclaimed, "What are you doing?"

"They'll kill you!" Jeff's white-ringed eyes couldn't blink. "Get out of the house! It's too dangerous!"

Like Pompeii in the shadow of Vesuvius, it grew too hot to breathe. A staggering weight drove Gage to his knees. "What did you do?"

Pressure increased like a cresting wave. Gage couldn't move. Mek vanished into the clutter as the pressure drove Gage to all fours.

"No!" Jeff lunged to the edge of the star, as far as the nearest candle. "Not him! I made the jinn solid for you! Take the jinn!"

The pressure was flattening. *Dear God.* It was so hard to pray. *Be my shield. Be my shield.*

The crushing eased enough for Gage to suck in a breath. Blinking to clear the tears, he still couldn't locate his oppressor. The angelic viewpoint had vanished now that he'd solidified, but he knew it had to be here. God always came when someone called.

"You idiot!" Jeff shouted. "What are you doing here? I wouldn't have called them!"

"You're not going to take me," Gage rasped to the nothingness. His throat ached from the heat, and the dry skin split on his lips. His eyelids felt like blisters. He could taste his own blood at the back of his throat, too thick to slake thirst, too fluid to gag back up. *God, be my shield.*

His fists tightened as he sucked in another hard-won breath, and as he did so, he realized he could still feel the staff in his palm.

He took another breath of the scorching air, then exhaled it with a smile. He couldn't see it, but every time he curled his fingers, he felt the iron-strength of that rod.

Not alone.

They can't harm the soul.

The whole armor.

Gage shoved himself to his feet, and he met Jeff's frightened gaze. Jeff's father would have died the same way. Now here was Jeff, watching it happen all over again.

Jeff started to step out of the circle, and Gage shouted, "Don't!"

Jeff's tears spilled over. "They can take me! This isn't your fault!"

"They're not taking either of us." Gage leaned on the staff so it would bear his weight. He imagined it like a lightning rod, pulling the heat from the room, drawing Satan as he plummeted, accompanied by booms of thunder. "You're safe in the circle."

Jeff raised his head. "Take the jinn! I offered you the jinn!"

I don't want the jinn. I want the boy.

The words crawled through their minds like a worm through moist earth.

Jeff said, "I get to choose! I called you. You'll obey me."

"They're not going to obey." Gage coughed, and blood spattered out of his mouth. "There's only one voice they'll obey."

Jeff folded his arms. "I'm playing by their rules. They'll obey."

I want the boy.

Jeff grinned at Gage. "They'll take the jinn."

Gage couldn't see Mek among the basement clutter. This would be a dragon's hoard for a jinn, if only the dragon weren't at home. Gage extended with his heart and felt the angelic vision snap on like a pair of sepia-toned goggles. The jinn was in the corner, studying something on the floor. Gage approached the corner as if drawn by a foul whispering. Instead of being able to make out the whisper, though, his heart heard words with the thickness of sludge.

I want the boy.

With his vision still brown and gold, Gage looked for the demon. It was more an impression than a vision, more a sense of its maw than actual fangs. The presence was a thousand tons of crushing emptiness. This was the weight Gage could feel pressing all over him, only now he could see it, too.

God, I can't do this! They'll break me! I'm not up to it!

I am.

Gage's breath caught. Even now he could still remember the feeling of the angelic mist resting over him, the weight of the armor, the grasp of the staff. Now he felt something else, like someone standing right behind him with hands on his shoulders. He could shrink from the inkiness into that supernatural grip for good.

Don't be scared. The feeling bubbled in his throat like hidden laughter. *You're so brave. I'm with you.*

With a calmness that surprised him, Gage spoke to the darkness. "You can't have me."

The bubbling warmth spread from Gage's stomach and

throat all the way to his hands and feet. For a moment Gage wondered if this was joy, and why on earth he'd be feeling it.

The demon slammed Gage, driving him back to the ground. Hard blows landed on his back, his head, his chest. He was being punched upward through the floor. But even as he curled like a pill bug, with eyes screwed shut and teeth clenched, the warmth stayed with him, the presence, the hands on his shoulders. The sensation rushed in with every haggard gasp. Even though they were beating him, crushing him, he could only think, *Stay with me. You're still with me.*

The maelstrom paused, as if reassessing. Gage struggled to rise, but the armor weighed him to the floor. No doubt he would be dead already if not for that, but it also kept him trapped. Floor-rooted, he tried to swallow past a thickness at the back of his throat that threatened to choke him.

Jeff was screaming. "You're supposed to take the jinn!"

I can take a jinn, whenever I want. Human blood sealed my pledge. The pledge always required a human.

Jeff dropped to his knees in the circle. Gage wrenched up his head and saw more in Jeff's expression than he'd ever expected to find—but mostly he saw that Jeff had been tricked. The poise of his mouth, the intake of breath, the flare of his eyes, the futile resolution to insist again.

Jeff had miscalculated in the worst possible way. If a jinn's life could fulfill the pledge, wouldn't Mir's life have already fulfilled it?

Gage coughed again, and blood sprayed over the floor.

Mek scampered up to him, right in front of his face. "You're sad. I'll stay with you just like God stays."

Gage rasped, "Go. They'll kill you."

Diamonds glinted in the jinn's eyes. "I left someone once. And that made me sad."

Gage pushed in futility at the jinn who should have had no body—only right now his hands connected. That would be Jeff's magic. "You've got to get away."

The jinn darted off as the weight crushed back onto Gage's chest. Light slipped away, scattering as if loathe to shine on such a struggle. Gage couldn't draw a breath anymore. He'd last as long as the oxygen he already in his lungs.

Hazy numbness cushioned him from the pain. He floated away from his consciousness little by little, away from the broiling air, away from the dark weight. But the laughter remained, waiting, abiding. Inexplicable joy. Gage reached for it, the only solid thing in a world going flimsier by the moment.

I am with you.

Inside his heart, Gage replied, *I know.*

Sense returned like the tingle of a limb fallen asleep. Gage could hear Mek, and he felt the jinn's small fingers touching his own. Daylight returned momentarily, and he again could feel the force of the darkness, only now he could breathe.

"Don't be sad," the jinn said.

Gage mouthed, *Run.*

"Take my treasure, and don't be sad."

Mek pressed something into Gage's hand, and the world lightened.

In his palm lay a silvery brown needle.

The weight vanished. Around his body, Gage once again sensed the rainbow armor. His curled hand still gripped the staff.

A needle, flecked with blood. The pledge object.

Within his heart, God said, *See?*

Mek jumped in place. "I made you happy!"

With his hands wrapped tight around the needle, Gage prayed as the laughter crescendoed within—

God, please, please—

The words weren't there, but Gage felt as if God answered the prayer anyhow. He tried with the angelic sight to find the demon. Mek darted up the stairs as the demon again swung around to focus all its attention on Gage.

"You don't have me." The needle sent cold spikes through Gage's hand, but he kept it clenched.

I have my pledge, the demon replied.

"No." Gage opened his hand and revealed the needle. "You don't."

God, please, destroy what offends you.

The world stilled as if creation were a painting. Etched into Gage's heart was the flare of Jeff's eyes, the demon's angry maw, the world shimmering white.

All the candles blew out on the protective circle.

The needle exploded in Gage's hand with a concussion that hurled Gage out of the world.

* * *

CHAPTER TWENTY-FOUR

* * *

Dad sat beside Gage while Gage played guitar with his eyes closed, the presence of God filling the room with the stillness of a midnight cathedral.

Dad sat with his Bible open, not even having the words for his prayer, but keeping his hands and his heart open while he waited.

He hadn't been able to wake Gage out of this ecstasy. The longer it went on, the more he knew he shouldn't.

Gage's skin was hot to the touch. His eyes watered. His lips were cracked, and he had a nosebleed. Still he kept playing the same song, over and over, and so help him—as a pastor, as a father, as a human—that song would never again sound the same.

Help him. Save him. Lord Jesus, remember your promises.

Gage took a huge breath.

Dad sat up. *Remember your promises!*

The guitar exploded.

Dad recoiled from the flying splinters and waving metal strings. Gage collapsed forward off the bed.

"Gage!" Dad caught him mid-fall, sweeping finger-sized bits of wood off his chest and lap. Gage gave another huge gasp, then coughed with blood-tinged, rib-busting jolts. "Are you all right? What's happening?"

Gage raised his head. "Jeff?" His voice was pained, and he blinked out tears. "Did I stop it?"

Gage tried to stand, but collapsed back onto his father. When he pushed back, his hands left blood on Dad's shirt.

"Taylor reached me just after you left school." Dad tried to lay him back down, sweeping wood shards onto the floor. "You were in a trance. What happened?"

Gage tried again to get up, then collapsed flat with his eyes closed. He rubbed his face and smeared more blood across his eyes. "Jeff. There was a demon. We need to get Jeff." He shuddered. "How did I get back here? Jeff's house. I was in the basement."

"I don't know what's happened to Jeff, but I want to know what happened to you." Dad brushed the hair back from Gage's forehead. "Let me get you a towel."

Gage rolled onto his side, covering his face in his hands. "I don't need a towel. We need to get Jeff."

He couldn't get up, though, so Dad ran into the bathroom and soaked a washcloth. A long splinter of walnut wood was jammed into the heel of his hand, and when he yanked it out, blood welled up.

By the time he returned with the washcloth, Gage had gotten to his feet. "We have to get him. I don't know if it's over."

"I'll get him." Dad started rubbing the washcloth over Gage's face. "You can't go anywhere. You're beaten up."

A crunch underfoot, and Gage stared at the slivers of wood coating the floor. The neck of the guitar. The unmoored strings. Gage closed his eyes, and now the washcloth was drinking up tears.

I know, Dad thought. *That could have been you. And it could be Jeff. But you're here now.*

Dad managed, "I think you worked a miracle."

Gage swallowed hard, then coughed. "I think God worked a miracle. But we need to go back. Jeff's still in there."

<hr>

Gage had his seatbelt unbuckled even before Dad finished pulling into Uncle Zack's driveway. The police tape was untouched on the front door, but Gage staggered around to the kitchen door with the square of glass Jeff had broken to get in. Ignoring the pain in his ribs, Gage flung open the door and ran in.

Not until he was at the basement steps did he remember that the last time he'd tried to enter the house, the evil of the place had pushed him back. Now he was all the way in, with no resistance.

Dad entered behind him. "Jeff?"

From the basement, glass crashed against metal. Gage called, "Jeff? Are you down there?"

The basement light was on, but the candles were out. Gage rushed down.

Jeff spun toward him, eyes wild. He paused, a box in his hand, then let it fall to his feet. Broken glass and torn books and assorted widgets lay scattered on the concrete. Jeff's chest was heaving.

With Mek crouching at his side, Jeff raised his arms to his chest. "Leave me alone! I didn't know! I didn't realize they wouldn't take the jinn!"

"You're an idiot." Gage pressed his ribs with the hand opposite the banister. "They'd already taken a jinn. Can't you count to two?"

Jeff looked terrified. Gage must be a sight—blood on his shirt and in his hair, his face probably bruised, and limping. Good—something ought to scare Jeff.

Jeff stammered, "All I wanted to do was save us both. You weren't supposed to be here."

Gage limped down the stairs—slowly, ow—and for every one he descended, Jeff took a step backward. "Your dad died trying to save us. The least you could have done was learn from his mistake and not do exactly the same thing!"

As Dad appeared on the steps, Jeff reached the back wall of the basement shadows. At the bottom, Dad rested a hand on Gage's shoulder. "Stop. Now isn't the time."

As Dad's hand landed home, Jeff gasped. "Wait! You're *alive*?"

"Of course I'm alive! Not that you did anything to help it!"

"But I saw you die!" Jeff's breath stuttered as he inhaled. "Mek saw it too. You were gone. They took you. It was the same thing—same as Dad—only you lasted longer. Then that explosion, and they left, and Mek couldn't even find you."

Jeff folded his arms around his stomach and bent forward, and with one foot he nudged at the candle burnt down to a white stop-action puddle.

Gage said, "I'm not dead. I'm right here, and it hurts too much to be dead."

Jeff managed, "I'm sorry."

Dad's hand tightened on Gage's shoulder, so he didn't mutter that his cousin ought to be sorry.

Jeff's voice was thin. "How were you even here?"

"Your bike was gone. It didn't take Sherlock Holmes to figure it out."

"You got here ahead of me."

All the burnt-out candles were in the same state as the first. "That was a miracle." Gage nudged the waxy remains with one sneakered toe, and it snapped off the floor. There was a scratch in the concrete, as if Uncle Zack had gouged out ahead of time where to place each one of them. "Dad says I was still at home at the same time. I prayed my way here."

Jeff frowned. "You said the thread was dead. You lied?"

With a sudden ache for his guitar, Gage lowered his gaze. "No, it's really gone. I guess we never needed a thread in the first place."

Dad said softly, "Or maybe the thread transfigured you the same way it transformed the guitar. Maybe it made you two into whatever a thousand generations of believers were destined to become all along." He stepped closer to Jeff and hugged his nephew as though Jeff hadn't nearly been the instrument of his own son's death. "If nothing else, right now, you're closer to the person God has always wanted you to become, and He loves you."

Jeff pushed back and swept his arm out, taking in the whole basement. "How can He?" He pointed to Gage. "How can *he*?"

Dad turned to Gage, who said, "Yes. I can. But you're still an idiot."

Dad said, "And if Gage can love you, then God can, too. But you're not an idiot. You just made a lot of mistakes." This time when he put his hand on Jeff's shoulder, Jeff didn't recoil. "Come on. Let's get back home. Get you both cleaned up."

They went back upstairs. The basement was a mess to fix some other day. Dad secured the house again, for whatever good it would do with a smashed window in the back door. Mek sat in the trunk of the car, occasionally poking out to tell Gage and Jeff about the tire iron. Long cables with rusty teeth. An old straw with a torn wrapper.

"Keep it out of my engine," Dad told Gage. "I don't need to replace four treasured spark plugs."

Gage sagged against the door, pressing his uninjured hand into his side. It hurt to breathe. Even the steps from the basement had left him dizzy.

A moment later, Dad said, "Jeff, I need you to make me a promise." He didn't look at the boy in the rear-view mirror.

"You've got to leave all the magic behind. It hasn't done you any good."

"I'm sorry, Uncle Matthew." Avoiding looking at Gage, Jeff traced his finger over the door handle. "I wanted to make things right. I thought if I moved the pieces the right way on the board, I could keep the game moving."

Dad prompted, "And now?"

"It's not a game. It's not about the rules." Jeff wrapped his arms around his stomach. "It's not even about blessings and curses."

When he didn't reply, Gage finally said, "Then what is it about?"

"It's about people." Jeff blinked hard, but he didn't wipe away his tears. "It's about all of us together in one big web. You and me and Grandpa and my mother and my grandmother, all of us together somehow working for one another. It's not about what we gain by playing the game. It's about staying together and who we become."

Gage laid back in the seat and closed his eyes, letting his ribs throb under his hand. That wasn't quite enough. But it was close enough for now.

Epilogue

Springtime in Vermont begins with mud season, a week of the high temperatures (40s and 50s) when teenage boys shuck their winter jackets and sometimes opt for shorts as the snow melts. Inevitably after two days of thaw, it teems with rain until the saturated ground can't hold any more, and incontinent lawns stand like marshes. Everyone tracks mud everywhere, and the world smells like sludge.

The streets looked filthy while debris got concentrated in the ever-shrinking piles of snow. The detritus lay on the sidewalks and even on the dead grass until new rain washed it away. Only then did the air lose its earthy scent to pick up the odors of pine and greenery.

It was his least favorite season of the year, but Gage had tired of winter. Uncle Zack had been dead for a month when Gage and Jeff went out with shovels and an icebreaker.

"You don't have to do that," Dad said. "It'll all thaw in a few more weeks."

Grinning, Gage said, "I'm killing winter."

Gage and Jeff hacked at the compressed ice along the tracks where Dad's car always pulled into the garage. The metal head of the icebreaker crashed into the ice with a crunch like cracking porcelain, then Jeff would skitter chunks of ice down the driveway, where Gage could shovel it into the street and the sun could melt it. The work warmed them, and they laughed as they took turns hammering the ice, shouting the names of invented martial arts maneuvers before each subsequent crash.

The ice opaqued after every blow, the cracks spiderwebbing as the tool chunked them apart. Leftover leaves absorbed the sunlight and created isolated spots of warmth, burrowing holes in the snow. Gage and Jeff tussled on the driveway, hurled snowballs at one another, and ran through the slush at the base of the driveway. They were killing winter.

Taylor biked into the driveway and dodged a snowball from Gage. "I thought you'd be inside loving your new guitar."

Jeff said, "He needed time to regrow his fingertips," and Gage shoved him.

"You've got to see it. It's a Martin." Gage beamed. "It's a little redder than the other one, but the inlaid wood is lighter. And the sound is awesome. You strike a D chord and you just want to keep hearing that D go on and on."

"And we do." Jeff snorted. "On and on and on."

Taylor was putting her bicycle into the garage when Jeff and Gage both pivoted. Mek came out of the house, staring at the horizon like a rabbit scenting the wind. The boys followed Mek's gaze toward whatever the jinn was looking at, and first one grinned, then the other.

"I was wondering when that would happen," Jeff whispered.

Taylor drifted up close to them, and Gage moved nearer as well. "Do jinn have to come in pairs?"

Jeff folded his arms, then shifted his weight to one leg. "Dad said they don't always, but usually."

Mek inched down the front steps, then advanced to the curb.

A second jinn had crested the hill across the road, standing atop the crusty snow with the same lightness as Jesus walking the Sea of Galilee. After a moment, Mek moved into the street, then stopped in the middle. Reflexively, Gage looked for oncoming cars, but he didn't have to. It was daylight. The second jinn came closer.

In spurts, the pair eventually got right up next to one another. Awkward and judgmental, they sized up one another with the unabashed appraisal of two children on a playground.

"This is stupid." Jeff went into the garage and returned with a Frisbee. "Let's get things started," he said, and he hurled the green disk into the field across the street.

Gage laughed as the two jinn watched it fly over their heads. When it slid to a landing along the snow top, they both ran after it, then crouched, poking at it with fingers as immaterial as daylight. All of a sudden they were chattering, laughing, gesturing. The new one was waving wildly at the air while Mek spun in circles, arms outstretched.

Jeff laughed. Gage jammed his shovel into a snowbank, then turned to Taylor to explain what was happening.

The pair of jinn scampered for the top of the hill, then vanished over the peak. Mek didn't look back.

The cousins stood for a silent moment, hearing nothing from the distance. No voices, no footfalls. Gage waited for the prickle of the jinn's returning presence, but none came.

Jeff set down his icebreaker. "I'll get the Frisbee."

"Leave it." Gage thrust his hands in his pockets. "They'll get it tonight as treasure, if they remember."

Jeff smirked. "They'll always remember treasure."

Gage returned his shovel and Jeff's ice-breaker to the garage. Inside, Jeff went into the kitchen for a soda, while Gage brought Taylor to his room to show her his new guitar. He played for her, fingers working their self-confident magic on six ordinary strings.

Thank you!

Thank you so much for reading about Gage, Jeff, Taylor, and my jinn! The jinn have a special place in my heart because they appeared in one of my earliest short stories ("Arrows" in Andre Norton's *Catfantastic IV*) and I hope my mischief-makers now have a special place in your heart, too. The next time your car keys go missing, remember—they make excellent treasure.

This book has been in process, in one form or another, for many years. It had a couple of close calls with publishers who in the end admitted they didn't understand it, and finally now here it is, out in the wild. I'd like to thank everyone who helped me with plot-storming and early reading, for the people who offered encouragement and suggestions, their time, and their faith.

Please consider leaving a review for the book at Amazon or Goodreads. Reviews really help so much, and they don't have to be complex. Just a star rating and a couple of sentences to say how you felt.

Please consider signing up for "Thursdays with Jane" at http://eepurl.com/dEJjI1 On most Thursdays, I share stories about my weird life as well as recommendations for books I've enjoyed or patterns I've knit. It's only once a week, and I'd love to see you there.

Thank you again for reading, and I hope we meet again soon!

If you enjoyed the angels and the jinn, please check out the **Seven Archangels Saga**! They're all available on Amazon in Kindle format, and the full-length novels are available in print, as well. Even better, the full-length novels are being released as audiobooks, so check Audible, Hoopla, Scribd, or wherever you pick up your audio. (You can ask your public library to pick up copies, instead, because then it's free for you and lots of people can enjoy them.)

www.ingramcontent.com/pod-product-compliance
Lightning Source LLC
Chambersburg PA
CBHW030747190726
48285CB00003B/735